QUESTIONS, QUESTIONS

"Did your son use drugs regularly?" asked Trace.

"I woulda busted his ass if he did," Nick Armitage snapped.

"I thought he might have gotten in with bad people," Trace said. "Drug dealers. Stuff like that."

"No, he didn't, and you can stop fishing. I saw you in my restaurant last night—with that little slope of yours."

"Mister Armitage, I'm going to do you two favors."

"What's that?"

"I'm going to make believe I didn't hear that crack because I didn't have a drink yet today and I'm not feeling so good and I might just have to pound it down your face. And second, I'm not going to tell the lady about it because you might just wake up one morning and find your intestines neatly piled on top of your chest."

"Yeah?"

Trace shook his head. If there was anything he hated before he had a drink, it was snappy dialogue. . . .

Exciting Reading from SIGNET

TRACE

WHEN ELEPHANTS FORGET

WARREN MURPHY

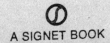

A SIGNET BOOK

NEW AMERICAN LIBRARY

PUBLISHER'S NOTE

This novel is a work of fiction. Names, characters, places, and incidents either are the product of the author's imagination or are used fictitiously, and any resemblance to actual persons, living or dead, events, or locales is entirely coincidental.

NAL BOOKS ARE AVAILABLE AT QUANTITY DISCOUNTS
WHEN USED TO PROMOTE PRODUCTS OR SERVICES.
FOR INFORMATION PLEASE WRITE TO PREMIUM
MARKETING DIVISION, NEW AMERICAN LIBRARY,
1633 BROADWAY, NEW YORK, NEW YORK 10019.

SIGNET TRADEMARK REG. U.S. PAT. OFF. AND FOREIGN COUNTRIES
REGISTERED TRADEMARK—MARCA REGISTRADA
HECHO EN CHICAGO, U.S.A.

SIGNET, SIGNET CLASSIC, MENTOR, PLUME, MERIDIAN
and NAL BOOKS are published by New American Library,
1633 Broadway, New York, New York 10019

First Printing, October, 1984

        3   4   5   6   7   8   9

PRINTED IN THE UNITED STATES OF AMERICA

MASKED STUDENT FOUND SLAIN ALONG HIGHWAY

The murdered body of Anthony Armitage, who had just completed his junior year at Fairport College, was found yesterday along a stretch of the Merritt Parkway, outside Greenwich, Connecticut.

Police said that Armitage, 22, had been killed instantly by a single bullet wound in the heart. When he was found, the youth was wearing a rubber mask bearing the likeness of former President Richard Nixon.

State police said Armitage was found in a small clearing off the side of the road, designed for motorists with auto problems. A passing driver spotted the body early yesterday morning when he pulled into the clearing to empty his car's ashtray. Armitage died near midnight, police said.

The student was the son of Mr. and Mrs. Nicholas Armitage of New York City. The elder Armitage is the owner of the well-known New York nightclub, Chez Nick, which is a gathering spot for people in show business and in other endeavors.

1

"I don't want to do it."

"What?"

"I. Don't. Want. To. Do. It. Should I repeat it in Latin? I used to be an altar boy, you know."

"No. Just explain it in English." Walter Marks did not seem so much puzzled as annoyed. His thin lips were pressed tightly together.

"All right," the other man explained. "To you, this Tony Armitage is just some young guy who got killed and had a big insurance policy with us."

"A half million dollars," Walter Marks said.

"Right. So you send in Devlin Tracy, your crack insurance investigator—"

"Hah. That's a laugh."

"Please, Groucho. Don't be hateful. So you send me in and you expect me to do what the police of seven continents haven't been able to do. Somehow solve this murder and prove it was suicide so that Garrison Fidelity Insurance Company doesn't have to pay off on the half-mill policy."

"So far that seems reasonable," Walter Marks said cautiously. Devlin Tracy thought that Walter Marks said everything cautiously. He was the vice-president for claims for Garrison Fidelity Insurance Company, and he lived cautiously.

"Yes. Very reasonable to you," Devlin Tracy

said. "All cut-and-dried. Did you ever think that that's a reference to flowers? Cut-and-dried. What has that got to do with facts and information? 'Tis a puzzlement."

"Trace, you're drunk again, aren't you?"

"No, I'm not. I took the pledge a long time ago."

"When?"

"Yesterday again," Trace said.

"Why do you have a drink in front of you right now? If you took the pledge?"

"This isn't a real drink. It's wine."

"Wine doesn't count?" Marks asked.

"No," Devlin Tracy said. "But if I did have a drink, no one could blame me. It's what you'd deserve for calling me in the middle of the night."

"I called you at noon," Marks said.

"Exactly. The digital clock in my bedroom had just flicked over from eleven-fifty-nine to twelve. I call the main observatory in Greenwich every three days to make sure the clock is right. When the phone rang at the last infinitesimal click to noon, I knew it was you. I just knew it. No one else would be so petty as to wait exactly till noon to call. I knew I was going to have a lot of trouble today resisting drinking."

"Please drop the subject and get on with your alleged thinking about this case," Walter Marks said. It was obvious that he did not like Devlin Tracy. Most of the insurance investigators who worked for Marks were on salary, real employees who trembled in terror at the sound of their boss's voice. But Devlin Tracy was on retainer. He worked when he felt like it, and Marks had very little control over him because Trace was a friend of Robert Swenson, the president of Garrison Fidelity, and that made him unfireable.

"As I was saying before you got off into this

insipid discussion of time," Trace said, "to you this case is cut-and-dried, but to me it's something different . . . something more."

"What different? What more?" Marks demanded.

"First of all, I don't feel like working. I'm here in Las Vegas and it's July," Trace said.

"This case would be in New York," Marks said.

"It's July in New York, too," Trace said. "I hate July in New York. But did you see who this kid's father is?"

Marks snatched up the newspaper clipping that lay on the table before them and read it again. "Yes. Nick Armitage. He owns a nightclub."

"With a French name," Trace said. "In New York," he concluded triumphantly as if he had just proved a point.

"So what?"

"That means he's in the Mafia."

"Why?"

"Every place with a French name is owned by the Mafia," Trace said.

Marks shook his head, woefully confused. "What about Italian restaurants? I thought they owned Italian restaurants, spaghetti joints, like that."

"No," Trace said. "Mafia bosses won't eat that crap. French restaurants only. Anyway, I know what you're up to, Groucho. You want me to go to New York. I hate New York anyway. I like Las Vegas and Hoboken. You want me to go in there and scout around and you know I'm going to get this Nick Armitage pissed off, and that's going to be it. When they drain the East River, I'll be standing up in a cement block. For eternity. Some things are more important than five hundred thousand dollars of dear old Gone Fishing's money. My life is indisputably one of these things."

"Please don't call Garrison Fidelity Insurance 'Gone Fishing,' " Marks snapped.

Trace looked around anxiously at the dark empty cocktail lounge. "Why? Is somebody listening?"

"Never mind," Marks said in disgust. "Just go check this out."

"You really want me dead, don't you?" Trace asked. "I mean, really dead. Like never to breathe again. Never again to smell the flowers. Even the cut-and-dried ones. I can't believe this of you."

"Just go check it out."

"No. My mind is made up."

"I'll have to tell Mr. Swenson. Then he'll ask you to go check it out and you'll do it."

"Why don't you ever want to pay up on insurance claims?" Trace said. "The kid got killed. Pay up."

"Not until you look into it."

"All right. It's solved for you. The kid was killed by the Sierra Club."

"What?"

"He was wearing this Richard Nixon mask, see. And you had these high Sierras out—they were high, that's what high Sierras means—and they were marching along the Merritt Parkway looking for edible marigolds and James Watt. And when they didn't see Watt, along came this kid wearing a Richard Nixon mask, so they settled for him. Question Jane Fonda. She had something to do with it."

"Idiotic. You are truly idiotic," Marks said.

"And I don't get any better. So now, if you'll forgive me, I'm going home," Trace said. "I'm sorry you wasted this trip to Las Vegas for no reason at all."

"Let me get this straight so I can be sure to tell it to Mr. Swenson correctly. You are refusing to take this assignment because you don't like July in New York and you are afraid this Nick Armitage is in the Mafia."

"I couldn't have said it better myself. Would you like another drink?"

"No."

"Will you be in town long?"

"Just until tomorrow. I've got to lay over a day to get some kind of super-economy fare. Something like that."

"Where are you staying?" Trace asked

"At the Araby," Marks said.

"A nice place. Have a nice time."

Atop the piano in their living room in a condominium high above Las Vegas's Strip, Trace found a note from his roommate.

"Had to go out. Sarge called. Wants to talk to you. Very important. Says your mother is coming to Las Vegas in a couple of days with her woman's club. I will commit suicide. Chico."

Trace read the note three times, poured himself a glass of Gallo Red Rosé wine from a three-liter jug in the refrigerator, then called the Araby Hotel and Casino and asked for Walter Marks's room.

He was relieved to hear Marks answer in his tight-lipped lemony sour vicious bitter way, as if he had just been interrupted biting the heads off live mice and wanted to get back to it right away.

"Who is it?" Marks snapped.

"This is Trace. I'll go to New York."

"Why? Why now?"

Trace thought of his mother coming to town. "Some things are worse than facing death," he said.

2

Michiko Mangini was the twenty-six-year-old product of an Italian father and a Japanese mother. She was barely five feet tall and weighed only one hundred pounds. Her body was the lissome physical machine of the dancer she had once been, and her fingers moved, even in casual conversation, with an elegant birdlike grace that deserved to be seen on a stage. Her hair was long and blue-black, a frame for the delicate features of her light-tanned face. Her mouth had been designed for smiling. Her voice was lilting and musical. Trace had never seen her do an awkward or ungraceful thing.

Until she fell on the floor.

She had entered their apartment on the Strip and had seen Trace at the stove in the apartment's small kitchen at the other end of the large living room.

She dropped her bag of groceries and swooned to the floor. Trace ran to her side. "Chico, what's the matter?"

"I must be tripping," she said. "I thought I saw you in the kitchen. Cooking." She clapped her hands to her chest. "This is it. The big one."

"Oh, for Christ's sake," Trace snapped. "You're going to make me burn my surprise."

"You don't have to burn it, whatever it is," Chico said. She was still lying on the floor, looking up at him. "You could take it out in the desert and bury it. That'd do too."

"Quiet, woman. This is important." Trace left her where she lay and walked back to the kitchen and the stove.

Chico got up and brought the groceries into the kitchen, where she peered over his shoulder to see what he was cooking. "God, what is that mess?" she demanded, looking into the frying pan in which Trace was stirring something vaguely green.

"You're so smart, you don't know?"

"It looks like swamp stew," she said. "Tell me. Where were you able to buy moss and lichen in Las Vegas?"

"You're lucky I semi-love you," Trace said. "Otherwise, I'd put you out of my kitchen."

Chico put the few groceries away, then poured herself a glass of orange juice from the refrigerator and took a cinnamon bun from a closed container and sat at the small breakfast table in the room.

"You're going to ruin your appetite," Trace said.

"Your cooking's ruined my appetite. Will you please tell me what that is and why you are perpetrating it?"

"All right. This is an original recipe. It's called Devlin Tracy's Green Pepper Veal Surprise."

Chico choked on the cinnamon bun and spattered orange juice and crumbs onto the table. She cleaned up the mess with her napkin and asked, "What's in it?"

"Green peppers. I found a green pepper in the refrigerator."

"Besides that."

"It's done now. You can taste it."

"Not without a list of ingredients first," she said. "In writing."

He ignored her and spooned some of the goo onto two plates and carried them to the table. He sat down facing her. He had already set the table with a knife and fork at each place. Chico got up and found the place mats, the cloth napkins, the spoons, glasses, cups, saucers, brought them all back, and swiftly and expertly arranged them.

"This way," she said, "we can at least pretend it's a real meal."

"I thought you'd be happy that I cooked for you," he said.

"Answer the question on the floor. What's in it?"

"Green peppers. I wanted to make it with veal too, but I couldn't find any veal in the freezer. Don't you ever buy veal?"

"No."

"So I had to use hot dogs instead. If this isn't right, it's because you made me cut up hot dogs instead of veal."

"What else is in it?"

"Vegetables. You had frozen vegetables. I think I used carrots and french fries. And asparagus. You keep a lot of asparagus in the freezer, you know."

"Not anymore. Not now that I know you're ready to violate it as soon as I turn my back."

"Ha, ha, ha," he said slowly. "We are not amused."

"What's the yellow goo that kind of holds this together into one big sodden mess?" Chico asked. She was pushing the food around on her plate, trying without much success to break it up into its component parts for physical analysis.

"It's cheese soup," he said. "I was supposed to use spicy cheddar and make a light cheese sauce, but I couldn't find any spicy cheddar in the house. All I could find was that can of cheese soup and I had to use that." He tasted a forkful of the food and chewed a long time. Then he got up and went to the refrigerator and took out a bottle of beer with an unfamiliar label, printed in vaguely foreign letters.

"I think it needs salt," he said. "Somehow I didn't remember to salt it."

Chico still had not tasted the food. "What's that you're drinking?"

"Imported Polish beer. I just found it."

"Is it any good?"

"I don't know. I never had it before. I just liked the label."

"What the hell is going on here?" Chico demanded. "First you make Green Pepper Veal Surprise, without veal. You destroy my kitchen with empty cans and plastic bags and you dirty twenty-seven dishes so you can fry things in one pan. Then you're drinking something you never drank before. Would you please explain?"

Trace sat down and twisted the cap off the beer bottle. He raised it to his lips and took a long swallow.

"Why are you drinking from the bottle?" Chico asked. "All these years, I've never seen you drink from a bottle. It's one of the few things I really liked about you." She looked down at the plate of Green Pepper Veal Surprise and picked up her cinnamon bun and took a bite.

"You're not even going to try my food," Trace complained.

"I don't see you packing it away."

"I kind of lost my appetite while I was cooking."

"I lost mine looking."

Trace let out a long sigh and pushed the plate back away from him.

"Ahhhh, crap. I'm not going to do this."

"Do what?"

"Be a detective." He saw her start to drum her fingertips impatiently on the table, and added, "It's Sarge."

"What does your father have to do with this purported meal?" she asked.

"I called him back. Remember when he was here the last time, we talked about maybe him starting a detective agency?"

"Yes."

"Well, I was just joking more or less. But he's gone ahead and done it. And now he wants me to go in with him and get a private detective's license and be a real gumshoe."

"I'm sure that this is all somehow going to lead to this kitchen and this plateful of placenta."

"I wanted to see if I was cut out to be a detective," he said.

"Keep going. I think we're getting warmer."

He took another long sip of beer from the bottle. His mouth pursed slightly in displeasure.

"Listen, there are things I know about. And I know about being a detective," Trace said.

"Umhmmm," she said, and nodded.

"It's tough being a big detective today," he said. "It's not enough anymore to track people down through the dark lonely rain-swept streets. You can't just give knuckle sandwiches to bad guys and shoot them in the belly so you can laugh, watching them die. All that stuff went out about twenty years ago."

"What do you do now? Kill them by food poisoning?" she asked. She pushed her plate away too.

"Being a private detective today is different. If you're going to be a big star, you've got to be a gourmet cook, for instance. You've got to be able to whip up things in the kitchen at a moment's notice. All the big detectives today are gourmet cooks. You've got to be able to separate eggs."

"Can you do that?"

"Sure. You put one here and you put one there, and then the eggs are separated. That's the one thing I do know how to do."

"How is that explaining this debacle?" she asked.

He ignored her. "And I just couldn't drink vodka anymore anyway. Anybody can do that. Even Finlandia vodka. It's imported beer all the way. Clever litle wines with a sardonic personality and imported beer. Even this Polack piss. You've got to find a beer nobody else drinks; then, when you're a famous detective, the distributor sends you a thousand million cases and you never have to buy another bottle."

"I get it now. You were practicing being a detective to see if you like it."

"That's right. Wait." He left the table and walked into the bedroom.

While he was gone, Chico took a forkful of food from the plate. Trace had once said that the woman would eat a dog-food billboard if she had to. She ate six thousand calories a day and never gained an ounce. It was one of the things he truly hated about her.

She chewed. The mess was unappetizing to look at, an ugly barbarian insult to her Oriental soul, but the ingredients were at least viable. Except for the hot dogs, which had wound up in her supermarket bag one day through a checkout clerk's mistake. She started to push the hot dogs aside on the plate and pick at the vegetables in cheese sauce.

She took another small bite.

Trace came back with a pair of Nike running shoes in his hand.

"What are those for?" she said.

"You've got to run if you're going to be a detective. Detectives today run a lot."

"Wouldn't pistol lessons be better?" Chico asked. "You haven't run since I caught you in my bed with that hatcheck girl."

"I wasn't running then," he said. "I was regrouping. Anyway, you've got to run. And, God, you've got to lift weights. I'll be pumping iron."

"You'll be pumping gas if you keep on this way," she said. Absently, she took a large forkful of the food and popped it into her mouth.

"And another thing. If I'm going to be a big detective, I've got to sit around and be dull and think big thoughts about the meaning of courage. And duty."

"How do you arrange to think big thoughts

when you have such a little brain?" she asked. "Why not think little thoughts and be a little private detective?"

"Please, lady. You're not the only smart one here. I tested out genius on my college boards. IQ 156."

"Your entire family doesn't have an IQ of 156. Cumulative. And that's counting your mother twice," Chico said. She pulled the plateful of food back to her. With her mouth full, she mumbled, "Speaking of which, you got my message?"

"Right. My mother's coming to town. With her woman's club. I think it's the annual chicken-soup tournament."

"And?"

"I'm leaving. I'm going to New York," Trace said.

"You're leaving me here alone? You know that woman's going to be sniffing around, trying to sell our furniture and replace it with something pretty in real wood-grained vinyl."

"Want to come to New York with me?" Trace asked. "Can you get off from the casino?"

"They owe me some time," Chico said.

Trace didn't bother to ask why, because he knew. Chico was a blackjack dealer at the Araby Casino, but she supplemented her income and her vacation time by occasionally "entertaining" high rollers as a favor to the casino. It was by her choice, and she and Trace did not talk about it.

"So you want to go with me?" he asked again.

"Yes."

"Thank God," Trace said.

"Why 'thank God?'"

"That's another thing about being a detective. You've got to have a funny-looking sidekick. Hopefully somebody who's a homicidal maniac. I can do that. I've got you."

"You'll pay for that, barbarian," she said. Her plate was empty and she pulled Trace's plate over and started eating from it.

He got up and took another beer from the refrigerator. "Eat up," he said. "There's plenty more."

Later they sat side by side on one of their sofas, listening to the intricate mathematical music of the Dave Brubeck quartet playing on their stereo.

Trace had abandoned the Polish beer but was sipping at a plain tonic water. Chico was drinking apple juice.

"So Sarge said that because he was a cop for twenty-five years, it was easy for him to get his p.i. license."

"Private investigator?" Chico asked.

"Right. And now he wants me to get mine. He really wants me to be a detective with him. So what do I do, Chico?"

"What do you want to do, Trace?"

"I don't want to do anything. I want to sit here with you and listen to music. I don't want to have to cook or run or lift big weights or think big thoughts. I want to sit here, empty-headed, with you, and listen to music and try to get you filled with passion for me so I can cop your nookie later. I quit drinking for you. I haven't had a drink of vodka since . . ."

"Yesterday," she supplied.

"Well, that was a mistake," he said. "It was forced on me. I hardly ever have a drink anymore. That's just to please you. I can't please you and Pop too. It's just too much obligation."

"Then don't be a detective," she said. "It's a license, but that's all. You already are kind of a detective for the insurance company. Do you need anything more than that?"

"No. That's the point. I take a case every so often. I save them a lot of money and they pay me a lot of money. I don't have to work any more than that. I like leisure. I don't like it as much as

18

I used to since you made me stop drinking, but I still like leisure better than work."

"Then do that," she said. "Be leisurely. Work when you feel like it or when you need the money. Tell Sarge no."

"I don't want to hurt his feelings," Trace said. "He didn't say, but maybe the only way he could con my mother into letting him out of the house was telling her that I was going to get involved in this agency with him."

"Find out."

"I will when I go to New York."

"When *we* go," she said.

"Yes," Trace agreed. "That's what I'll do." He lighted a cigarette and took a long drag. "You know, everybody's always talking about the responsibilities of being a parent. But children have responsibilities to their parents too. Maybe even bigger ones. Parents end their responsibility when you get to be eighteen or twenty-one or something, but after that, all the responsibility is on the kids. And it can last for years. It's the nature of the parent-child responsibility."

"What insipid shit," she said. "Why are you talking that crap?"

"You think it's crap?"

"Most definitely."

"See? I was trying to be a deep thinker. It doesn't work."

She took his hand and put it on her breast. He could feel her nipple, hard and puckered, through the thin eggshell-colored silk of her blouse.

"Think about this for a while," she said.

"Will it make me deep?" he asked.

"Very deep."

"I hope so," he said.

"If it doesn't, I will," Chico said.

3

In their dark bedroom, Trace smoked a cigarette and let lazy plumes of smoke drift upward toward the ceiling. He thought that cigarettes had no taste in the dark. You had to see the smoke to taste the flavor. Maybe someone, he thought, should invent a cigarette for people who liked to smoke in bed in the dark. He thought about this for a while and decided that, for safety reasons, it would probably not have much market potential. He thought about coupling the sale of those new cigarettes with a fire extinguisher for when the bed, inevitably, caught on fire.

He finally rejected the idea. That was all right, he thought. He had a lot of good ideas.

Chico said softly from alongside him, "I've got a deal for you."

"I'm listening."

"You still drink too much," she said.

"I've virtually stopped."

"You've virtually stopped drinking when I'm looking. So instead of drinking a fifth of vodka a day, you're drinking a gallon of wine and I don't know how much vodka."

"Don't forget the Polish beer. It may be my new favorite drink," he said.

"You drink too much and you smoke too much," she said. "You should exercise. You're forty years old and you look all right, but your heart and lungs have to be ready to give out."

"Does this conversation ever assume a cheerful direction?" Trace asked. "Or do we start taking bets on how many days I've got left?"

"You don't have to lift weights," she said. "But a little running wouldn't hurt. A little calisthenics. Anything to get your heart pumping and your blood flowing."

"That's why I have sex," he said. "If it doesn't get the blood flowing, what good is it?"

She ignored him. "I think you should try to get your life going in a new direction," she said.

"As soon as you propose one that I don't find totally repulsive, I'll be glad to," Trace said.

"You should talk to your children. They're growing up, Trace, and you haven't spoken to them in two years."

"Don't tamper with success," he said. "I haven't talked to What's-his-name and the girl for two years and they're still thriving. Leave well-enough alone."

"Here's my proposal," Chico said.

"Go for it."

"We go to New York. You really slow down on the drinking. You cut down to one pack of cigarettes a day. You exercise some every day."

"You mean, besides sex?"

"Yes. And no casual extracurricular sex."

"This is really getting nasty," Trace said.

"Do you think you could do those things?"

"Of course. If I wanted to."

"You do it, and I'll give you five hundred dollars," she said. "A five-hundred-dollar bet."

"If I lose, I give you five hundred dollars?"

"No. If you fail, before we leave New York, you call your children and talk to them."

"I'd rather give you five hundred dollars," he said.

"Is it a deal?" she asked.

"Who'll be the judge of whether I win or lose?"

"I will. But you'll be on your honor."

"I'll take the bet," he said instantly.

"No cheating," she said.

"I've changed my mind," he said.

"Too late."

"I don't have to join Sarge in the detective agency?"

"No," she said.

"I don't have to think big thoughts?"

"Only if you want to," she said.

"Can I cook?" he asked.

"As infrequently as possible," she said.

"You've got a deal," he said. "Shake." A moment later: "I meant my hand."

4

Trace did not like the flight to New York. He decided he had better get into training for his bet with Chico, so instead of ordering vodka to drink, he ordered beer. That annoyed him.

He did not like either of the dinner choices on the menu and he asked the stewardess if he could whip up a batch of his Green Pepper Veal Surprise for everyone on the plane.

"Sorry, sir, we don't have any veal," the stewardess said.

"That's all right. I don't need veal. That's one of the surprises."

Chico shook her head at the stewardess.

"Well, I don't really think so," the stewardess said. "Regulations, you know."

"No wonder airlines are going broke," Trace groused. "You've lost your spirit of adventure."

"That's right," chipped in a bald-headed man seated across the aisle from Trace. "Everything's dull and the same. Take off and land. Take off and land. Take off and land."

"Sounds good to me," Chico mumbled. "I kind of like an unbroken pattern of take off and land when I fly."

"Quiet, woman," Trace said. The stewardess walked down the aisle. Trace said to the man in the opposite seat, "That was a good offer I just made. I'm a gourmet chef, you know."

"Really?"

"That's right. I'm a private detective. We're all great cooks."

"I didn't know that," the man said.

"You probably don't read enough," Trace said. "Right from Nero Wolfe on. We're all good cooks. Hell, even Sherlock Holmes. Except he mostly cooked up cocaine."

"I read Mike Hammer. I don't think Mike Hammer ever cooked," the man said warily.

"Well, that was Mike Hammer. What did he know? I'll tell you. If he cooked, he'd still be going strong. Instead of being reduced to beer commercials."

"I heard you ask the stewardess for beer before. What kind was that?"

"You've heard of Miller High-Life?"

"Yes."

"That was Polish Low-Life. They didn't have it, though. I only drink imported beers. It's part of my image as a big private detective."

"Trace, will you be quiet?" Chico said, pulling on his sleeve.

"I pump iron too," Trace told the man. "And I run forty-seven miles every day. Wear out a pair of track shoes a week."

"That's a lot of miles," the man said. "How long does that take you?"

"About sixteen hours," Chico interrupted. "That's why he's not a very successful detective. He's always either running or sleeping."

"She's just on the snot because they wouldn't let her bring her wok on the plane to cook for me," Trace explained, and winked at the man. "But I'll calm her down. You know women."

"Sure do," the bald man said.

"I've been well served by many women. But

this one is the best," Trace said. He tried to put his arm around Chico, but she slapped it away.

"What'd you do that for?" he asked.

"What was that supposed to mean?" She imitated him. " 'I've been well served by many women.' "

"Oh, that. I heard a big mystery writer say that once on television. I didn't know what the hell it meant either, but I thought it had a ring to it."

"Yes. A stupid sexist ring," Chico said.

"There you go, bringing sex into it. Sex, sex, sex. I'm tired of sex all the time."

"Remember that," Chico said. "When I am being well served by many men. None of them you."

Trace was still grouchy when they landed at Kennedy Airport in New York. He put on a terrible fake French accent when they got into a taxicab, trying to convince the driver that he was a French diplomat. He whispered to Chico, "Then he'll try to charge us a hundred dollars for the trip into the city and I'll have the bastard arrested for gouging."

The driver charged them twenty-one dollars and fifty cents.

Trace gave him twenty-five dollars.

"Give him another five for his honesty," Chico said.

When the driver pulled away, Chico said, "I guess he wasn't fooled by your accent. Better luck next time."

"Next time, I'll try Japanese," Trace said. "Maybe they only gouge Orientals."

Trace left Chico behind to unpack, bathe, and unwind, and he took a taxi to the office that retired Police Sergeant Patrick Tracy had opened above Bogie's restaurant on West Twenty-sixth street.

On the second-floor landing, he saw a door on which a white oak-tag sign had been inscribed with black plastic stick-on letters from a hardware store. In block capitals, it read:

TRACY DETECTIVE AGEN Y

Trace found the missing letter c on the floor and stuck it back onto the sign, then walked inside. The office was one large room that had once been an efficiency apartment. Off to the side was an open bathroom door. Sarge was sitting, facing the door, behind a small desk that looked as if it had been used in a kindergarten class. A beaten-up green metal filing cabinet was behind the desk. The walls had three *Playboy* centerfolds and a calendar. Trace was about to say that the calendar was open to the wrong month when he saw it was also for the wrong year.

Against the wall next to the door was an old brown velvet sofa. Most of the velvet's nap had worn away and white threads were visible.

Sarge got up as Trace entered.

"Nice place," Trace said. "Trezz chick."

"Hi, son," Sarge said cheerily, and shook Trace's hand. "It'll be nicer when I get some money to decorate. When'd you get to town?"

"Just now. Mother leave yet?"

"This morning," Sarge said.

"Praise be," Trace said, extricating his hand from his father's viselike grip. Trace, at six-foot-three, was two inches taller than his father, but the older man was broad and muscular. His hands looked like small canned hams. He had a thick pile of white hair and there was a faint road map of Irish bars imprinted lightly in the skin on his nose, but hidden mostly by his healthy tanned complexion.

Trace looked around the office and said, "I'm surprised."

"About what?"

"I thought you'd have a waiting room filled with women with legs from here to here," Trace said.

"That's only in books," Sarge said. "Truth is, women with legs from there to there don't have problems. Least, not the kind that detectives can solve." He went to a closet, removed a folding chair for his son, opened it, then brushed dust off it with a handkerchief. "Took this from the basement," he said. "You'll be the first one to use it. Want a drink?"

"No."

"You sick?"

"No," Trace said. "How long have you been here?"

"Just since Monday," Sarge said.

"Any action yet? Any cases?"

"Not yet, but I've got all my old friends in the department keeping an eye out for me. They'll be sending me stuff after a while. I printed business cards."

He took one from his wallet and handed it to Trace, who read aloud, "Patrick Tracy, Private Investigator." The card gave the office's street address and telephone number.

"Good. Looks professional," Trace said. "So your old cop friends are going to help?"

"Well, cops run into a lot of stuff where people can use p.i.s. Maybe." When Trace sat in the folding chair alongside the desk, stretching his long legs, Sarge sat down too. "Only trouble with old friends is that . . . well, they're old. A lot of them retired. A lot more are dead. There aren't many guys working in squad rooms anymore that I remember or who remember me. Most of my friends are deputy chiefs or captains, just hanging around waiting to retire."

"They can still help," Trace said hopefully.

"They deal with papers now, not cases. They're all freaking statisticians," Sarge said. "Reading computer reports and stuff. No wonder nobody ever goes to jail in this town anymore."

"What does Mother think of your office?"

"She hasn't seen it," Sarge said. "I told her it was in Harlem."

"Why?"

"I didn't want her here trying to decorate. I like it the way it is. Well, maybe a little bit better, but pretty much like this. Anyway, so I told her it was in Harlem. I knew she wouldn't pester me that way."

"She's going to find out," Trace said.

"I know. But this way, at least I got some peace and quiet until she does."

"You've only been open since Monday. You'll get some cases soon," Trace said.

"I expect so. Anyway, I like this place. The rent's only a hundred and fifty a month, the restaurant downstairs has a good bar and they send up food when I want it. So are you going to be my partner?"

"I don't know yet, Sarge. I've got to think about it."

"What's to think about? You apply, take your test, get your license, you get to carry a gun, you can't beat the hours." He stood up and pulled back his jacket to show a large Police Special revolver inside a shoulder holster. "You know how good it feels to carry this gun again? Anyway, you can handle all the stuff in the West. After a while, when I get a reputation, I'll be getting a lot of work all over. And I can handle the stuff in the East."

"I know. But it's a commitment. I don't like commitments," Trace said.

"I've noticed," the white-haired man said dryly.

"I was an accountant and I didn't like it, so I walked away. Then I was a degenerate gambler in Las Vegas, and when I got tired of it, I walked away. Now, I work for the insurance company when I feel like it, and when I stop feeling like it, I'll walk away. I think if I get involved with you, I won't be able to walk away. That scares me some. How do you walk away from your own father?"

"Same way you walked away from your ex-wife and two kids?" Sarge asked.

"You going to start on me too?" Trace said.

"Not me, pal," Sarge said. "Anyway, I can't browbeat you into it. But it's something I always thought would be good. You and me together."

"Give me a chance to think about it some more."

"All right. Is Chico in town?"

"Yes."

"Where are you staying?"

"We're at the Plaza. With Mother out of town, why don't you come up and we'll have dinner later?"

"A drink anyway," Sarge said.

They agreed to meet at five P.M. When Trace left, Sarge told him, "Hang on to that business card. It's the only way you'll get this phone number. It's unlisted."

"An office phone, unlisted?" Trace asked. "How come?"

"If I list it, your mother will find it out," Sarge said.

"How's Sarge?" Chico asked.

"Depressed. *I'm* not drinking and *he's* depressed."

"Why? Your mother's out of town."

"It's more than my mother. It's the agency. He opened up on Monday and he hasn't gotten a case yet."

"He's just started, for crying out loud. What's he expect?"

"Sure," Trace said. "That's logical, but it's got to be scary anyway. He's had this dream for years about opening up his own agency, and now his dream's coming true and it might turn out to be a nightmare. I don't like it. When your dreams die, sometimes you die along with them."

"Is that another one of your big thoughts?" she said. "Should I say, 'Gee whiz, that's deep,' and pretend that you're really an intellectual?"

"No, it's really the way I feel. Sarge is sixty-seven and he's healthy as a horse—"

"He'd have to be, to live all these years with your mother," Chico interrupted.

"But people can get old fast when bad things happen to them."

"What are you going to do about it?" Chico asked.

"I don't know," Trace said.

"Yes, you do," she said. And uncharacteristically, she kissed him.

They were supposed to meet Sarge at five P.M. in the Plaza's Oak Room for cocktails. Trace took a leather shaving kit into the bathroom. From it, he took a small tape recorder, not much larger than a pack of cigarettes. Into it, he plugged a two-foot-long wire on whose other end was the replica of a small golden frog, an inch high. The frog figurine's mouth was open, and the gap was covered by a thin golden mesh, behind which was a small powerful microphone. Trace inserted a cassette into the tape recorder, and taped it to his right side with long strips of surgical adhesive. When he finished dressing, he pulled the wire around through his shirt button and connected the frog figurine to it as a tie clip.

Through his shirt, he pressed the small tape device's "record" button and said, "Lawrence Welk, with you, for New Year's testing. And a vun, und a two, und a tree . . ." He stopped the tape, rewound it, then pressed the "play" button. He heard his test message repeated clearly. He turned off the recorder, put on his jacket, and went outside.

Chico was sitting naked in front of the bedroom mirror, putting on her makeup.

"Why don't I go downstairs and meet Sarge?" Trace asked.

"What time is it?"

"Ten to five."

"I'll be ready," she said.

And she was. It was one of the many nice things Trace liked about her: she was always ready on time. Putting on makeup took her five minutes when she was dawdling, sixty seconds when she was in a hurry, and the result of the two sequences was indistinguishable. She made up her mind what she was going to wear even before she opened her closet, and then she wore it. No last-minute looks in the mirror and suddenly deciding that a dress that she had worn and looked wonderful in for three years suddenly was just "not right" for her.

They left the suite at three minutes to five and arrived at the same moment as Sarge at the lounge.

Sarge greeted Chico effusively, hugged her, then demanded a table "pronto."

When the waiter seated them, Trace and his father ordered beers, and Chico, whose body could not metabolize alcohol, ordered Perrier water. "Make it two rounds right away," Sarge told the waiter.

"No special Polish brew?" Chico asked Trace.

"No. I've given that stuff up. It was making me dumb."

"Sure," she said. "And why spend the money on that when plain water would work just as well?"

"If we play our cards right," Sarge told her, "maybe we can get him liquored up, and you and I can go off cavorting."

"I'm ready anytime," Chico said. "Let's play kneesies."

"Good idea," Sarge said. "You know I'm a big private detective now. I carry a gun and everything. You can be my moll."

"I didn't know private detectives had molls," she said.

"I'm breaking new ground," Sarge said.

"Whenever you two are finished," Trace said. He took the newspaper clipping from his inside pocket and handed it across to Sarge.

As he took it, Sarge asked Chico, "Don't you think he ought to join up with me?"

"Why would you want him?" she asked.

"Just father and son, it'd be nice."

"Well, if it's true that private eyes are all deep thinkers, I don't know," she said. "Trace is about as deep as a rain slick."

"I'll teach him, though," Sarge said. He looked toward the far side of the bar for a moment, wistfully, and said almost to himself, "Your mother said I was just throwing away good money. If I had to work, I should get a job in a bank somewhere as a guard."

"That's the stupidest idea I've ever heard," Trace said. "Even from my mother." He glanced at Chico and she shook her head slightly as they shared the same thought. His mother was a thoughtless, hardhearted, unloving emasculating kvetch.

"Read that clipping," Trace told his father. "Come on, I don't have all year."

Sarge read the clipping quickly, then handed it back. "I saw this story," he said. "I know the family. Armitage's got a bad reputation. A bad guy with a bad temper."

"Well, that's what I'm working on. And I need your agency."

"What do you mean?"

"There's going to be a lot of legwork in this," Trace said. "And I don't have any contacts in New York. I need you on this."

"This one of your insurance cases?" Sarge asked.

"Yeah, we had the kid's policy. How do you know the family?"

Sarge looked across the bar as he answered. "I know the kid's mother, Martha, from a long time ago, when I was a cop in Brooklyn." He turned back and looked down at his beer.

"Think she'd remember you?" Trace asked.

"I imagine so," Sarge said. "I guess so."

"Then I double need you. You're an in to the family. You ever meet this guy?" He looked at the clipping. "Nick Armitage?"

"No. But I've heard of him."

"The paper kind of hints that he might be a mob guy. Do you know anything about that?"

"I think he moves dope. He used to move a lot of it," Sarge said. "But maybe he's gone straight. I could find out."

"How straight would he be, owning a nightclub?"

"Not too," Sarge said. "But I'd find out."

"All I'll pay you is a hundred a day plus reasonable expenses."

"My usual fee is two hundred a day," Sarge said.

"How the hell do you have a usual fee when you haven't had a client yet?" Trace demanded.

"If you set your price cheap, people don't appreciate the work you do. I thought that was one of the things I taught you when you were little."

"Okay, okay. How about a family discount?"

"For you, a buck and a quarter a day. Nothing less." Sarge nodded at Chico. "Unless she works with me. Then I'll do it for nothing."

"Nothing doing," Trace said. "She's on my team. I need her brains."

"I'm not working with anybody," Chico said. "I've come to New York to shop. Bloomie's gets my brain and body and soul."

"A hundred and a quarter a day," Sarge said.

"You've got it," Trace said. He nodded for a moment, then grumbled, "Maybe I will go into business with you. You're a goddamn thief, and it might be my only way to get rich."

5

Sarge turned down their invitation to join them for dinner.

"I'll pass. I want to be home when your mother calls from Las Vegas. She worries if I'm not home."

"When does she call?"

"Never know. Usually late. She forgets about the three-hour time thing."

"Horseshit," Trace said. "That woman forgets nothing. She calls that late just to wake you up and annoy you and bust your chops. I know that woman."

"Afraid I do too," Sarge said. "I think I'll be home when she calls. In case she calls early."

"Have it your own way. I'll see you in the morning."

He left them and Trace told Chico, "First thing we have to do is find excuses to keep Sarge out all night. Screw this pussy-whipped bullshit about being home in case my mother calls."

"Don't bet that hand too high," Chico said.

"Why not?"

"How long's she supposed to be gone for?"

"Eight days and seven nights," Trace said. "You know, somebody ought to offer a special gambler's package. Eight days and six nights. The last day you're there, you've lost all your money and you can sleep in the gutter."

"Mess around with her phone calls and she might come back early," Chico warned. "She might get here before we leave."

Trace thought about that for a moment, then nodded. He called out softly after Sarge's departing figure, "Hurry home, Sarge. Hurry. Man the telephones. You're the last best hope of civilization."

Trace told Chico that she was much too beautifully turned out to waste, so he would take her someplace fancy for dinner. She was impressed until they got into a cab and Trace told the driver to take them to Chez Nick.

The cabbie grumbled about losing his place in line at the hotel and Trace understood why when he found out the restaurant was only six blocks from the hotel. The afternoon humidity had finally broken, and on the warm pleasant night, they could easily have walked, Chico pointed out to him.

"What? Walk with you? Down all these mean streets where violence dwells? Where muggers and white slavers and pimps and pornographers are just waiting to scoop you up and take you away from me. Not a chance, girl. I am your man, and to prove you're a man, you may not live like one, but you have to be prepared to die like one."

"What the hell does all that mean?" Chico asked.

"Listen to him, he's right," the cabbie said, hoping to earn a big tip.

"See?" Trace said trimphantly. "He recognizes a big thinker when he sees one. You know what they always say. You want to know anything in New York, ask a cabdriver. Or a private detective. Keep your door locked so nobody breaks into the cab if we stop."

Trace gave the cabbie five dollars and told him to keep the change. Outside the restaurant, under the canopy that reached to the curbside, he told Chico, "It's annoying, having this restaurant so close to the hotel. I could really have run up the expenses if it were far away."

The tuxedoed maître d' turned toward them from his station as they entered, and Trace jumped forward and shook his hand and greeted him effusively. "Pierre, good to see you again. How's the family, Pierre?"

"Very good, sir," the man said chillfully. "I'm George."

Trace snapped his fingers. "Of course. Pierre's your twin brother. Give him my best. Do you have a table for me and the lady?"

The maître d' made a pretense of checking his reservation list, and when he turned back, Trace shook his hand again and put a twenty-dollar bill into it.

"I think we can take care of you. I've forgotten your name, sir. I'm sorry."

"Rascali," Trace said. "Luigi Rascali."

The maître d' nodded. Trace noticed a set of double doors that led to a stairwell. The doors were marked simply "TO THE DANCE." He thought if that was the disco entrance, the restaurant's soundproofing system was wonderful because he heard no music at all where he was standing, except the unobtrusive playing of a piano in the far corner of the dining room.

George took them to a table in a corner of the room, and when they had been seated, Trace told Chico, "I like this place a lot."

"Why? You haven't been here three minutes yet, Mr. Rascali."

"Because it's not like New York restaurants. We're sitting by ourselves. Usually in a New York restaurant, they jam you shoulder and jowl with other people and they're always talking about the stock market. Or what's in *New York* magazine. Who gives a shit? And then they always order smelly disgusting food. They're sitting so close you have to smell it, and it's awful but they wolf it down anyway, splattering juice everywhere. New Yorkers all eat like pigs. I think they give out stars on how many people a restaurant can jam into one room without any of them being comfortable."

Chico leaned over and said softly, "You said it's a Mafia place. Maybe that's why. Maybe the Mafia doesn't like people listening in on their conversations."

"You kidding? That's what they like best. That's why they do all that ring-kissing and that phony yap-yap. 'I am honored, Don Duck, that you have chosen to grace my humble establishment with the eminence of your august presence,' and 'It is a mark of the high esteem in which I hold you and your family that after many years, it is good to return to such a place of warmth and friendship,' and they go on like that forever. They *want* everybody to hear them."

"How do they get any business done, then?" Chico asked.

"On the telephone, the way everybody else does. They come here at night and they talk all that crazy shit, and the next day they get on the phone and they call Louie McGurn-Gurn and they say, 'Louie, go shoot Pasquale in the fucking head. Right. He owes me forty dollars and I'm tired of waiting for the cheap bastard. Plug him.' That's why they're always getting arrested. The FBI has all their phones tapped, but they wouldn't waste three cents tapping a joint like this. Nobody ever says anything that means anything."

"I didn't know you were such a big expert on the Mafia."

"I know everything," Trace said. "The real Mafia decisions, they're made by some guy eating fried peppers out of a paper bag in a plumbing office somewhere. The stuff they do here at night is just for show. It's to impress each other."

It was still early in the evening but most of the restaurant's tables were filled. The room held about one hundred diners, Trace figured, but the walls were covered with heavy fabric and tapestries that muffled sound. Even the piano player at the far end of the room was unobtrusively muted. Most of the groups that were eating were four men, no women, and a lot of the men spent a lot of time glancing across the room at Chico.

Trace was used to it, and whenever his eyes met theirs, he smiled a lot and shot his sleeves so that his cuff links showed.

"I wish I had worn my nine-pound cuff links with the engraved map of Sicily," he said. "That'd get us some respect around here."

The waiter seemed disappointed when Trace ordered only a beer and Chico Perrier water, and was crushed when Trace said he would pass on the wine list for now and they would just like to look at menus.

As was normal, Chico seemed to order one of everything. Trace settled on a salad and a steak. He noticed a man in a tuxedo who was working the room like a politician, going from table to table, smiling, talking, shaking a lot of hands, then moving on.

The man was average height, but even the well-cut tuxedo did not hide the fact that he was lumpily muscular. His neck was that of a football player and his chest was thick. His hair was black, streaked with gray; he was well-tanned, well-manicured, and his smile was so white his teeth looked as if they had been sandblasted to an almost inhuman level. Killer Dobermans wouldn't mind having teeth like that, Trace thought.

Trace picked at his salad while Chico polished off her spiedini appetizers, soaking up the anchovy sauce with a lump of bread the size of her fist. Then she attacked her salad. Halfway through hers, she saw Trace had not eaten the cherry tomatoes in his, was in fact nibbling his way around them, and she speared them quickly with her fork and put them into her own salad bowl.

"I was saving them for last," Trace said.

"Too late. He who hesitates is lost," Chico said. She quickly gulped down the tomatoes before he could argue about them. "Digestion is nine points of the law," she said.

Trace saw the husky man in the tuxedo reach the maître d's station and engage George in quiet conversation, while looking at the seating chart and the reservation book. When he glanced in their direction, Trace looked down at his salad. A few minutes later, the man was standing in front of their table. Trace reached under his jacket and turned on his recorder.

He waited for Trace to look up, then flashed a very wide white smile and said, "I don't plan to interrupt your meal, Mr. Rascali. I just wanted to welcome you to Chez Nick. I'm Nick Armitage."

"Call me Luigi," Trace said, and extended his hand. "This is Miss Mangini."

Chico looked up, nodded imperceptibly, and went back to her salad.

"Your first time here?" Armitage asked.

"Yes. A beautiful place. I am always pleased to be in such a beautiful place when I come in friendship," Trace said.

"It's beautiful now that Miss Mangini's in it," Armitage said.

Chico smiled. "Thank you." She bent over her salad again.

"Have you come far?" Armitage asked Trace.

"It is never too far to come to spend an evening in warmth, among people to whom living is all." Chico kneed him under the table, hard, and Trace added, "From Los Angeles. I was sorry to hear of your troubles."

"Troubles?" Armitage looked puzzled.

"The tragedy in your family. I read about it."

"Oh. Yes, thank you. I appreciate your concern." He nodded several times slightly, more to himself than to Trace.

"A terrible thing," Trace said.

"Yes." Armitage gripped the edge of the table with both hands.

"And no knowledge of who committed this odious act," Trace said.

"None. But someday," Armitage said. He smiled broadly again and said, "If there's anything I can do for you, please let me know, Mr. Rascali."

"Thank you. We will. And it's Luigi," Trace said.

"Luigi."

After he left, Trace told Chico, "Doesn't seem too broken up."

"I don't know," she said. "He looks to me like he's on a very tight string, the kind that snaps. Please. No more of that Mafia dialogue nonsense. I almost choked."

"Okay. I wanted to show you how it was done, was all."

"And why'd you tell him we were from Los Angeles?"

"Because Las Vegas is too small a town. If he got curious about us, he'd be on the phone in a flash, and twenty minutes later he'd know everything there is to know about us. Vegas, everybody knows everybody. It's got the small-town syndrome."

Chico paused later, during their entrées, and

said, "By the way, don't think I haven't noticed that you're hardly smoking."

"I'm going to win that bet," Trace said. "Five hundred smackers for no excessive smoking, drinking, sexing, and exercise every day."

"We'll see. But if you want, you can smoke tonight. Start your new life tomorrow."

Trace immediately lighted a cigarette. He noticed Armitage talking to two men sitting at a small table in the far corner of the room, near the piano. The two men were young, apparently in their late twenties and each was wearing a dark-blue pin-striped suit. Both had wavy hair and acne-pocked coarse features. And both were big. Trace noticed one of them glance at him as Armitage was talking to them.

Outside, walking back to their hotel in the pleasant summer evening, Trace asked, "How was the meal?"

"Mock French. Average. How were the prices?"

"Real French. Average freaking outrageous."

"That's what you get for making believe you're taking me to dinner when you're really working," she said. "I knew when I saw that silly frog tie clip you were wearing."

"Sorry about that. Thought I might as well get the lay of the land."

When they started into the Plaza Hotel, Trace glanced back and saw the two young men in the pin-striped suits standing on the corner watching them. They had followed him from the restaurant. He thought about it for a moment, then decided not to tell Chico. At least not until he knew why they were being followed.

6

Trace's Log:
Tape Recording Number One, Devlin Tracy in
the matter of Tony Armitage murder, one A.M.
Thursday, Plaza Hotel in my least favorite city
in the world, the Big Wormy Apple.

Although it's better than usual. My mother's
out of town.

Chico is sleeping in the other room and, dammit,
I am going to have a cigarette, or maybe a lot of
them. I'll cut way down tomorrow, enough to
win my bet.

But I've figured out something really important.
If you're listening, Groucho, no, this doesn't have
anything to do with the Armitage case. I said
important, really important.

I've figured out why people always gain weight
when they quit smoking. This is a breakthrough.
Fatties around the world may someday thank me
for this.

See, it takes time to smoke a cigarette. You
figure, fishing around in your pocket for your
smokes, then finding an ashtray and a match,
and then lighting it, and flicking it, and stubbing
it out, maybe it takes you like two minutes a
cigarette that you're really involved in the act of
smoking.

So what, you say? Hah! Just wait and listen.

So I smoke, on my good days, maybe four and a half packs. Ninety cigarettes. You take two minutes a cigarette times ninety, and you're talking about 180 minutes. Three hours.

That's three hours that you used to be occupied doing something and now you don't have anything to do with that time. It's enough time to take up a hobby or something, but most people who quit smoking don't know this and don't anticipate it. So they wind up with all this extra time, but they don't really know they've got it and they're bored and they don't quite know why, so because they're not doing one natural thing, like smoking, they just automatically start doing another natural thing, like eating. And then, whammo, fat, diabetes, heart disease, and ugliness.

This is the way it works. I can tell you out of personal experience and pain, and I think all those organizations that try to tell you how to quit smoking ought to warn you about this. And whoever is listening to this tape, in case I've gone to my final reward, I want you to know that this is a gift to humankind. I don't expect royalties or any financial consideration at all. Consider it a donation from one real sweet guy that everybody liked and respected, and if you don't believe me, ask Walter Marks, who sent me to New York to get involved in this stupid case.

So where are we? All right. I'm just into town and already I've been to see Nick Armitage. This is a fast start on a job and I hope Groucho is duly impressed.

Armitage looks like a weight lifter and Sarge says he's got a reputation as a bad guy, so I'm going to keep an eye out and not cross him. At least, not any worse than I already did. I don't know why he sent his two bookend bodyguards to follow us from the restaurant. Maybe my name,

Luigi Rascali, didn't fool him. It was probably Chico's fault. He probably looked at me and said, Sure, this guy's Luigi Rascali, but there's no way that little Oriental woman is named Miss Mangini. It's all her fault.

Everything's her fault. Tomorrow, I've got to drink less, and smoke less, and exercise, and stay away from fast women. Well, at least I don't have to do gourmet cooking. I've pretty well decided not to go into Pop's detective agency with him. If I did, my mother would just find a lot of excuses to be on the telephone with me, busting my chops. It'll be a miracle if Sarge can make the agency pay. It's tough when you have to have an unlisted phone for your business to keep your wife out of your hair.

Speaking of which, I hope Sarge got her telephone call tonight. I don't want her nosing around my apartment in Vegas and finding out I've gone to New York, and then calling Bruno, the ex-wife, and letting her know that I'm here, because as sure as God made green, yellow, and red apples, she'll be here, sniffing around, whining and complaining about something. I can't take that.

I've got to win this bet with Chico. Losing is just too horrible to contemplate. Having to call What's-his-name and the girl. I can't do that. No way can I do that. Never.

Sarge says he knows the Armitage kid's mother. Well, maybe he can find something out there I'm pretty proud of myself and I know Groucho will be too. I need a private detective agency to help on this case, and by hard long negotiations I got one to help us for a hundred and twenty-five a day. They wanted two hundred, but I got them down to one-twenty-five. I'm nothing if not economical.

And that brings us to expenses. Hotel bill and the car I rented for tomorrow and so forth are on credit card. Counting tip, and twenty-dollar bribe to Pierre, the maitre d' who thinks his name is George, Chez Nick cost me a hundred and forty. My usual one hundred and fifty expenses for the day for miscellaneous stuff. And one-twenty-five for the detective agency. That adds up to . . . let's see, four hundred and fifteen dollars. I'm starting to like this case better already.

Oh, by the way, there's a tape in the master file. It's my brief meeting with Nick Armitage at his restaurant tonight. I have a hunch I'll be seeing him again. Good night to all of you from all of us here in Gotham. Devlin Tracy signing off.

7

Trace woke up to find Chico kneeling astride his body. She was naked and beautiful and he pulled her down to him and kissed her for a long time.

"You come here often?" he asked.

"That's kind of up to you, isn't it?" She rested her cheek on his shoulder. "It was nice of you to get a suite of rooms, really nice."

"Suites for the sweet," he said. "Besides, Groucho's paying for it. Money is no object."

"Until you try to collect," she said.

"Live dangerously."

"I will. I'm calling room service and having breakfast sent up. Do you know how long it's been that I didn't have to get up and make you coffee and a piece of toast and a quarter of an egg and watch you pick at it, then go inside and throw up?"

"I haven't been doing that since I stopped drinking. Almost stopped drinking."

"That's why I almost stopped nagging you. You want breakfast in bed?"

"I thought you were going to have food sent up?"

"You have a lewd and lascivious turn of mind," Chico said. "I was talking about room-service breakfast in bed."

"Is our bed big enough for your breakfast? Will

we get a suckling pig and five thousand pancakes to fit on this mattress?"

Chico was gone and on the telephone, and Trace went back to sleep. When he woke, he was covered by a food tray. Chico was eating from another tray while she sat on the edge of the bed. Crumbs flew into the air from her direction.

With her mouth full, she said, "Eat. Eat. You've got to go to work today."

"Yeah. The Mysterious Case of the Richard Nixon Mask Murder. When I'm a big detective, it'll be the one case that everybody remembers and talks about."

"Shouldn't you solve it first?"

"Oh, I'll solve it," Trace said. He nibbled at the corner of a piece of cold toast and decided, once and for all, that he didn't like toast. Intellectually, he regarded this as a big breakthrough. All his life, he had been trying to eat toast because everybody was always putting it on his plate, starting with his mother, who always burned hers and then scraped the charcoal from it with the edge of a kitchen knife. And because everybody always put toast on his plate, he had always assumed that he liked it and should try to eat it. But now he had faced up to the truth. He hated toast. He liked a bite of Danish once in a while and sometimes a hard seeded roll with a lot of butter. But he hated toast.

"From now on, hold the toast," he told Chico, waiting for her to ask him why.

"Sure," she said cheerily, without argument. "More for me. Why was he wearing that Richard Nixon mask?"

"I don't know. You think it's important?"

"It would seem like it, wouldn't it?" She was chewing away remorselessly at her food, as if she were a mouse and she had to tunnel her way through a mountain of food to get home by nightfall. "Was he wearing the mask when he got killed?"

"I don't know. Why?"

"I guess they can tell those things when they do autopsies and stuff. If the murderer put the mask on him, then it means one thing."

"Like what?"

"I don't know yet," Chico said. "Don't interrupt, I'm thinking. If the murderer put the mask on him, it means a ritual, a joke, a warning, I don't know. But if he was wearing the mask on his own when he got killed, then it means something else."

"What something else?" Trace asked.

"I don't know," she said. "I don't know anything about this whole thing yet, except that stupid clipping you're carrying around. Maybe he was wearing a disguise, maybe he was going to a masquerade party, what do I know? It just means something else if he put the mask on himself. I think."

"I guess that's logical, so I guess I'll have to find out, won't I?"

"Put your little mind to it."

"Big mind, please. I'm going to be a big detective someday. Maybe." He took the tray off his body and set it on the end table. "Aren't you done eating yet?" he asked.

She had a faint smile on her lips. "Not quite yet."

"Stay away from me, you wild, disgusting beast," he said. "I've got to exercise."

The telephone rang.

"Saved by the bell," Trace said.

"You think so?" Chico said, and vanished under the covers.

Sarge said, "What are you up to, Dev?"

"Fighting off a kamikaze assault on my virtue," Trace said. "Why?"

"I thought you were coming down here to the office. Don't fight, surrender. I would."

"Get out of there, you animal," Trace yelled.

"What?" Sarge asked.

"I wasn't talking to you," Trace said. "What's up?"

Chico giggled, and Trace slapped the back of her head through the blanket.

"I got to thinking last night about Martha," Sarge said.

"Martha?"

"Martha Armitage. So I called her."

"What'd you do that for?" Trace asked.

"I figured it would be all right. I thought, What the hell, her husband's probably out working at the nightclub. If a man answers, I hang up."

"Okay, so?"

"I told her that I was involved in looking into her son's death. She seemed excited by that."

"She remember you?"

"Yes. Anyway, she's coming down here today."

"Here where?"

"To my office, at one o'clock."

"Good. One o'clock. I'll be there," Trace said.

"If he's done," Chico said, her voice muffled by the blanket.

Trace hit her on the head again. "One thing, Sarge," he said.

"What's that?"

"Can we get some police reports on the killing? Like was he wearing the mask when he got killed or was it put on later? That kind of stuff."

"He was wearing it when he was killed," Sarge said.

"How do you know?"

"I already got the reports. I was up at headquarters this morning."

50

"Good. I'll see you in a bit," Trace said as he hung up.

"When do you have to be there?" Chico asked.

Trace glanced at his watch on the end table. "Couple of hours."

"Good. We'll be done by then."

Trace lifted up the sheet and looked at her perfect smooth golden body. "Maybe," he said.

8

The first thing that Trace noticed was that the three *Playboy* centerfolds had been removed from the wall behind Sarge's desk, and the second was that two large robust green plants now stood on the sill of the front window, overlooking West Twenty-sixth Street, where the implacable July sun beat down on them.

Atop the file cabinet was a hot plate with a pot of coffee on it, and a pile of newspapers that had been roughly stacked on the floor had been removed. Two more chairs had been set out in the office. A window air-conditioner hummed.

"Looking a lot better, Sarge," said Trace after he entered and looked around.

"More middle-class, I thought," Sarge said. "Attract a better class of client. Here are those police reports. You want coffee?"

"No. It's too hot," Trace said. He took the reports, which were in a manila folder, and leaned against the wall near the front windows to read them, but before he started, there was a faint tapping on the office door and Sarge jumped to his feet and hurried to go open the door.

Martha Armitage was a tall, elegant brunette. She was simply dressed in a white blouse and dark plaid skirt, and the garments showed her figure to be full and lush. She had large sparkling dark eyes, but her makeup looked as if it had been hurriedly applied, because Trace thought it was a touch too thick. Her lipstick, too, seemed a little excessive and Trace thought it a shame because her lips were sensual and full and needed nothing added to be beautiful. Trace got the feeling that she had applied her makeup as if she were going to a tony nighttime party at which she wanted to be the most spectacular woman there, instead of to a daytime meeting with a private detective in a seedy office in downtown New York.

Sarge took her hands and pecked her casually on the cheek. Trace reached behind him to turn on the tape recorder under his shirt.

"Hello, Patrick," she said almost shyly.

"Good to see you again, Martha," he said. He led her to the sofa, where she sat primly, her legs crossed at the ankle, her feet together on the left side of her body.

"Coffee?" Sarge asked.

She shook her head, then noticed Trace by the window.

"This is Devlin?" she asked Sarge.

"Yes. My son."

She nodded to Trace. "I've heard your father speak of you a lot," she said with a smile.

"Good to meet you, Mrs. Armitage."

Sarge poured himself coffee and Trace noticed that he was using a real cup with a real saucer. Yesterday it had been styrofoam all the way.

"Your office is nice," the woman told Sarge.

"A few more plants and furniture, it'll be all right," Sarge said. "I was a little surprised bv your reaction on the phone, Martha."

"Why?"

"Because I thought you'd think that Dev and I were pests. But instead . . ."

Mrs. Armitage glanced at Trace again. She said,

"Instead, I want you to look into my son's murder. That's right."

"Why's that?" Trace asked.

Before she could answer, Sarge said, "I didn't get a chance to tell you, Martha, but Devlin isn't really my partner in this agency. He's on assignment from the insurance company that insured your son."

"I see. So you'd be looking into this matter anyway?" she asked.

Trace nodded and Sarge said, "That's how I got into it. I help Dev on his New York work."

"You were going to say why you wanted us to look into it," Trace prompted.

"Isn't it obvious? My son's been murdered," she said.

Trace noted a faint undertone in her voice, a little hint of nervousness, of insecurity. "A lot of people still might not like private detectives around. They'd prefer to leave it to the police," he said.

"My son's been dead over a month. The police haven't found out anything yet. I don't even think they're looking anymore," she said. She looked at Sarge, as if for approval, then said to him, ignoring Trace, "Nick, my husband, hasn't been the same since the killing." She paused, but both men were silent, encouraging her to continue. Then she looked at Trace as if explaining and said, "My husband is not an easy man." He nodded.

She seemed to have difficulty getting more words out and Sarge said to Trace, "What Martha means is that her husband knows a lot of people who aren't nice people. He makes his living a tough way."

"A lot of us do," Trace said. "I understand."

The words, when they came, spilled out in a torrent. "I want somebody to find out who killed my son and have them arrested. I want them in jail for it. I don't want my husband to find out first. Because if he does, he'll kill them, and then the police will be after him, and I've lost my son and I don't want to lose my husband too. I want you to find out who killed Tony."

Trace recognized the errant look he had seen in her eyes. It was fear. Not the kind of frightened panic that came from confronting a sudden danger or obstacle, but a kind of numbing, grinding fear that came from insecurity. It was a look that alcoholics often developed, just as, he thought, women alcoholics all too often put their makeup on too heavily because it took too steady a hand to apply light, delicate daytime makeup.

He glanced at her fingers, folded in her lap, and saw that they were moving spasmodically, fingertips pressing against fingertips. Trace felt like offering her a drink. He knew she would accept.

"Is your husband looking for the killers?" Trace asked.

"He doesn't talk about the ... the tragedy anymore," she said. "But I know he is. You know, there was a man once." She paused and looked off into space, as if trying to remember. When she spoke again, she spoke to a point on the wall on the far side of the room, looking at neither of them.

"They were bad times for us. We didn't have any money and Nick was trying to borrow money to open a tavern in Manhattan. He went to the bank manager to try to get a loan, and the man laughed at him because Nick didn't have any collateral. Well, Nick got the money somewhere else and he wound up making a lot of money. But he never forgot that man at the bank, and one day, years later, I read in the paper that the man had been arrested in some scheme to defraud the bank. When I told Nick about it, he said, 'I know,' and I knew right then that somehow he had set it up to happen that way. Nick has a memory like an elephant. He doesn't forget. I know he's looking for those people who killed our son."

"You keep saying people," Trace said. "Were there people? Or could it have been just one person?"

She shrugged. "A figure of speech, I guess. It could have been just one person."

"Any idea what one?" Trace asked.

"I don't know."

"Tell us about your son. Was he a good student?"

"I'll have that coffee now, Patrick, if you don't mind," the woman said. She stopped wringing her hands in her lap, but it seemed to Trace as if it had taken her a conscious effort of will to stop.

As Sarge poured coffee for her into another clean cup, she said, "Tony was a good student. A B student. His first couple of years up at Fairport, he got A's, but this last year he slipped a little."

"Kids do," Trace said. "They discover women, social life, partying."

Mrs. Armitage nodded and took the coffeecup from Sarge.

"Did your son live on campus?"

"There isn't any campus housing," she said. "He lived in a small private house off campus, with two roommates."

"Do you have their names?" Trace asked.

"Yes. Phil LaPeter and a girl, Jennie Teller."

"Two guys and a girl," Sarge said.

"All very unromantic," Mrs. Armitage said. She took a slow sip of coffee. "When I heard about it, I thought, Oh-oh, trouble. Jealousy, fights, arguments."

"And now your son is dead," Trace said.

She stopped as if she had been hit, and carefully put her cup back onto the saucer. "No. It wasn't anything like that. The three of them were just friends. I don't know who might have done it," she said again, softly. "I don't know. That's what I want you to find out."

"What about your son's habits?" Trace asked.

"What do you mean?"

Trace shrugged. "You know. Was he a big drinker? Did he use drugs? Did he travel around with a lot of bad company?"

She shook her head. "Tony was going to be a lawyer. Nick didn't even let him come to the nightclub. He didn't want him hanging around that kind of atmosphere. He'd get upset if Tony ever showed up."

"And drugs?" Trace asked.

"There was, I don't know, some kind of drug. There were traces found in Tony's body. But he didn't do that on his own. Whoever killed him must have given him drugs," she said. "He was a good boy, Mr. Tracy."

Trace listened desultorily as Sarge asked a few more routine questions, then finally looked at his own son with a question mark on his big red Irish face.

Trace said, "Just one question, Mrs. Armitage."

"Yes?"

"Why did you have half a million dollars' insurance on your son?"

She seemed to wince and took a deep breath before answering. "Tony wasn't our only child, Mr. Trace . . . Devlin. We had another boy before him. He died when he was a year old. Nick said that if God ever played a dirty trick like that on us again, somebody was going to pay for it. After Tony was born and grew up a little bit, Nick took the insurance on him."

"I see."

"I guess that's all for now, Martha," Sarge said. "Did you drive?"

"I took a cab."

"I'll walk with you to one," he said.

As they were leaving the office, Mrs. Armitage paused, then turned back to Trace. "Do you think we'll be seeing each other again?" she asked.

"Probably," Trace said.

"I . . . I don't want my husband to know what you're doing for me, or that I ever talked to you."

"I understand," Trace said. "We never met."

"Thank you, Devlin," she said.

Sarge took her arm and led her out.

When they were gone, Trace moved out of the sunlight that poured through the window, and sprawled on the couch, reading the reports in the folder Sarge had given him.

There were photocopies of a string of reports, including a number from Connecticut. It surprised Trace for a moment to see Connecticut State Police printed on the top of the forms, until he remembered that Tony Armitage's body had been found in Connecticut. He had been thinking of this as a New York case.

Trace remembered Chico's question from the morning and rapidly read through the reports. Young Armitage had been wearing the mask when he was killed. He had been shot in the heart at close range with a .38-caliber pistol, and death had been instantaneous. The mask had been partially removed from his face, but it was splattered with blood, and intricate analysis showed that it had been on his face when he was shot. The mask was a common-enough kind, made of latex, sold in novelty shops nationwide, and there was no identifying mark to determine what store it might have come from.

The Connecticut reports were very thorough, Trace thought, and they used very unpolicelike phrases such as "consistent with" and "raised implications."

He had been shot between midnight and one A.M.

The Connecticut investigation had been under the control of a state police officer named Lt. Shriner, and Trace put his name in his personal memory bank to keep. He would probably have to talk to him before the case was over.

The Connecticut cops had also taken statements from Armitage's two roommates, LaPeter and the young woman Jennie Teller, but neither had been able to cast any light on the killing. Both had been out of town that weekend, LaPeter in Pennsylvania at a concert with a half-dozen friends who were good for alibis, and Teller at a psychology seminar in Atlantic City. Neither had seen Armitage since two days before the killing, and had learned of his death only when they returned to the campus. There were no reports that Armitage had any enemies, had been heavily into drugs, or that he had been depressed or acting strangely in the days before his death.

The autopsy report showed that the young man had a quantity of methaqualone in his body, consistent with having taken two capsules three hours before his death. Trace recognized the drug as the generic name for Quaaludes. There were no other drugs in his system.

The New York police reports were brief, dealing with their having notified the Armitages of the death of their son. Notification was made at the couple's apartment on the Upper West Side, about ninety minutes after the body had been found.

Trace snapped the folder shut just as Sarge came back into the office after having seen Mrs. Armitage to a cab.

"Well, what'd you think?" he asked.

Trace shrugged. "Nothing to think yet."

"How come you're not smoking?" Sarge asked.

"You noticed?" Trace asked.

"You spent the whole meeting drumming your fingers on the windowsill. How the hell could I not notice?"

"Christ, I didn't even know I was doing it," Trace said honestly. "I'm going to hell in a bucket. Do you know before I left the room today, Chico made me do a dozen pushups?"

"Can you do a dozen?"

"No. I did one. Twelve separate times. She said they get easier."

"They won't," Sarge said. "You ready for lunch?"

"Yes," Trace said.

"Good. You grab one of these plants. We've got to bring them back downstairs to the restaurant."

"You borrowed them from the restaurant?"

"Sure. Why not?"

"Why didn't you buy some like normal people do?"

"Because any plant I own dies," Sarge said. "You can go into the biggest forest in the United States and find the biggest, strongest freaking oak tree in America and put a sign on it that says, This Tree Is Owned by Patrick F. X. Tracy of New York, and five minutes later the tree's freaking leaves will start to wilt and fall off. A week later, the tree'll be nude; a month later, it'll be dead. It'll look like year-old celery. I tell you, I'm a human defoliation program."

"It must be in the genes. I am too," said Trace.

"Anyway, that's why I don't buy plants, because if I buy them, they die, and then I'll get pissed and want to get my money's worth anyway, so I'll leave them here, hoping they come back to life, and they won't and they'll look like shit and so will this office; so instead, if I have to impress somebody, I borrow the plants from the restaurant downstairs. The woman who owns that place, now, *she* can grow plants. Grab one."

"By the way," Trace said, "did you charge Mrs. Armitage a fee?"

"No."

"Why not?"

"Because I'm charging you. How can I charge her for the same work? It'd be unethical."

"It'd be good business," Trace said.

"Grab a plant," Sarge said.

9

"Why's that woman so nervous?" Trace asked his father.

"Martha Armitage?"

"Yeah."

"I don't know. I guess she's just a nervous woman," Sarge said.

"That's a great answer. For a bill and a quarter a day, I get 'because she's a nervous woman'? Should I pay you now or later?"

They were sitting in a corner of the bar in the downstairs restaurant with the jukebox behind them and the long bar stretched out before them. Trace was drinking white wine and Sarge was sculling down a mug of beer and manfully attacking a large cheeseburger. Lugging the plants down the stairs, he had kept busy touting Trace onto the scungille salad, how it was big enough for dinner for two and the price of an appetizer for one, the best bargain in New York City, and then the restaurant was out of the scungille salad.

"That's the only trouble. They're always out of it," Sarge said.

"That's how they can afford to sell it so cheap," Trace said. He spun around on his stool so he could look out the window at the girls passing the restaurant.

Sarge nodded at his son's wineglass and said, "No more vodka?"

"I've kind of given it up," Trace said. "I've been drinking for more than twenty years like a real rumdum and I've still got my heart and my lungs and my liver. So maybe it's time to walk away before God sends me a due bill. And Chico doesn't like my drinking so much. She said it was making my brain into mush. So I drink this and beer. Except once in a while I slip."

"How often is once in a while?" Sarge asked.

"Every day," Trace said. "But only a little. Not like the old days."

"So now you stopped. Is your brain any better?"

"That's what I'm worried about. It's still mush," Trace said. "And it kind of annoys me a little bit to give up vodka just because Chico wants me to."

"How's that?"

"It's a bad precedent. What's next? She's already starting to badger me about my smoking. We've got a bet that I'll really cut down this time. So that's bad enough. And then, maybe I'll have to start wearing boxer shorts because she doesn't like briefs? Or eating whole-wheat bread. And washing my hands every time I finish reading the newspaper. It could get bad."

"Chico's all right," Sarge said.

"Sure. Now she is. But what happens once she gets power over me? Who knows what rotten thing she might want me to do next? I don't trust women."

"Not a bad rule generally," Sarge said.

"So I don't trust Martha Armitage either."

Sarge did not answer but instead hunkered down over his cheeseburger.

Trace sipped his wine and glanced at a bank of photos along the top of the wall separating the bar area from the dining room. The restaurant was decorated throughout with photographs and posters of Humphrey Bogart during his film career, and Trace wondered if this strip of photos represented villains in Bogart's movies. He thought he had never seen a more degenerate-looking group in his life. Obviously, Central Casting had been asked to send over photos of candidates for the roles of pervert, bank robber, child molester, poorbox thief. Evil was written all over their faces. Only one picture was relieved by anything resembling beauty or sanity, and Trace would be willing to believe that the man might have been framed for whatever crime he'd been charged with. But the others were guilty. No doubt about it. Guilty of crimes and guilty of being ugly.

Trace had not been hungry, but if he had been, his appetite would have vanished when he saw that row of portrait photos. He wondered if they could stop Chico from eating. If they could do that, the powers of those photos was immense. They might become the nation's newest dieting fad, redeemed by the fact that it worked. Men, women, all would drop pounds like snake scales in molt season.

It might finally be the way that he'd make his fortune without working. Another brilliant idea.

His trouble, he often thought, was that he had just too many ideas. You didn't get rich by having a lot of ideas. You got rich by having just one good idea and then doing something about it. Allen Funt, for example. Trace was fond of thinking about Allen Funt. As far as he knew, Allen Funt had not had a logical thought in his life, save one. Conceal a camera, catch people off guard, and call it *Candid Camera*. That was it. One idea. But it was enough and Funt was rich. Trace had too many ideas and he was poor.

From now on, he was going to isolate just one good idea and then refine it and never let go of it. And this group of degenerates' pictures as a diet aid might be just the ticket. He'd need a selling slogan: "Nobody every got fat barfing."

Or "Upchuck your way to slimness and beauty."

Maybe he could get pictures from a photo service. Buy the rights to reprint pictures of the ugliest people ever to walk in front of a camera. Trace looked again at the collection of portraits on the restaurant wall. No. That group was perfect. Just perfect. Except for the one face near the right side. It had to go. The man in it looked almost normal.

Sarge had retreated from his cheeseburger. "So why don't you trust Martha?" he asked.

"I don't know. Something. I thought you might know."

"Can't help you, Dev. Everything she said seemed right to me. Not knowing who might want to kill the kid. Wanting to find out before her husband finds out. It all seemed right."

"Yeah, that was right enough. But it was her attitude or something. Something was going on there in that office that I just couldn't put my finger on."

"I don't know what it could be," Sarge said. He ordered another beer.

"You know," Trace said, "I read those police reports and nobody ever asked if the kid was killed in some kind of hazing prank. Or some kind of thing for some lunatic club. Wearing a Nixon mask. Doesn't that sound like a prank?"

"I guess so. But what'd those police reports say from those Connecticut pansies? The kid was wearing his mask when he was shot? Why, I don't know."

"Me neither. Why do you call them pansies?"

"You read those reports, you have to ask me that? They used words like 'inferred' and 'apparently.' I've seen them before from Connecticut.

They call criminals 'actors.' " He pronounced it in two sharp syllables with the accent on the second: act-OR. "For Christ's sakes, you get some guy mugging some little old lady at night on a dark street, he ain't no act-OR. What he is is a mugg-OR."

"Oh, for the good old days, when you booked poipetrators," Trace said.

"Damn right," Sarge said without a glimmer of humor. "Afterward is when the world went to hell. When they started taking away our language. Do you know that in police reports now they say gay. Gay? Would you believe that? Gay?"

"What did you say? Dirty stinking faggots?"

"Dev, you do me a disservice. You know that I am a man without prejudices as long as the low-lifes of the world stay away from me. No, we did not refer to them as dirty stinking faggots. We called them exactly what the language dictates that we do: homosexual perverts. I defy you to find a prejudice in that phrase."

"It'd take a better detective than I am," Trace admitted cheerily. "What do you think the chances are that the kid was killed, I don't know, as a lesson for the father? To warn him or keep him in line or something?"

"That won't wash, I don't think," Sarge said. "Nick Armitage is a tough guy, from what I know, but he's not really a mob guy. Not anymore. Maybe he was once, but not anymore. He runs his nightclub and I'm sure he moves drugs around up there, but I don't think he's any threat to anybody. And if he was, if somebody had a beef with him, they'd go after him. Not after his family. Families are always kept out of mob beefs. Didn't you see *The Godfather*? Pacino went nuts when they almost killed his wife and kid."

"Sometimes life isn't the movies, Sarge," Trace said. "His mother says this kid didn't use drugs, but he had Quaaludes in him. Why? Where the hell did that mask come from? Why, why, why? I don't know."

"You're not supposed to know. You're supposed to find out. That's your job," Sarge said.

"Maybe you ought to nose around with your cop friends. Find out if Armitage has been having any problems with bad guys. Maybe some of your cops have heard something. Maybe—"

"Hey, Dev. I was doing this work before you were born."

"Not quite, but you're right. I apologize. You know what to do."

"What are you going to do?" Sarge asked.

"I think I'll go up to Connecticut and see what's going on with Armitage's two roommates."

"Anything special in mind?"

"I don't know," Trace answered honestly. "I just don't know."

10

Trace called the Plaza to see if Chico wanted to go for a drive in the countryside and escape New York City's blistering July heat, but there was no answer, so he picked up his rental car at the parking garage two blocks from the hotel and started for Connecticut alone.

He drove up the West Side Highway—carefully, because he always expected more sections of it to fall down—then got onto the New York Thruway and then the Cross Bronx Expressway, finally getting off at the dual exit to the Hutchinson and the Merritt parkways.

Even without seeing a sign, he knew when he had passed into Connecticut. The highways around New York City were littered with the entrails of automobiles, hubcaps, tires, old wheels, pieces of fenders, the wreckage of what was once transportation. The roads looked as if they had never been cleaned, as if some fleet of giant ptero-dactyls had flown over them, dropped stolen cars on the road shoulders to crack their shells, pulled out the meat, and left the husks. But somehow, the big car birds of death didn't fly over Connecti-cut, and the roadways there were unlittered and clean.

The Merritt Parkway was particularly pretty, Trace thought, and totally out of date. It was tree-lined with a broad center mall between the two directions of traffic. In the early spring, it glistened with dogwood trees. It was one of the few roads in the East that Trace thought was pleasant to drive on.

But he knew that someone, somewhere in Washington, was drawing plans to make it efficient. Efficient. The big buzz word of the age. Make it efficient. Put tractor trailer rigs on it. Let them drive ninety miles an hour and terrify sane people. Get rid of the trees and flowers and the mall. Put in extra lanes of traffic. Let's get it rolling. Onward and upward, America. Right smack dab to hell.

First, they'd make it efficient. Then it would turn out to be almost as efficient as the Connecticut Turnpike, where one of the bridges had fallen down a few years before. Or the West Side Highway in New York, which was always semiclosed because it was a hazard.

Cast one small vote, Trace thought, for inefficient. For pretty, old-fashioned, outmoded, and kind of wonderful. If you had to pick a highway to get murdered along, pick the Merritt, he thought. Good going, Tony Armitage.

He passed through one of the vaguely British-looking toll booths in Greenwich, wondered why everybody in Connecticut wanted to think they lived in England, dropped a quarter in the toll box, then pulled off to the shoulder of the road to check the police report on exactly where the young man's body had been found.

He checked his ashtray and saw that he had smoked only one cigarette since leaving New York and was pleased with himself, because normally, the ashtray would be filled and spilling on the car's floor mats by now. He lit another as a reward.

The spot where Armitage's body had been found was about eleven miles down the road. It was an open spot alongside the road, an emergency stopping area, with a large mesh trash basket marked LITTER.

He pulled off the road and got out of the car to look around, but there was nothing really to see and he asked himself what he had expected. Tire tracks leading right to the killer's house? A painted outline showing where the young man's body had lain? He realized that it had never done him any good to visit the scene of a crime, but he did it out of habit anyway. The only thing he learned was that litter baskets somehow managed to survive alongside the road in Connecticut and he saw why: it was cemented to the ground.

He got back onto the roadway and drove along until he passed the road sign for a college whose Latin name translated roughly into English as Fat Albert's. The next exit was for Fairport, the town and the college.

The buildings of Fairport College looked like an exhibit of American garden-apartment architecture, all new and polished and dull. The town around it was run-down and ramshackle unlike some of the neighboring towns like Westport and Weston and New Canaan.

Just off the college campus there were sleazy-looking commercial sections that seemed to specialize in karate classes and triple-X-rated videotapes. He found that Tony Armitage's last address had been a rickety-looking one-family frame house about six blocks from the campus.

He sat in his car and put a fresh tape into the recorder fastened behind his right hip, then walked across the street and rang the doorbell. No one answered, and no one answered his pounding on the door, but Trace had not expected anyone to, because the house literally vibrated with noise. He could feel the door humming under his hand from music that was being played inside at a volume high enough to loosen the fillings in his teeth.

Trace opened the door and was in a living room that was so neat that he was instantly impressed. In his limited experience with this generation, he had found their college kids usually lived in hovels, rutting in dirt, rolling in filth, learning the skills that would enable them to apply later on for welfare.

The noise was coming from a closed door at the end of the hallway. The door bore a KEEP OUT sign. Trace knocked, and when there was no answer, he opened the door and stepped inside.

His back to Trace, a tall thin man knelt on the floor at the end of a small bed, working on a loudspeaker with a screwdriver. Trace quickly counted seventeen speakers in the room, all of them blaring "She Works Hard for the Money." There was enough assorted sound equipment—tape decks, turntables, radios, tuners—to make Crazy Eddie feel the hot breath of competition searing the back of his neck.

Who would want so many speakers? A sound engineer? But who else? And why? Trace wondered. And while he was at it, to hell with sound engineers. Trace could not tell the difference between a supermarket record played on a seventy-nine dollar stereo system, and one played by midgets, piloting laser beams, on a system made entirely of platinum. They were all the same to him. The only people who seemed to be really interested in sound were rock musicians and they talked knowingly about balance and mix and tremulous occupation and autofellatio or whatever the hell it was, and they all nodded a lot as if it were art, and then they turned the volume up three times too high for human ears and took dope so that they didn't have to listen to it.

It gave Trace a headache and he was getting one now.

He walked forward and touched the young man's shoulder. He twitched his shoulders as if Trace's touch was the lighting of a fly and he was trying to shoo it away.

Trace clapped a big hand on the young man's shoulder, and he turned around, looked at Trace in surprise, then rose to his feet.

He was almost seven feet tall and seemed to Trace about seven inches wide. A shock of unruly tannish hair made him look like a blade of meadow grass.

Over the din, he shouted, "It's a hundred a month."

Trace shouted back, "I'll give you a thousand a month to turn off this shit."

He looked around the room at the mixers and speakers and tape decks, then back at the young man.

"What?" the young man yelled.

Trace stuck his fingers in his ears. The young man still didn't move.

Trace said, "I have a friend at the Connecticut Power and Light Company. I'll have him cut your power."

"What?"

"That means disable this fucking noise or I'll disable you," Trace shouted directly into the young man's ear.

"Oh."

The young man wasn't too sure himself where the noise was coming from because he looked around the room a few times, checking out different units, before nodding to himself and walking over to turn off a cassette deck.

The room slipped into immediate silence. Trace could hear the air pulsate and could make out the faint swish of hair on his arms as the air molecules, still vibrating from the sound, brushed across his skin. He could hear the young man's pulse, even from halfway across the room. He knew what it was like now to be an Indian yoga. He hoped nothing would happen to change it. Silence. It was wonderful.

The young man talked, and that ruined everything. He had a nasal whiny gulp that mixed adenoids and a terminal case of Southern accent.

"So. You came for the room, you came? A hundred a month. You're kind of old."

"Are you Philip LaPeter?"

"Yeah. A hundred a month, I said."

"I'm not interested 'n your freaking room," Trace said.

"Then why you here? The sign, the door, keep out, it said."

What kind of language was he speaking? Trace wondered.

"I couldn't read the sign. The sound waves distorted my vision," Trace said.

"All right, I don't need funny from you, I don't even know who you are, doing here, what you want?"

Perhaps the way to deal with him was to respond to the last clause of the sentence, Trace thought. "I want to talk about Tony Armitage," he said. He watched the young man carefully; there was just a touch of apprehension about his eyes as he said, "He's dead, he got killed. That's why I'm renting his room, a hundred a month. You here from the father?"

"No. The insurance company."

"Oh," LaPeter said. "We go outside, I make some joe, you want to talk."

Trace had not heard coffee called joe since he was in the army and sergeants called it that when they were trying to impress recruits into believing that they had been in the army since the Spanish-American War.

LaPeter led the way to the kitchen, a large room in the back of the house. Trace thought that LaPeter and Armitage probably had gotten a good deal when the female roommate moved in because the kitchen was sparklingly clean, as was the living room and all the rest of the apartment he had seen, save LaPeter's sound studio and bedroom.

"Where's the girl?" Trace asked.

"What girl, you say, the girl?"

"Hold on. Is there another language we can speak?" Trace said. "We don't seem to be doing so well in this one. Latin? Spanish? I talk a little Yiddish."

"Only English I talk."

"Well, then, talk some," Trace said. "The girl, Jennie something."

"She's been away for a while, away."

It wasn't quite a Southern drawl, Trace realized. It sounded more like hillbilly talk, taught to LaPeter by a Chinese grammarian.

"Do you know where she went?" Trace asked.

"Oh, she didn't go anywhere. She's staying off with somebody is where she went. She's around."

"But she's not here, is that it?"

"Right. Like you said, right, she's not here. Joe's ready."

He poured water over instant coffee, gave Trace one black without asking if he wanted cream and sugar, then sat down across from him at the kitchen table.

"So what is it that you want, can I do for you?"

"I'm looking into Tony's murder for the insurance company."

"You got a card with your name on it, like a card?"

"Right here." Trace took a business card from his wallet. "My name's the thing in the middle there with the capitals. Devlin Tracy. I'm not the Garrison Fidelity Insurance Company. That's who I work for."

LaPeter looked at the card for what seemed to be a long time, then turned it over and looked at its blank back. He nodded as if it contained everything he had expected to find there.

He handed the card back. "Tell me what I can do for you. I'll do it."

"Was Tony Armitage a good friend of yours?"

"Sure. A good friend."

"How long did you know him?"

"We lived together here almost two years, since sophomore year, we got close."

"Pals," Trace said. "Drinking together, going out to eat, like that?"

LaPeter nodded.

"Doing women together, drugs, hanging out?"

"Yeah, like that. We were friends."

"What about the girl who lives here? What's her story?"

"She moved in last year only. Jennie. She's going to be a headshrink."

"You romancing her?" Trace asked.

"Not me." His nose wrinkled slightly as if he thought the idea altogether in bad taste.

"What about Tony?"

"What about him? He's dead," LaPeter said.

"I know he's dead. But he wasn't always dead, was he? Were he and Jennie getting it on?"

"I don't know I ought to tell you anything like that. All you got is this card, no badge. Do I have to tell anything like that to somebody, no badge?"

"No, you don't *have* to. The problem, though, is that after me will be a lot of guys and they'll have badges and you'll have to tell them all over again, over and over. You tell me and maybe I'll get this all straightened up and you won't have to tell anybody again."

"I don't know if I trust you."

"I'm hurt," Trace said, "really hurt. In all my life, you're the first person who didn't trust me. Except my ex-wife. And my mother. But she doesn't trust anybody."

"Hey, don't be hurt," LaPeter said. "It's just that, well, it's hard, sometimes, man, it's hard, real hard."

Trace had no idea what the young man meant, but he said, "I can attest to that." He wondered if he should do his Richard Nixon impersonation and repeat the line. It was the perfect Richard Nixon–imitation line. He decided to do it.

"I can attest to that," he said again. He twisted his head awkwardly off to one side, lowered his brows, and rolled his eyes up into his head. As he spoke, he nodded as if to himself and held his mouth open as if the words would be followed by a dribble of spit.

LaPeter applauded and laughed. "I love it," he said. "W. C. Fields. All his movies I see. Do it again."

"I don't want to spoil it. Everybody loves my W. C. Fields," Trace said. "So was Tony banging Jennie or not?"

"Last year," LaPeter said. "That was why she first moved in. They got hooked up last summer and then she was here, we were all juniors, but it didn't last long and she stayed on anyway 'cause she pays her piece of the rent, but romances are bullshit."

Trace tried again. "I can attest to that," he said, and waved his arms over his head, his fingers in two V's, again imitating Nixon.

"Love it. That's the best W. C. Fields ever. Again?"

"No. It'd only spoil the fragile beauty of the

moment," Trace said, miffed. "How long did their romance last?"

"Like I said, not long, month or two maybe."

"And no nookying afterward?" Trace said. "I can't believe that anything breaks up clean that way."

"Well, maybe once in a while, but they weren't regular together, sleeping together anymore. That's why my room looks like shit moved in to stay. That used to be my studio, where work was. Tony had one bedroom and I had one, then we got Jennie in here and she got my bedroom and I had to move into the studio with all my stuff, and everything it fucked up."

"Women are always doing it," Trace agreed. "So where were you when Tony got iced?"

"Iced. Good word," LaPeter said.

Trace did not know if he should be complimented or insulted by having his vocabulary praised by one who talked like this.

"One of my very favorites," he said. "So where were you during the ice job?"

"Like that one too. Ice job. I was at a concert in the Poconos. Megan's Friends. You ever hear of them?"

"Of course. And I've heard of the Beatles and the Stones and Janis and Pegasus."

"I never heard of Pegasus," LaPeter said.

"I just made it up to see if you were still listening," Trace said. "Where in the Poconos?"

"At the theater in Stroudsburg they were. A friend of mine works for them down there, with the sound system, so I wanted to see how it all works. I'm into sound systems, I guess you figured out."

"You're joking. Really?"

"Yeah. That's why I got all that equipment in there," he said, pointing vaguely toward the bedroom that housed his noisemakers.

"Was Tony into sound equipment too?"

"No. Into junk he was. Gadgets. Phone machines and things. Tape recorders. Bugs. Stupid stuff. He liked toys."

"Who'd you go with?" Trace asked.

"I told this to the cops, the family and everybody, you know, and they checked out everything, and if I need like an alibi, I got like an alibi because I went with these guys and that's what the cops got told by them."

Trace took a small notebook from his pocket and pushed it and a pen across the table toward LaPeter. "Write their names down there in case I need them."

LaPeter wrote slowly, laboriously, and Trace said, "Were tickets expensive?"

"What tickets?"

"For Megan's Friends? Were they expensive?"

"Yeah. Twenty-five bucks and they weren't either good seats."

"Everything else was sold out, though, right?" Trace said.

"That's what my friend said, the one who works there. I wasn't going to go, but Tony lent me the money at the last minute, so I went with my friends. Those are the names there." He pushed the paper back.

Trace put the notebook and pen back in his pocket without looking at the list. "So what do you think happened to Tony?"

"I think he got killed." LaPeter chuckled softly.

"Why did you do it?" Trace asked.

"What, what?"

"Calm down. I just wanted to get your attention again and see how you'd act and stop you from acting smart. Now why do you think he got killed?"

"I don't know."

"Try harder. Who hated him?"

"Nobody hated Tony. He was just, well, he was just Tony. He was okay."

"You ever meet his parents?" Trace asked.

"Just at the funeral."

"What family did you talk to?"

"Huh?"

"Before, you told me you talked to the cops and the family about where you'd been when Tony was killed. What family did you talk to?"

"I told the father. He was up here after the funeral to talk to me. Him and a couple of guys, like big guys."

"Look like ugly twins?" Trace asked, and LaPeter nodded. "And Armitage wanted to talk about the murder?"

"I don't know," LaPeter said. "Like he wanted to talk, but it wasn't the murder so much. He wanted to talk about Tony and his other friends and stuff like that, more than the murder."

"Did Tony belong to any clubs or anything like that?"

"No. I don't think so. He was in a prelaw program, and not much for clubs he wasn't. Neither was I. Why?"

"Because of that mask he was wearing," Trace said. "I thought it might have been an initiation or something. It wasn't that?"

"No. I don't know of anybody that'd initiate Tony into anything. He didn't join things."

"You never saw that mask before?"

LaPeter shook his head.

"Would you say you two were close friends?" Trace asked.

"Yeah. Sure."

"How close?"

"To what compared?"

"Well, was he your best friend at school here?"

"Yes."

"Now we're getting to it. Was he the best friend

79

you ever had in your whole life? The bestest goodest friend any boy ever had except for his dog?"

"No. Ernie Wisniewski was my best friend ever. He taught me how to jerk off."

"Were you Tony's best friend in the school?"

"I don't know. Tony had friends. He had money and people wanted to be his friends, so he let them be."

"Did you know each other before school here?"

"No. We met in a lit class when we were freshmen and we were okay, friends like, and then there was an ad in the paper for this house and we wound up, both of us going here at the same time, not knowing the other one was, and that's how we got this place and became really good friends like we were. Are we going to do this a lot more because if we are, I'd like some more coffee? It keeps me awake."

"I'll be going soon," Trace said. "What kind of drugs did you and Tony use?"

"What do you mean?"

"People are always asking me what I mean when I think I talk in perfectly clear sentences," Trace said. "What kind of drugs did you and Tony use? Now, don't say 'what do you mean?' because what I mean is, before, I asked you if you and Tony hung out together and did women together and did drugs together and you said yes, and now I wonder what kind of drugs."

"All right, no big deal. We did grass sometimes."

"Nothing stronger? No coke or pills or like that?"

"Just some smoke. That's all we did. Just because I do music sounds don't mean that I'm some kind of drughead. Those days, good-bye, are gone. You wind up like Hollywood Henderson, all bullshit and criminal charges. The world's different now, Jack Kennedy ain't president anymore."

"I thought that Tony might do more drugs than that. You know . . ." He smiled and lowered his voice as if someone might overhear. "His father being in the nightclub business, you know, Tony might have access to drugs."

"Not that I know about. Smoke only he used."

"Did he sell anything maybe?"

"No."

"You never saw that?" Trace pressed.

"Hey, we lived right here. Sure, most of the time he wasn't around a lot and all, but I never saw nothing."

"But you smoked pot?"

"Yeah," LaPeter said.

"Whose pot?"

The gaunt thin youth thought a moment, then said, "Tony's."

"Always Tony's?"

"Yeah. He always had smoke on him."

"Did he have a black suit? He was found in black pants and a black shirt? Were those his clothes?"

"Cops showed me pictures," LaPeter said. "Yeah, they looked like Tony's regular clothes."

"That place where he was found on the Merritt Parkway. Does it mean anything to you? Anything special?"

"Like what?" The young man seemed really interested.

"Like it's a place where you and Tony met somebody sometime. Or where you transferred cars or had a flat. Or were stood up by some girls. Something. Anything."

"No. Nothing like that. I wouldn't even know the place."

"When did Tony give you money to go to the concert? And please don't ask me what I mean."

"I don't know. I told Tony about I wanted to go to the concert. About the money, I guess, I was complaining, and then that day he gave it to me."

"The day he died."

"Right, and he gave me twenty-five dollars and I went with my friends and then we hung out in the Poconos and we slept in a parking lot, then we came back."

"When did Jennie know that you were going to be out of town?" Trace asked.

"I don't know. Why?"

"Just curious," Trace said.

"I don't even know if she knew," LaPeter said. "I don't think I told her I was going. I didn't like tell her too much, 'cause, well, I didn't see her all that much."

"Not your friend?"

"Kind of a friend she is, but what I do isn't really any of her business, if you know what I mean. So I don't think I told her. Maybe Tony did."

"Where will I find this Jennie?"

"I don't think she'll be here. She takes some summer classes and sleeps around somewhere else right now and I don't know where. She works as a waitress at a diner a little bit from here."

"What diner?"

"Cochran's. You go out the door and you turn left and you go like six blocks and it's there. But I don't know when she works, if she works, or like that. You going to go there?"

"Probably."

"Well, you see her, you talk to her, you be sure to tell her talk to me. We've got to figure out what we're going to do about the rent here."

"I'll tell her. Show me Tony's room."

"Sure." LaPeter led Trace down the hallway toward his room, but opened the door immediately to its left. The room was furnished with a bed and dresser, but the closets were open and empty and the only sign that it had ever been inhabited was a paper shopping bag near the door filled with electronic-looking gadgets.

LaPeter said, "That's Tony's junk. His family didn't want it. Probably I sell it." He picked the bag up and put it outside the door to his own room.

Trace backed away, then opened the door on the other side of the hall. "This Jennie's room?" he asked.

"Yeah."

The room was decorated a little more than Tony's had been. Posters from the Alvin Ailey ballet company were on the walls. The sliding doors to the closet were open, but all Trace could see hanging up was a pair of blue jeans and a thin yellow sweater. A pair of winter boots were propped in a corner of the closet.

"Thanks a lot," Trace told the young man. "You've been a big help."

"Okay. Do what you got to do. If you find who killed Tony, then it's a good thing to do that."

"Where are you from anyway?" Trace asked.

"West Virginia. Why?"

"Just wanted to know. Thanks again."

11

"You Jennie Teller?"

"Who you?"

"Friend of Phil LaPeter's. You Jennie?"

"Yeah."

"He didn't tell me you were black."

"Maybe he thought you'd figure it out on your own. Some people do. Right off."

"Ho, ho," Trace said.

The woman waited.

"So I was just talking to your roommate."

"'Bout what?"

"About your other roommate."

"Un-uh," the black woman no-ed. "Already told it all to the fuzz. No more. You a cop?"

"I'm with the insurance company. Come to help the poor family pick up the pieces of their shattered lives. Money can't do anything to ease the sorrow of a loved one's passing, but isn't it nice to know that you don't have to be a burden on your family when you die? Do you have insurance? I'll sell you some."

"Don' need no insurance. Ain't got no family to be burdening. Just put me in a pine box and lower me into the ground. No muss, no fuss, no bother. And no talk. Good-bye."

"Can I have coffee, then? While I think of something else?"

"Yo' dime."

She swished away to pour him coffee from the large metal urn in the center of the diner's long counter. She swished nicely and was good to look at.

She put the cup down in front of him and moved containers of milk, sugar and Sweet'n Low in front of him.

"Forget the insurance. I just want to find out who killed Tony Armitage."

"I tell it all to the police." She pronounced it PO-lice. "I got nothin' to say to you. Get it from the PO-lice."

"I read what you told the cops. I didn't seen it say anywhere that you two were lovers."

"Nobody asked. I'm not talking to you no more."

"What soured it up?" Trace pressed.

"Who said something did?"

"Your other roommate. Jack and the Beanstalk."

"Phillie talk too much."

"Just tell me what busted it up and I'll leave."

"Nothing busted it up. We met, we liked each other's looks, we crawled into the sack. It was good for a while and then it wasn't good anymore, so we crawled out of the sack and moved along. Don't have to be mo' than that, you know."

"I know," Trace said. "It's one of the endearing things about feminism."

"What is?"

"It made it so much easier to get women into the bed."

"A typical, dumb, narrow-minded, sexist view," she said.

"Good," he said.

"What's good?"

"That you finally stopped shucking and jiving and talking to me like some Harlem street urchin. I knew if I worked at it long enough, I'd get you talking English."

"It's a shame sometimes to shatter people's illusions," the tall light-skinned woman said. "They like to hear me all cool and jazzy with hidden darknesses in my daytime soul. Yassuh, yassuh, yassuh, indeed. Help send that little pickaninny to college, gets her that edjOO-cation. Gets big tips. Oooooh, thank yo', Mr. Charley."

"Well, stow it with me," Trace said.

"Don't have to, since I'm not talking to you anymore anyway." She walked away.

Trace noticed a black man in a booth at the diner's far end, watching him. The man was big, with a shaved skull; he looked like a brown bullet.

A young man came into the diner and sat at the far end of the counter. He must have known Jennie because she leaned over and talked to him for a few moments. She poured him a cup of coffee, then took two packs of Sweet'n Low from the pocket of her light-green waitress's uniform and set them in front of him.

Trace concentrated on drinking his coffee. He had certainly screwed up this interview, he thought. Usually he had no trouble making people talk to him, but somehow he had rubbed the young black woman the wrong way. Dumb, he thought to himself. He had just been dumb.

He looked up as the young man took a sip from his coffee, then got up and walked from the diner. He had left several bills in front of him and Jennie picked them up, tucked them into the top pocket of her uniform, and cleaned up the space where he had been sitting.

She looked at Trace when she was done, shrugged, then walked back to him.

"You want more coffee?" she said.

"No. Here." He took a business card from his wallet and on the back of it wrote his room number at the Plaza. "I'm there if you change your mind and want to talk to me. Might save everybody a lot of trouble."

"I don't have any trouble," she said. She took the card.

Trace said, "LaPeter says talk to him about the rent."

"Thank you. I will."

"When you call me, if a woman answers, don't hang up. That's only my mother. We always travel together."

"That's sweet," she said, and slipped the card into the top pocket of her uniform along with her tips. "Tell her not to wait up for my call."

The black man rose from the booth and walked down the counter to them.

"Jennie. Everything all right?"

"Sure, Barker, sure."

"This face bothering you?" he asked, nodding toward Trace but not deigning to look at him.

She shook her head.

"Then why he jawin' so much?" Barker demanded.

"He just one of those who like to talk."

"That's right," Trace said. "I'm just one of those who likes to talk."

"I wasn't talking to you," the black man said.

"Too bad," Trace said. "We might have had a nice conversation and wound up being real good friends. Friends are forever, don't you think?"

"I think you some kind of wise ass. Ain't you, boy?"

"That's right. Boy," Trace said.

Barker started toward him, but Jennie stretched across the counter and grabbed his sleeve.

"He's leaving, Barker. Right now."

Barker looked at her, then at Trace. Trace took out his wallet again and dropped a dollar onto the counter, then took his time about standing up.

"Well, if he's leaving . . ." Barker said.

"For now," Trace said. "Just for now. See you, Jennie."

"No, you won't."

"Don't you come back here," Barker said.

"I'll see you again too," Trace said to him.

Driving back up the Merritt Parkway, Trace opened his pack and counted his cigarettes. There were six left. He had smoked only fourteen so far that day, when normally he would have smoked forty by then. He was very proud of himself and stopped at a roadside pay phone to call Chico and tell her.

She answered the phone after a couple of rings and told Trace she'd been in the shower.

"I only smoked fourteen cigarettes so far today," he said.

"Is that good?"

"That's a reduction of two-thirds in my normal amount."

"All right. Fair. I expect better tomorrow," she said.

"Pain in the ass," he said. "Hold on." He lit another cigarette for spite. "Hear from Sarge?" he asked.

"No. And no messages."

"Did you spend a lot of money today?"

"Not too bad. Less than I'd spend back home. Eighteen guys tried to pick me up at Bloomie's. That's the biggest singles bar in the world, Trace."

"Any of them get lucky?"

"All eighteen. I made a dollar eighty. Six of them are still here."

"Are we going to have dinner tonight or did you already make a date?"

"We'll have dinner, you and me. I don't think any of these guys would be prepared to see me eat at this stage of our relationships."

"I'll be there in a little while. Clear the room before I get there."

"We'll all be done by then," she said.

Chico insisted that Trace exercise some more before they went to dinner, but he held the day by insisting that twelve pushups were certainly ample for a man who had not exercised in fifteen years. He promised to do thirteen the next day.

Sunset had brought another break in the day's stifling heat and they walked the half-dozen blocks to Chez Nick. The maître d' smiled at them as they came in and Trace said, "Pierre, it's good to see you again."

"It's George, sir."

"That's right. Pierre's your twin brother."

"Do you have a reservation tonight, Mister . . . Mister . . ."

"Tell him my name," Trace told Chico because he couldn't remember the name he'd used before.

"Rascali," she said. "Luigi Rascali."

"Right," Trace said. "We don't have reservations yet."

"I'm afraid there'll be a little wait tonight," George said. "Perhaps an hour."

"That's fine," Trace said. "We'll wait in the disco. I find the music very soothing before meals."

"Very good, sir."

"Good," Chico said as they walked down the stairs. The thumping sound swelled as they got nearer the bottom double doors. Trace thought it was like being a bacterium traveling toward the nerve of a tooth. "I love discos," she said. "I'm even dressed right."

"You planned this, didn't you? You checked and found out there would be a long wait and so you wore your Disco Dolly dress so you could drag me on the floor and embarrass me, in front of my inferiors. Tell the truth."

"You're a suspicious thing," she said. Trace pushed open the doors. His ears were pounded by noise that seemed to come from everywhere. Lights flashed around the walls and the ceiling and the floor. Throbbing along in counterpoint to the thump of the electronic music was a general din of people shouting, trying to be heard.

They stood inside the door.

Trace said, "How can you stand this place with all this noise?"

"What?" Chico said.

"How can you stand all this noise?" Trace asked again.

"I can't hear you."

"I know. You've got a banana in your ear. Never mind." He began to pantomime. "Me. Drink. Lots of drinks. Get sick. Throw up. Hide in toilet. Quiet there maybe."

"Let's dance," she said, uncomprehending.

"You dance. Me drink," he said very slowly. "Drink. Now. Dance. Later."

She nodded and pointed toward a raised platform at the far end of the room where there was a bar and a scattering of cocktail tables.

As they walked toward it, Trace swiped two cocktail napkins from an empty table, wadded them up, and stuck them in his ears.

They folded their bodies around a small table, and before they had a chance to take a breath, a waitress stood in front of them, demanding their order. "Wine for me. Perrier for the lady," Trace shouted. The waitress seemed to have no trouble hearing. She nodded and walked away.

Trace talked right into Chico's ear.

"How can you stand this noise?"

She tried to talk back into his ear, saw the cocktail napkins stuck in them, and pulled them out.

"Idiot. I grew up in them," she said.

"Why didn't it affect your brain?" he shouted.

"I don't know. It's nice sometimes to come to one of these places and do something like this. Mindless. Turn off your brain. Dance. Do drugs. You don't have to talk to anybody because you can't hear them."

"People who go every night"—he waved toward the dance floor—"they're zombies, right?"

"Right. But some of them dance real well."

"Oh. Well, that's all right, then. As long as they dance well, who cares if they're vegetables or not. Chez Nick, the home of the dancing rutabaga. Really, woman, where's your taste?"

"Trace, I dance with them sometimes. I don't take them home to Mother."

Their drinks came. A glass of wine and a bottle of Perrier cost twelve dollars. Trace gave the waitress fifteen.

"Nice place you bring me to," he told Chico. "Twelve dollars for two drinks and one of them that water that Frenchmen do unspeakable things to." He sipped his wine. "God, I hate this shit."

"Have a real drink if it'll make you feel better. I'm tired of your being grouchy. Have a cigarette too."

"No way. You're just trying to weasel out of having to pay me that five hundred dollars when you lose your bet. You notice anything going on?"

"Besides the drug dealing at the bar?" she said.

"How the hell did you spot that so fast?" he asked.

"Generation gap," Chico said. "People my age were born with the knowledge of how to score drugs."

Trace was watching a man at the bar. He had long dark hair and a Fu Manchu mustache. He wore bright plaid trousers and a matching vest, and a white shirt, open at the throat, with puffy ballooning sleeves.

A blonde had just walked up to him and he had slipped his hand into her purse. She, in turn, put a bill on the bar, then walked away.

Chico said softly into Trace's ear. "Another transaction completed. I love a guy who knows how to close the deal."

"I don't want to hear about it."

The man at the bar turned back to his drink. Less than a minute later, the scene was replayed, this time with a young man in multicolored matching pants and shirt, with an army bush jacket over them. Again, the money onto the bar, as if to buy a drink, and then Fu Manchu's hand slipping into the pocket of the bush jacket.

Trace watched the young man walk away, but lost him as he blended with the mob of people milling about the dance floor in wild gyrations that reminded Trace of the sacrifice scene in the original *King Kong*.

"Lost him," he said.

"Going to the men's room," Chico said.

"If everybody who buys stuff is in that men's room, it's a fire hazard."

"That's why they have big bathrooms in these places. Didn't you ever notice? Well, no, you've never been here. They have all kinds of counter space and room, so all the nose-candy people have room to work."

"I hate it when you know more about things than I do," Trace said.

"Your days must be filled with nothing but unending grief," she said.

Trace looked around the dance floor for a while, then brought his gaze back toward the bar. As he did, a door in the corner behind the bar opened and he caught a glimpse of a black man walking inside. The heavy door closed quickly behind him.

The waitress came up to their table and Trace ordered two more drinks.

"Is that the office back there?" he asked, pointing.

The waitress nodded.

"Who's the black guy who just went in?"

"I don't know," she said, and walked quickly away.

Their drinks came. The music continued to crush against his skull.

"Want to dance?"

Trace looked up. The man standing at their table was one of the two men he had seen sitting upstairs, talking to Armitage the night before, and who had then followed him and Chico back to the hotel. He was wearing another striped three-piece suit and was standing close enough so Trace could count the acne scars on his face.

The other man was standing, with his back to the bar, ten feet away, watching them. When his eyes met Trace's, he smiled and cracked his knuckles.

"Not really. Thanks anyway," Chico said.

"People usually come here to dance. I thought maybe your friend here was too old to dance." He nodded at Trace but didn't look at him.

"No," Chico said again. "I just don't feel like dancing."

"I bet you could dance real good with me if you wanted to. I'll get them to play slow music, so we can hold each other."

Chico turned away from him, toward Trace.

"Come on, lady," the man said again. He turned to Trace, "Come on, old-timer, help me out."

"The lady said she didn't want to dance."

"That was with you. Not somebody younger," he said.

"Buzz off, beanbag," Trace said.

"What? What'd you say?"

Before Trace could answer, Chico slid out from her seat. "Come on. Sure, we'll dance. Right now. Let's get it on." She grabbed his arm.

He tried to pull away, but she held tight and yanked him toward the floor. "I'll be back to continue our conversation," the man said to Trace in a half-shout.

"I'll wait for you," Trace said. He saw the other man leave the bar and come over toward his table. He stood there looking down at Trace.

"I heard what you said to my brother."

He was wearing an identical suit and his face was as swarthy and as scarred. Maybe they were twins, Trace thought.

"Well, if it isn't Tweedledee. Or are you Tweedledum? Or don't you remember?"

"I heard what you called my brother. I don't like smartasses. You better stand up."

"What for? You're just going to try to knock me back down, so why get up?"

"Because if you don't, I'll hit you while you're sitting down."

Trace sighed. "Well, then, I guess maybe I ought to get up." He started to his feet, just as Chico returned.

"Time to go, Trace," she said.

The man at the table turned toward her, and as he did, Trace punched out his lights. A hard left in the belly doubled him over and then a chopping right hand onto the side of the temple pitched him forward onto his knees. He hit the floor, the top half of his body lying across the seat of a chair.

"Your right hand's getting better," Chico said as she took Trace's arm and led him away.

"That one was pretty good," Trace said. "Where's his clone?"

"Last I saw him, he was rolling around on the floor, holding the family jewels."

"You didn't."

"I did. I kneed him in the groin. Hard. Teach him not to try feeling up a dancer," Chico said. "But I still think we ought to get out of here before the cavalry arrives."

"Hai, Michiko-san," Trace said.

On the steps going upstairs, leaving the loud raucous music behind, Trace said, "On the whole, I think we might plan on eating elsewhere tonight."

"It'd better be soon. I'm starved," she said. "Fighting always brings out my appetite."

Upstairs, Trace told the maître d', "Pierre, please cancel our reservations tonight. And my best regards to your brother, George."

They started to walk back toward their hotel, but when a cab came down the street, Trace hailed it.

"In case our friends follow us," Trace explained to Chico.

The driver grumbled when Trace said he wanted to go to the Plaza. "For Jeez sakes, buddy, it's only six blocks."

"That's right. In only six blocks, you won't have us to kick around anymore."

"You don't make no money on no six-block fare," the driver said.

"Usually you make more than you do with an empty cab. Look at it this way. Don't consider us fares. Just think of us as old friends that you just happened to meet on the street and we're spending a few happy moments together before we all go our separate ways again, okay?"

The driver said, "Aaaaaah."

Trace said to Chico, "Some people just can't stand being cheered up."

"Cheer me up by feeding me. God, I'm hungry."

"Must be two hours now since your last feeding," Trace said.

"Don't complain. Think how tough it would be

if I were a drinker. God, that'd eat up the money, wouldn't it?"

"You gonna get out or not?" the driver snapped as he stopped across the street from the Plaza.

Trace told the driver that normally he was a big tipper, but since the driver was so rude, Trace was tipping him only a small amount. He asked Chico, "What's five percent of two dollars and forty cents?"

"Twelve cents," she said.

"All right. Two forty and twelve. Two-fifty-two. Driver, do you have change of a nickel?"

"No."

"Well, here. Take the whole two-fifty-five."

"Thanks a lot, pal," the driver said sarcastically as he took the money.

"Hold on. You got a receipt? This is tax-deductible."

The driver snarled again and drove away.

Trace yelled after him, "I've got your license plate, mister. You won't get away with this."

Chico said, "Why do you bust people's chops like that? Is it because you're not drinking and smoking so much anymore?"

"No. It's New York. It brings out something in me. They're all such assholes in this city. They're surly and rude and stupid, but they believe their own press agents. The Big Apple. Wow, man, like wow, so they think they're better and smarter than anybody else, and that's crap. They're jerk-offs and I like to remind them of it once in a while. Just repayment for all the poor little people from Dubuque that they terrorize."

"Enough of the big thoughts for the evening," she said. "Feed me."

"My delight and my pleasure," he said.

They walked a block and a half away from the Plaza to a small corner restaurant. Trace left Chico to order for both of them while he found a telephone and called Sarge's home. When there was no answer, he called his father's office. No answer there either, and on a hunch, he called the restaurant downstairs from the office, but Sarge had not been in since lunchtime, he was told.

When he returned to the table, Chico had finished the rolls in front of her and was eating Trace's. The woman ate like a tapeworm farm, Trace thought, wondering how she did it and still managed to stay tiny and thin. She had been a dancer most of her life, and exercise kept her body supple and strong. But a normal person could exercise twenty hours a day and still get obese on Chico's diet. It must be genetic, he thought, some secret message stamped into her genes that dictated that her furnace burn hotter and brighter than anyone else's and burn up food before it turned to fat. Maybe he would get her to pose for a before-and-after photo, to promote his new diet plan using those pictures of all those degenerates he had seen on the wall of that restaurant near Sarge's office. Get a picture of some fat Japanese woman and call it before. Take a picture of Chico and call it after. It'd make him a million.

"Couldn't reach Sarge," he said. His voice must have sounded depressed, because she said, "Not much of a day for you, I guess." Her voice was sympathetic, but not so much that she would let go of the last of the rolls she held in her hand.

"Not much," he agreed. "It started off bad with Sarge getting me up in the middle of the night, just when I thought I was going to make it with you. And then there was that woman. She just rubbed me wrong somehow."

"What woman?"

"Martha Armitage. The one Sarge set up the meeting with."

"You don't know why she rubbed you wrong?" Chico shook her head. Her long black hair splashed about her shoulders.

"No."

"You're not terribly smart, are you?"

"As a general rule, no, but specifically in this case, what are you talking about?"

"How did Sarge treat her?" Chico asked.

"He went downstairs and borrowed plants for the office, for crying out loud. He swept and threw out the old newspapers. The *Playboy* girls came off the wall. He went and bought a real coffeecup."

"Sounds like a boy getting ready for a date, doesn't it?" she said.

He looked at her for a long while before wrinkling his brow quizzically and asking, "What are you getting at?"

"Sarge and Martha Armitage," she said.

"Oh, come on, Sarge is my father."

"Since when's your name Jesus and his Joseph?" she said.

"Nonsense. She's too young for him anyway. I don't know where you get these ideas," Trace said.

"Have it your own way," Chico said with a lighthearted shrug of the shoulders. "It doesn't mean anything to me."

They fell silent when the waiter came with their food. There were two appetizers, a shrimp cocktail and fried mushrooms.

"The shrimp cocktail goes to Madame?" the waiter asked.

Chico nodded. The waiter put down the plate, then stepped over to put the mushrooms in front of Trace.

"I'll have those too," Chico said. "He's on a diet," she explained.

"Very good, ma'am," the waiter said, setting down the dish.

After he left, Trace said, "So just what do you have to base that ridiculous theory on?"

"If I start to answer you, you're going to complain that I'm talking with my mouth full again."

"I will not."

"You always do."

"This time I won't," Trace promised. "Talk. Eat but talk."

"Okay. Yesterday at the Plaza, when Sarge mentioned that woman's name—what's her name, Martha?—I saw his face. I saw right away from the look on his face."

"What kind of a look?" Trace asked.

"It wasn't a macho look," Chico said. "That's what you'd usually see with some guy when an old flame's name was mentioned. It's the way men are. They always talk about being able to keep secrets, but what they mean is that they don't say anything. They don't have to. Their faces give everything away. Everybody knows everybody that any man has ever slept with. That's a fact and that's the way men are. You too. I always know. But Sarge is ... well, he's a better man than most. There was kind of an embarrassed look on his face when her name came up, maybe a little guilty. It was different, but it was just as foolproof. He and whatever her name is were a thing, sometime, somewhere. I've seen that look two hundred times."

"Got guilt on his face? He ought to have guilt on his face. If you're right, he was cheating on my mother."

"Hey, pardner, save that," Chico said. "I've met your mother. I'd be on Sarge's side for anything up to and including homicide. Want a shrimp?"

"No."

"Good," she said as she plunked the last in her mouth and pulled the plate of mushrooms toward her. "I'm going to ask you now if you want a mushroom."

"I don't," Trace said. "You've just told me that my father is a philanderer and now you're trying to talk me into a mushroom?"

"One. I didn't say that Sarge is a philanderer. I said he had an affair with Mrs. Armitage. Two. I want to know now if you want a mushroom because I know you and you'll ask for one just when I have only one left and I hate to give the last one away."

"I won't ask for any," Trace said. "You're sure, aren't you?"

"I'm sure. It's my special field of study," she said. "And today, that whole act in the office—plants, clean cups, sweep—what do you think that was all about?"

"Well, I don't like it," Trace said.

"It's not for you to like or not like. What the hell's wrong with you? Did you think you were the product of immaculate conception? Don't you think your father ever crawled into the sack with anybody?"

"I don't have your cavalier attitude toward extramarital sex, I guess," he said.

She sputtered mushroom bits over the table. "You sanctimonious hypocrite," she said. "I can give you the names of at least a dozen married women you have bopped in the last twelve months."

"That was different," he said.

"Why?"

"Because I'm not my father."

"I give up," she said.

"You're spoiling my meal. What did you order for me anyway?"

"A grilled cheese sandwich."

"I hope you didn't get tomato on it. I hate

tomato on grilled cheese. Only Philistines mix tomatoes and cheese."

"No tomato."

"What are you having?" he asked.

"I'm having a steak and things."

"Okay. Let's stick to food and drop that other subject."

"Fine. I'd much rather eat," Chico said.

Trace had a terrible desire to order a double vodka on the rocks, but he ordered a carafe of wine and drank it by himself while watching Chico eat. He nibbled at his cheese sandwich but had lost his appetite.

When they got back to their room, Trace again called Sarge's home and office numbers but got no answer.

"No answer from Sarge," he said. "I'm starting to worry."

"So he's out. He's a big boy," she said.

"What did you mean by that?"

"Mean? I mean that he is big and grown up and why are you worrying about him as if he's a child?"

"Because, dammit, he's probably out getting laid. With women he picks up on the street. I don't know what he's up to, but I'm sure it's no good."

Chico sighed. "I'm going to sleep," she said.

Trace sighed, too. "Maybe I will later. If I can."

12

Tape Recording Number Two in the murder of Tony Armitage, Plaza Hotel, midnight, Thursday.

Something hangs heavy on my heart, Miss Crabtree. I feel about as much like making this report as I do running and weight lifting and doing pushups and gourmet cooking and not drinking enough and not smoking enough to even sustain a morning cough. My life has gone to hell in a hand basket.

Trusting other people's judgment is not good. Like I trust Chico's judgment and she says Sarge and Martha Armitage had an affair, and I guess she's right and I don't like it one little bit.

And where is he now? He's never home anymore when I call. While my poor mother is suffering away the days and nights in Las Vegas, losing money at her specified rate of two dollars in nickels each and every hour, no more than five hours a day.

I'm very disappointed in you, Sarge.

I guess somehow I never thought of my father being involved with anybody physically. Except my mother. And that doesn't count. That's a romantic act, I don't know, kind of on a par with docking a steamship in New York. A series of intricate maneuvers to be accomplished as rapidly and with as little excitement as possible.

I guess I'm overreacting. Do other people think about one of their parents making it with somebody? I don't know. Maybe people don't. Maybe I'm just one of the few, cursed by being half-Jewish, condemned to a life of worrying about things that are none of my business. Maybe it's part of my becoming a big thinker with big thoughts about life and love and parenting and family.

My two kids. What's-his-name and the girl. Do they ever think of me in bed with somebody? Do they ever consider that I'm off rutting around with some Eurasian beauty? Yeah, I'm sure they do. I think that Madame Defarge doesn't miss a chance to tell them that their father is a degenerate. Maybe they're too young to care about degenerates. How old are they anyway? I don't know. The girl is something and What's-his-name is older. Or at least he's bigger, the last time I saw him. I wish I knew their birthdays, if they have birthdays. Maybe they're a year older on January first, like horses. I'll have to ask my mother. She keeps track of trivia like that. What else does she have to do beside being a cuckoldette?

I'm going to put this out of my mind. I'm not going to think of my father, the philanderer. Instead I'm going to do what I'm supposed to be doing here. Working.

So I met Martha Armitage today at Sarge's office. I'm glad I was there because if I hadn't been, they probably would have groped each other on the office floor. Splinters would serve them right.

I've got a whole bunch of tapes in the master file. Not one of them tells me a damn thing. First one is Martha, sweet Martha, flirting with my father in front of my very eyes. So she wants us to look into her son's murder so we can find the killers before her husband does, 'cause he might get into trouble. Okay, I'll buy that. So far so good. What'd she say? That Nick has a memory like an elephant? And he's looking for the killers. Well, I wish he'd find them fast so we could get the hell out of here and Martha can get back the hell out of Sarge's life. That lady drinks too much. I can tell. First it'll be sex and then she'll have Sarge swilling booze again the way he used to.

So Tony Armitage was a good prelaw student but slipped a little bit last year. I would too. That might have been the year that his roommate bought nine more speakers for his stereo. How the hell could anybody study with that racket going on? Tony had the right idea. Buy junk and gimmicks and gadgets. Telephone taping machines, nonsense that breaks right away and nobody wants. Anything but that screaming rock music. It's funny, I used to kind of like rock 'n' roll. But I must have liked the roll part because now they just call it rock and I hate it all.

Anyway, so Tony and Phil and Jennie led a very platonic existence, his mother said, which Phil told me was a lot of bullshit because Tony was porking Jennie for a while. And then it stopped. Why? Well, I'll get to her.

Nick didn't let Tony come to the nightclub and Tony didn't use drugs, his mother said. And again, bullshit. Phil said that he and Tony used grass. At least, that's what he admitted to. Who knows what else they might really have used? Maybe the murderers didn't load Tony's body up with that Quaalude crap. Maybe he took it himself.

Parents don't know crap about their children. And considering the revelations of the last couple of hours, maybe children don't know anything about their parents, and especially their wayward fathers.

Get off that, Trace. Stick to business.

Tony was wearing the mask when he was killed, but nobody knows anything about that mask.

Dead, one bullet through the heart. And the mask could have come from anywhere. Shot between midnight and one A.M.

And the Connecticut faggot cops said that Tony had no enemies, no reports of using drugs, and that both his roommates had been out of town. How convenient.

Sarge says that Armitage isn't really a mob guy, or at least not anymore. So he doesn't think the kid was killed as some kind of move in a mob game. I believe him too. They wouldn't put Richard Nixon masks on the kid. It'd be, you know, bullets in the eyes and mouth, the mark of the squealer. Anyway, Sarge is going to keep checking with cops around to see if anybody's got it in for Nick Armitage. We'll see. That's if Sarge drops the romance long enough to work.

The scene of the crime in Connecticut told me nothing. It never does. I don't know why I bother.

I've got a tape of Phil LaPeter, Tony's roommate, impresario of noise and first person I ever met who didn't have a first language. I will never, ever go to West Virginia for any reason. I could spend years there and not understand a word anybody said.

LaPeter is renting Tony's room. Nothing wrong with that, I suppose. The rent's got to be paid. They were friends, he said, and I guess so because they lived together in that house for a couple of years. So Tony played around with Jennie for a while and then it didn't last long, LaPeter said. A couple of months maybe. LaPeter gave me the names of the people he was in the Poconos with, but I'm not going to check them.

That's FBI work. They've got thousands of people who can do that stuff. If he gave them to me, they're real enough. I won't waste time. But Tony gave him the money for the concert at the last minute. I wonder if that meant anything. Why didn't he give it to him before when LaPeter was grousing that he wouldn't be able to go because he couldn't afford it?

I don't know.

LaPeter met Nick and the two bookend goons from Nick's place. What'd he say? Let me think. Nick wanted to talk about Tony and his other friends and stuff like that, more than the murder. I find that passing odd.

And LaPeter never saw that mask and Tony didn't belong to any clubs.

I got the feeling that LaPeter didn't really care all that much for Jennie, and for more reason than that her moving into the apartment cost him a room for his studio and now he has to work in his bedroom. When I saw that she was black, that explained it. I think LaPeter is a little too much of the hillbilly soil to welcome living in close quarters with a black woman.

She has, by the way, been staying somewhere else. There's nothing much in her closet at the house. Unless she spends all her time in waitress uniforms, she's got her clothes stashed in some other apartment.

Unfortunately, I was unable to find out where because the lady in question seemed to take an irrational dislike to me and refused to talk to me.

She said she told everything she was going to tell to the PO-lice. Well, at least I got her to stop using that Stepin Fetchit accent with me. Maybe that's a first small step. If I keep after it, winning her confidence slowly, maybe in five or ten years she'll give me the time of day along with the little container of Sweet'n Low for my coffee.

I will be satisfied, however, if she does not give my name to that big dude in the diner who wanted to crease my skull because I was talking to her. I don't want to see him again. Although I think, maybe I did. Tonight, at Nick Armitage's disco dump and drug supply house.

Anyway, there was some black guy walking into the office and not five minutes later there were those two morons again, trying to pick a fight with me. The nerve of that one. Insulting my dancing. He's lucky he didn't see me on the floor. DISCO DEVLIN RETURNS TO ACTION. WOWS CROWD AT CHEZ NICK. ROBBINS OFFERS LIFETIME CONTRACT.

I'd show him.

Unfortunately, I didn't get much of a chance to before Chico disabled him with a well-placed knee to the gentles. And I cold-cocked the other one. Somehow I don't think Luigi Rascali is going to get a warm reception at Chez Nick's anymore, not even from Pierre, the maître d', or his twin brother George.

I got the two goons on tape and Jennie Teller too.

So then we got out of Chez Nick and I fed Chico and she filled my head with all that crap about my father and Martha Armitage, and I don't want to talk about it anymore.

I think tomorrow I'm going to talk to the Armitage family. I am tired of pussy-footing around. I'm turning this tape off and going to bed. It is two A.M. and I don't know where my father is.

13

The Armitages lived in one of those Upper West Side apartment houses that rich people were always being assassinated in front of.

A uniformed doorman detained Trace in the lobby while he called the Armitages' apartment on the intercom.

"It's a Mr. Devlin Tracy. Something to do with insurance," he said. He put his hand over the mouthpiece of the phone and told Trace, "You'll have to wait for a minute."

"You don't have a bottle of vodka around, do you?"

"No, sir."

Trace shrugged. "I thought it'd make the time go faster." He really felt like a drink. As part of his self-improvement program, he had done one pushup thirteen times and delayed his first morning cigarette until after he had gotten out of bed; he had decided that the change in life-style was making him cranky and miserable. Perhaps he was trying too much too fast. Perhaps he should spend all the years until age fifty cutting down on his drinking, and then the next ten getting his smoking under control. Plenty of time after that to worry about exercise. He would suggest that to Chico when he saw her next. Then he thought of the five-hundred-dollar prize she had offered him if he stuck to the regimen. It would be the first time he had ever, in any way, gotten any money out of her. He decided he would stick with the plan a little longer.

He heard the doorman say, "Very well. Thank you."

He hung up and handed Trace back his business card. "You can go right up, Mr. Tracy. It's Penthouse Suite A." He looked at Trace as if wondering why he had gotten through where others had failed and Trace said, "I give away free digital stick-on clocks with every insurance policy. Nobody can resist them. You want one?"

"No, thank you."

"Your loss. We're down to our last seven million, and when they're gone, that's it. Taiwan's not making them anymore."

"Oh?"

"They're going back to making Taiwanese."

"Oh."

The door to the apartment was opened by a pretty, young blond maid wearing a milk-chocolate-brown uniform. She had little laugh lines in the corners of her eyes and a broad expressive mouth and bright brown eyes whose makeup matched the color of her uniform. Her accent when she greeted him was crisp, clipped, and British.

"I'm Devlin Tracy. I was piped aboard," he said.

"Mrs. Armitage is expecting you." She closed the door behind him. "Would you walk this way?"

She led him down a long hall and Trace looked at her hips and said, softly so only she could hear, "If I walked that way, I'd dislocate my hip."

She looked over her shoulder and smiled at him, the well-practiced smile of a young woman used to being appreciated.

"Thank you, I guess. Madam is on the balcony."

"If we hurry," Trace said, "maybe we can get there in time to save her."

The maid giggled. She turned left from the hallway into a theater-size living room. It wouldn't have surprised Trace if a string and flute quartet had been practicing in one corner of the room. Next to the living room was a formal dining room, only half its size, but still bigger than the first floors of most private homes.

This was one of the only two ways to live reasonably in New York, he decided. Be very rich, where you didn't have to worry about parking fees for your car or where to buy gasoline or get your snow tires changed, and could afford to have people do it all for you. The very rich could live in Manhattan. And so could the very poor because the government made it possible for them to survive. Everyone in the middle lost. He reached behind him and turned on his hidden tape recorder.

They made another left turn.

"Should I leave a trail of beans so I can find my way back out?" Trace asked, then saw Martha Armitage. It was like a scene from a Hollywood movie. She sat at a glass-topped table on a large balcony that overlooked Central Park and Trace's hotel a half-mile or so in the distance. New York's broad avenues, from this distance, removed from the horn honking and the creative swearing, looked beautiful and Parisian instead of maniacal and ugly.

Mrs. Armitage was wearing a satin robe in the color of Homer's wine-dark sea. A breakfast plate was laid out in front of her. Trace again thought she was very beautiful and she responded to his thought by giving a very beautiful smile to him and the maid.

"This is Mr. Tracy, ma'am," the maid said.

"Thank you, Cheryl."

"Yes, thank you, Cheryl," Trace said.

"How do you do, Mr. Tracy? Please sit down. Would you have some breakfast?"

"Just coffee," Trace said.

Mrs. Armitage nodded to Cheryl, finished her orange juice, and handed the maid the glass. "Coffee for Mr. Tracy and would you please make me another orange juice?"

Cheryl took the glass and was off like a shot as Trace sat down across from Mrs. Armitage. He wondered again if Chico had been right. Had this woman and Sarge gotten it on together? She was certainly beautiful enough to have been worth the effort, he thought. Her beautiful eyes looked around warily.

Martha lowered her voice. "I'm glad you came, Devlin. Of course, this is the first time we've met."

He didn't like her calling him Devlin, as if she were already a member of the family, but he just nodded and said nothing. He noticed she was wearing a lot less makeup than on the previous day, and her hands had ceased their nervous fluttering.

"How are you doing?" she asked. "Any progress?"

"Not much. Is your husband here? It's really him I was hoping to see."

"He's sleeping. He generally works late hours, you know. But if he's not up soon, I'll call him, although I don't know exactly what kind of reception you're going to get."

"Warm, I think," Trace said. "I usually get warm receptions. People like me a lot."

"I wouldn't have thought so. I'm happy to be proved wrong," Martha said.

Cheryl swished back onto the balcony with a small porcelain coffeecup and saucer and a matching pot of coffee which she placed in front of Trace. She put down a large water tumbler of light-colored orange juice in front of the woman. Martha picked up the glass and drank half of it greedily, then said, "That'll be all, Cheryl."

Trace wondered for a moment what he was doing there. It had seemed important the night before to talk to the Armitages, but he began to think that maybe he had just wanted to see Martha again, just to satisfy his curiosity. He was about to ask her when she had met Sarge when Nick Armitage, wearing trousers and a white shirt opened at his thick bull neck, came onto the balcony.

"Who's this?" he asked his wife brusquely.

"Oh, Nick. I'm glad you're up. This is Mr. Tracy from the insurance company."

Armitage looked coldly at Trace, then said, "I know you, don't I?"

"We met at your club the night before last," Trace said.

"You didn't call yourself Tracy then."

"No."

"What'd you call yourself?"

"I forget," Trace said honestly.

"Why? Why use a different name?"

"I thought it'd get me a better table," Trace said.

"I don't think I like you," Armitage said.

"You made that clear when you sent your two morons to follow us back to our hotel."

"Oh." Armitage was obviously surprised that Trace had spotted the men. "Well, what do you want here?"

"Mr. Tracy is looking into Tony's death," Martha interjected.

"Let him talk for himself, Martha," Armitage snapped. The man had made no attempt to shake Trace's hand and now he pulled a chair back

112

from the table as if to keep his distance, turned it around, and sat with his arms folded against the back of the chair, staring at Trace.

"What do you want here?" he repeated.

"You like some coffee?" Trace said. "Maybe it'll improve your mood."

"My mood's fine. Or it will be as soon as you get out of here. I'll ask you only one more time. What are you nosing around for?"

"Insurance," Trace said. "Before we pay, we look into the death."

"So, you've been looking into. You find anything with all your looking into?"

"Not much."

"I didn't expect so," Armitage said. "Cops didn't find anything, you wouldn't find anything."

"You never know. Sometimes we get lucky."

"Look. I don't care what you people do. Pay the money, don't pay the money, I don't give a damn. My lawyer handles that crap anyway. But why don't you just get out of our lives? My wife doesn't need this and I don't need it. Someday I'll find out who killed Tony."

"And?"

"And I'll take care of it my own way."

"What does that mean?" Trace asked.

"Anything you want it to mean."

"Until then, why don't you humor me? Let me ask a couple of questions."

"Go ahead," Martha said quickly.

Trace glanced at her. The food on the plate in front of her was cold and untouched, but she had finished her glass of orange juice.

"And then you'll get out of here?" Armitage said.

Trace nodded.

"Go ahead. Make it quick."

"That mask your son was wearing. Did either of you ever see it before?"

113

"No," Mrs. Armitage said.

Her husband looked disgusted and shook his head.

"You never heard him mention it?" Trace asked.

"No."

"Not even in a joke?" Trace said. "Chuckles. Ho, ho, costume party, guess-what-I'm-wearing kind of talk?"

"I said no," Armitage said. "Move it along." He took an untouched cup of coffee from in front of his wife and sipped at it.

"Did your son hang out in your nightclub?"

"No. I didn't like him there."

"Why not? I thought you ran a clean business."

"I run a clean restaurant upstairs. Downstairs is for degenerates. How clean can degenerates be?" Armitage said.

"You don't think much of your customers," Trace said.

"Just enough to take their money."

"You think they're sex fiends? Druggies? Like that?"

"I don't let drugs in my club," Armitage said quickly. "But anybody who wants to be with orangutans jumping around to some kind of weird noise, I don't want my kid hanging out with. So I told him to stay out of the club."

"What did you think of Tony's roommates?" Trace asked. He noticed that Martha Armitage had moved back slightly from the table and folded her arms across her bosom, content to watch and listen, a small placid smile on her face.

"What's to think about?" Armitage said. "The guy's some kind of hillbilly whacko. The *mulanyam*'s all right for a *mulanyam*."

"You didn't like her because she was black?"

"Take it or leave it," Armitage said with a shrug.

"Is that why you dumped on Tony, because he was sleeping with her?"

"Who told you that?"

"It doesn't matter," Trace said.

"Well, it's not true. He wasn't going to marry her, was he? He wants to dip his wick anywhere he wants, let him. That's how you grow up," he said.

"You went up and talked to both of the roommates after Tony died. Why'd you do that?"

"Because it looked like the cops weren't getting anywhere. I wanted to know if they knew anything."

"Did they?"

"Not so's you'd notice," Armitage said. "They were both out of town."

"You didn't think that was strange?" Trace asked.

"I don't know. It could have been strange. Maybe not. They both went where they said they went. I checked. Is this getting us anywhere."

"Maybe. Did your son use drugs regularly?"

"What the hell kind of question is that?" Armitage snapped.

"Did your son use drugs regularly?"

"I woulda busted his ass if he did. And I think you've maybe asked enough questions."

"He had Quaaludes in him when he died."

"Somebody put them there. Tony didn't use anything."

"I thought he might have got in with bad people," Trace said. "Drug dealers. Stuff like that."

"No, he didn't and you can stop fishing. I hope you're done now because that's all you get here." He hesitated. "You were with the little slope in the restaurant the other night."

"Mr. Armitage, I'm going to do you two favors."

"What's that?"

"I'm going to make believe I didn't hear that crack because I didn't have a drink yet today and I'm not feeling so good and I might just have to pound it down your face. And second, I'm not going to tell the lady about it because you might just wake up one morning and find your intestines neatly piled on top of your chest."

"Yeah?"

Trace shook his head. If there was anything he hated before he had a drink, it was snappy dialogue. "You might ask your two house idiots."

"What are you talking about?"

"They came after us in the disco last night. She left one of them lying on the floor. He may walk with a limp for a while."

Armitage looked confused and Trace realized he had not been told what had happened the night before. His two muscle men had probably been too embarrassed to let him know.

"Oh," he said.

Cheryl came onto the balcony and handed Armitage a note. He read it, nodded, and put it into his pocket.

"You're going now, Tracy, right?"

"I guess you're not going to invite me to spend the weekend," Trace said.

"You guess right," he said as he rose to his feet. Without a word to Trace or to his wife, he walked from the balcony.

Cheryl still stood there. "I'll show you out, Mr. Tracy," she said.

"Thank you." Trace stood and looked at Martha Armitage. Her face had a confused expression on it, as if she had been subjected to an information overload and was having trouble processing all of it.

"I'll see you again, Mrs. Armitage," Trace said, but the woman just nodded, without looking up to meet his eyes.

As he followed Cheryl through the living room, Trace noticed that a door in the room, disguised to look like one of the room's walnut wall panels, had been left partially open. He moved over toward the center of the room, and when he glanced through the door's opening, he saw reflected, in a mirror on the wall inside the room, the image of Nick Armitage. He had his arms around a woman and was kissing her. He released her and they both stepped out into the living room. The woman looked at Trace with open curiosity.

Trace thought she looked like a younger version of Martha Armitage. She had the same large, wide-set eyes, and although her hair tended more toward red, she had the same snow-white complexion. She was a little shorter, a little more bosomy, and had a wider, fuller mouth.

"Hi," she said.

Trace stopped. "Hello."

She turned to Nick. "You going to introduce me to your friend?"

"He was just leaving," Armitage said.

"Devlin Tracy," Trace said.

"I'm Anna Walker." She reached forward and shook his hand vigorously. "Sure you have to leave? Nick says you're a very interesting conversationalist."

"I think it's leave or be thrown off the balcony," Trace said. "I don't think Mr. Armitage likes me."

"Just go, will you please?" Armitage said.

"Sure. I'll be around." Trace nodded to the woman and followed Cheryl out into the long hallway that led to the front door.

He stopped alongside a small Chippendale table and lighted a cigarette. While he was dropping the match into the ashtray, he noted the number on the telephone atop the table and repeated it softly so that his microphone could pick it up.

"What'd you say?" Cheryl asked.

"Sorry. Just clearing my throat. Who was that?"

"Miss Walker. That's Mrs. Armitage's sister," the maid said.

They were at the door. "I guess this is good-bye, then," Trace said.

"It seems that way, doesn't it?" the maid said.

"What a pity."

"Life is filled with tragedies," she said, biting off the words with her brittle British accent. But she was smiling.

Just then, Martha Armitage came down the hall. "I'll show Mr. Tracy to the elevator, Cheryl."

"Very good, ma'am. I want to finish the grocery list."

She left and Martha walked into the outside hallway with Trace.

As she spoke to him, he realized her voice sounded a little thick, muffled, and slurred.

"Was that true?" she said. "Was Tony sleeping with that black girl?"

"Yes."

"Did Nick break them up?"

"I think so."

"Nick is . . . well, he's very bossy. He pushed Tony very hard," she said. "*He* wanted Tony to be a lawyer."

"What did Tony want to be?"

"I think he just wanted to be young for a while. A lot of people never are." They were at the elevator and she seemed to be looking past Trace, gazing off into space.

She came back to him and said, "It didn't go so well, did it?"

"He's got a short fuse," Trace said.

"I gather you do too," she said.

"Sometimes. Before a morning drink," he said.

She nodded agreement.

"I hope you won't let him stop you," she said. "Please try hard, Devlin. I don't want him to be the first to find out who . . . who killed Tony. It'll be real trouble."

"I know. A memory like an elephant. I'll try to find out. My father and I both will."

"Patrick promised me that last night," she said. "But I wanted to hear you say it."

"You look a lot like your sister," Trace said.

"Anna? Everybody says that."

"Except you're more beautiful."

"They don't all say that," she said.

"What do they know?"

He heard the elevator approaching their floor. A woman came from the floor's other penthouse apartment, hurrying toward the elevator. She was holding a miniature poodle in her arms.

"Thank you, Mr. Tracy, for your trouble," Martha said loudly. "Mr. Armitage and I appreciate it." She turned to the woman and said, "Hello, Mrs. Bentley."

"Hello," the woman sniffed.

The elevator door opened. The dog snarled at Trace as he backed carefully into the elevator.

The July heat slapped across Trace's face as he stepped from the air-conditioned lobby out into New York's humid air. He walked a few steps away from the canopied entrance to the apartment building, then leaned back against the fender of a car to wait. The fender was uncomfortably hot through the fabric of his trousers.

He lit a cigarette and thought that there should be a way to impregnate cigarettes with liquor, so that a person could smoke and drink at the same time. He gave this vision ninety seconds before regarding it as hopeless. If God had wanted there to be a product like that, He never would have invented marijuana.

He heard high heels tapping on the flagstone walk from the apartment building, and a moment later, Cheryl turned up the sidewalk toward him. He tossed his cigarette away, turned on his tape recorder again, and walked over to her. Under her arm, she was carrying a folding grocery basket.

She smiled when she saw him. "Well, well," she said. "Fate's been kind, after all."

"I was just in the neighborhood and thought I'd drop by," Trace said. "Did you know that eighty-one percent of all the women who go grocery shopping in this neighborhood are mugged? And it goes up to ninety-two percent if they're pretty? With you, that makes it a certainty. You're lucky I'm here to protect you."

"I won't be able to pay you," she said.

"Your company is payment enough."

"Keep it up. I love it."

As they strolled down the street, Cheryl asked, "Just what is it you do, Mr. Tracy?"

"My friends call me Trace," he said. "I'm an investigator. I'm looking into Tony Armitage's death."

"I'm afraid I can't help you. I don't know anything about it," she said.

"Well, then, we'll just walk. Did you see Tony much at the apartment?"

"Not generally," she said. "But I work days and I guess he'd be in school most days."

"I guess. Did you like him? When you did see him?"

"He was nice," she said.

"Friendly?" Trace asked.

"Yes."

"Overfriendly?"

She hesitated, then said, "No. Not at all. I have this terrible suspicion that I am being, how do you Americans say it, pumped?"

"I'm sorry. I didn't mean to give that impression," he said. "I'm just trying to find out what kind of a young man he was."

They turned left at the corner. "He seemed to be a nice, friendly young man," she said. "I didn't know him well," she said, but her eyes called her a liar.

"Like his father," Trace said, but the young woman did not comment.

The supermarket was in the middle of the block. Cheryl said, "I'll have to leave now. I have a lot of shopping to do."

"I was going to offer to take you to lunch," he said.

"I'm afraid not."

"Dinner?"

"Perhaps sometime," she said.

"Good. That's better than a 'no.' "

"Have a nice day, Mr. Tracy," she said, turning away.

He touched her arm gently. "How do I reach you?" he asked. "For dinner?"

"Just wait in front of that car by the apartment. I pass by every day," she said with a smile.

"Fine," he said. "If you need me, I'm in room thirteen-seventeen at the Plaza."

"Very good."

"It's Devlin Tracy," he said. "Call me Trace."

"I'll remember," she said, and walked into the store.

Sarge was at the bar in the restaurant below his office. The dining room was filled with a lunchtime crowd from a fashion-design school a block away, and Trace grumbled that it looked like a punk rockers' convention.

"Keeps you young," Sarge said. He was eating a roast-beef sandwich on rye and had a large mug of beer before him.

"I'm used to Las Vegas," Trace said. "Pushup bras, see-through blouses, black mesh stockings and garter belts. Wholesome Americana. This ripped sweat shirt and painters' pants kink is more than I can take. It's downright unwholesome."

"Downright upright," Sarge said. He introduced Trace to the bartender and said, "This is my son. He wants to throw out all the degenerates in the place."

"Not until my notes are paid off. Please," the bartender said. He was a wiry man with a bushy mustache and warm, but watchful, owner's eyes.

"Well, okay," Trace said. "Just until then." He ordered a glass of wine and Sarge said, "Still not drinking?"

"Still just beer and wine. I've got a bet with Chico."

"You impress the hell out of me. I always worried about your drinking."

"It's a pain in the ass," Trace said. "I keep waiting to see some dramatic proof of how not drinking vodka anymore is improving my health. Making me stronger. Making me live longer. And I don't see anything. My pulse is still as fast as a cheap clock ticking. I still wake up in the morning with sewage in my mouth."

"I know," Sarge said. "And every two days you run across an article that says a little drinking is good for you. Keeps the blood flowing, helps your circulation, prevents stroke. It made me take the pledge."

"What pledge?" Trace asked.

"I pledged not to read any more articles," Sarge said. "Anyway, I've got the booze under control now, so I don't feel too bad."

"How'd you do it without going buggy?" Trace asked.

"It didn't have anything to do with what was

good for me. It was what was good for the rest of the world. I found out I was turning into a Wild West cowboy, rip-roaring, rooting-tooting drunk. And I was afraid that some night I'd turn into a rooting-tooting *shooting* drunk and get somebody dead that didn't deserve to be dead. Although that might be hard in this city. So that's when I quit for real."

"It's been a long time," Trace said.

"Ten years now. And once in a while I cheat—I think a man's got to be allowed to cheat once in a while—but when I do, I drink home so the only person likely to be a victim is your mother. And that woman's indestructible, as you know."

"How is she, by the way?" Trace asked.

"I didn't talk to her yesterday, but she's fine. She couldn't reach me last night, so she called seven neighbors and made them all come over to the house to make sure that it wasn't on fire or that I wasn't lying dead in the kitchen."

"What did you do?"

"I knew she'd do that. She always does. So I left a note on the door."

"What note?" Trace asked.

"It says, 'Dear neighbors, I am all right. I am just out. Patrick Tracy.'"

"That should take care of it."

"No," Sarge said. He bit into his roast-beef sandwich, washed it down with beer, and said, "No, it never does. After your mother calls the seven neighbors who are still talking to her, she decides that they're trying to shield her from the truth, so she calls the police precinct to report me missing or dead. Mind you, this is all by long distance from Las Vegas. She carries a Rolodex with her of the people she can call to harass me."

"What do the cops do?"

"I'm an ex-cop. They cover for me. If I'm going to be out, I let them know, and whatever time

Hilda calls, they tell her I was just there but I left and I'm helping them out on a case."

"And she buys that?" Trace asked.

"What choice does she have? The only alternative is for her to fly home, and if she did that, she might miss the million-billion-zillion dollar jackpot on the nickel slot machine."

"I tried calling you last night too," Trace said.

"You should have tried the police precinct. They would have told you I was just there but I left."

"Where were you? What'd you do? Have a big date?"

"Some big date," Sarge said. "You asked me to nose around with the cops about Armitage. See if anybody's got it in for him. So I prowled around the city last night talking to every cop I still know who isn't senile."

"So, what's going on?"

"Nothing. Armitage is running his nice, neat small protected narcotics business in his club. Nothing big, nothing troublesome. Everybody knows it but everybody leaves him alone. He apparently has a pretty large payroll wearing blue. But nobody's been mad at him, nobody's been moving in, and he hasn't been trying to take over anybody else's business. There wouldn't be a reason for anybody to hit the kid as a lesson to him."

"That's right. And you said the mob wouldn't do that anyway," Trace said.

"Not the mob. But remember, Armitage is mostly dealing cocaine and you're not talking the mob anymore. You're talking Colombia and Venezuela and all those countries, all those Latins, and they're all nuts. They'd blow up a school in session to erase a blackboard. But as I said, no sign of that. Everything's peaceful."

Trace waved for another wine. He asked the owner if he had any scungille salad.

"Not today."

"I told you, son, they never have it. That's why it's the cheapest thing on the menu."

"Next week, we're advertising squab for a dollar," the owner said. "That'll take your mind off the scungille."

When the wine came, Trace asked his father if he had any word about what Nick Armitage might be doing.

"That's one of the things that's funny," Sarge said. "Armitage always had this reputation as a guy who takes out his own garbage, without anybody's help. But there's no word out on the streets about anything he's doing about the dead kid. Nobody's looking for the killer for him and there's no money out on the street for a tip and not even a sign that he gives a damn. I heard he wouldn't even go with the Connecticut cops to see the murder scene."

"Maybe he didn't like the kid," Trace said.

"He's got to save face, though," Sarge said. "Hell, he could hate the kid, but it was his kid and somebody dropped him and he's got to even the score. A very Italian trait. Well, you know that, you live with half an Italian."

"It's the Japanese half that makes me miserable," Trace said. "I was up in Connecticut yesterday. I saw some guy hanging around one of the kid's roommates, and I think he might be one of Armitage's men. I'm not sure, but I think I saw him in Nick's club last night."

"Well, that's something anyway. Does the roommate know anything, do you think?"

"I've got to keep working on it. She wouldn't talk to me," Trace said. "So that's all you did last night?"

"Yup." Sarge gulped his beer and pushed the

empty glass back across the bar. "Do it again," he said to the bartender.

"Make it fast," Trace said, "or he'll steal your plants again."

"We only leave the dead ones out for him to steal. He's harmless," the bartender said.

Trace told Sarge about his trip to the dead youth's college, and then his and Chico's adventures the night before in the Chez Nick disco. Sarge was laughing aloud when Trace finished telling him how Chico had left one of Armitage's hired muscle men writhing in pain on the dance floor.

"I love that woman," Sarge said. "I truly do. Don't let her get away, son."

"More her choice than mine," Trace said. "If she ever decides to change career fields, maybe the two of us'll have something to talk about. Anyway, I saw Martha Armitage today."

"Oh?" Sarge turned on his seat to look at his son.

"I went up there to talk to the husband. How'd she get involved with him anyway? He's a nasty bastard."

"Don't know. Just somebody from the neighborhood, I guess. A kid's romance, and then it gets to be a marriage and then somehow he gets to be connected and rich. It happens that way sometimes, even to nice ladies, and before they know it, they're mobster's wives."

"Enough to make a woman drink," Trace said casually.

"Yeah. I guess so," Sarge said.

"How well do you know her?" Trace asked.

"I think I told you. I met her once on a case. You sound really interested, Dev."

"I met her sister too. Anna Walker?"

"I don't know her."

"She was up at the apartment. I saw her and Nick in a clinch."

Sarge sipped at his beer. "That's interesting, but I don't think it's got anything to do with the kid's murder, do you?"

"I don't know," Trace said. "I don't know anything anymore."

14

"I've got bad news," Trace said.

Chico was lying naked on the large bed in the bedroom of their hotel suite. Her long, tapered fingernails were drying under the fifth coat of blood-red nail polish, and she waved them about her head like an out-of-synch orchestra conductor. The movement of her hands and arms created corresponding waves of motion in her breasts which Trace found very erotic.

"Please stop staring at my tits," she said.

"You need only cover them to prevent that," Trace said.

She reached for the edge of the sheet and he said, "Don't you dare. Will you stop worrying about whether or not I like you shamelessly flaunting your body and listen to me? I said I've got bad news."

"Well, try this for bad news," she said. "The answer is no. No matter how you beg and plead, I am not getting involved in this murder matter of yours. I already did more than I wanted to when I kneed that gorilla last night at the disco. No more. I am in New York on vacation. This town is made blessed by the fact that your mother is absent from it. I intend to enjoy these days. I will not work. Repeat, will not work."

"For your information, that isn't the bad news I had in mind," Trace said.

"Oh? What is?"

"I wanted to tell you that I would not be able to spend this evening with you. I have to go out with Sarge. I didn't want you to be hurt or feel left out or neglected. I wanted to make sure that you wouldn't be bored."

Chico began to giggle. She was a tiny woman and all of her was tiny, in perfect proportion, but for each day of the last three years, Trace had found her more beautiful than the day before. Except for her giggle. It was the dirty snicker of someone with an evil mind.

"Bored?" she said. "Because you won't be with me?" The giggle became a deep-throated laugh.

Trace felt that his potential absence from her side did not actually call for such hilarity. "I don't see what's so terribly funny," he said.

"Trace. I am perfectly capable of amusing myself in New York City."

"But you won't have as much fun as you'd have with me," he said hopefully.

She laughed again. "That is one of the most idiotic statements I've ever heard you make," she said. "For instance. I love to go to the ballet. The last time you went with me and snored through the entire performance."

"I told you. Somebody must have put something in my drink before the show."

"Yes. Alcohol. You drank eight doubles during dinner."

"I was tense. I needed relief," he said.

"You didn't have to spell relief v-o-d-k-a-d-o-u-b-l-e."

"I didn't snore loud," he said. "It was just a little snore."

"And then, remember, we went to the opera? Remember the opera? You insisted upon singing along." She waved her arms over her head again. Her breasts moved. He wanted to jump on her. "You mistake Pavarotti for Mitch Miller. 'Sing Along with Luciano.' I thought you were going to get us arrested."

"I regard opera as one of the last strongholds of participatory democracy," he said. "And I don't sing. I hum. I like to hum along."

"Let's analyze that," she said. More arm-waving, more breasts. Chico had always felt that her breasts were simply too small. She had always demanded to know the chest sizes of all the other women he slept with. She was sure that he went to other women, only in search of pneumatic fulfillment. The fact was that he thought her bosom was, like the rest of her, perfect, but as many times as he told her this, she refused to believe him. Frustrated, he finally realized that a late-blossoming bosom in childhood could scar an adult for life.

"You say you hum," she went on. "That's more or less true, only because you can never remember lyrics. The words to every aria are not 'Oh, dolce, oh, screamo, insufferato.' You hum. The trouble is, Trace, that your range is only three notes. And they're not consecutive. You hum an A, a D, and an F."

"A perfect D chord."

"D minor, idiot. Be that as it may. I do not mind one fractional bit of an infinitesimal iota that you will not accompany me wherever I choose to go tonight. There is ballet, opera, dance recitals, all the things that they don't do in the desert in Nevada, so you can do whatever you like with Sarge. As long as you stay sober. I like you a lot more now that you're sober."

She looked up from her nails and saw that Trace had taken off his shirt and was unzipping his trousers.

"Why are you taking off your clothes?"

"Why do you think?"

"I think that *you* think you're going to climb into bed here and jump my bones."

"I think you're right," Trace said.

"Not a chance."

"Why not?"

"I have just bathed and powdered and perfumed myself."

"I don't care if you're clean," Trace said. "I can deal with that."

"I would have to do all that again," she said.

Trace snickered. "I just wanted to show you how self-centered you really are. The reason I'm taking my clothes off is so that I can exercise. It's time for me to do my daily half-hour of aerobic exercise. Dancing in place. Calisthenics. All part of my self-improvement program."

"You mean those thirteen times you fell down this morning and called them pushups, that wasn't all?" she said.

"That was just part of it. This is the new me. I'm not drinking anymore. I haven't had a cigarette since I came back to this room and I'm already two packs behind my daily average. I'm exercising like a whirling dervish. I've sworn off self-abuse. I haven't scored a woman for the longest time, except for you, and I wouldn't have you now on a bet. It's the new me, Chico."

"Some people will do anything for five hundred dollars."

"Some people will do anything not to have to call What's-his-name and the girl," Trace said. "Suppose the ex-wife answered the phone. What would I do then? What could I say? 'Hello, Bruno, let me talk to Thing One and Thing Two? This is their alleged father'? No way I'm going to lose that bet."

He lay down on the floor to do a pushup. He

got halfway up and fell forward onto his face. "But I'm not joining Sarge's firm," he gasped, lying on the floor, panting. "I can't do all this stuff and think big thoughts too. And I'm not really that hot for gourmet cooking either."

He tried another pushup. This time he was able to straighten his arms completely before he collapsed and fell onto his face.

"Come on, Trace," Chico said cheerily. "I'm proud of you. On your feet and do toe-touches. I'll call out cadence for you. Come on. Stand up. You're terrible at pushups."

"I lack incentive. If I had something under me besides this rug, I might amaze you."

"Don't hold your breath. On your feet."

He slowly rose to a standing position.

"All right," she said. "Bend over and touch your toes."

He bent over once. His fingertips reached halfway between knee and ankle.

"I can't touch my toes," he sniveled.

"Practice. You'll get better. All right, now straighten up and reach high over your head. Don't just hang there like that, you look like a rag doll with an empty belly. Come on. Up, down, up, down, one, two, three, four. Up, down, dammit, not just down."

"I'm stuck. I can't go down and I can't get up."

"Your back?" she said.

"Yeah. Help," he said softly.

She rose from the bed and walked to him. She put her right hand flat, palm side down, on the small of his back and cradled his chest across her left arm. Suddenly, he straightened up and threw his arms around her.

"A miracle. A miracle. Call Lourdes," he yelled exuberantly. "The power of your healing body next to mine."

He squeezed her tight to him and tried to kiss her.

She turned her face away. "Conniving, horny mutt," she grumbled.

"Tell the truth. You love being wanted," he said.

"Not by you," she said, but she turned her face back and let Trace kiss her.

Later, feeling good, Trace called Walter Marks, the insurance company's vice-president for claims, at his home.

"Hello, Groucho."

"Where the hell have you been, Tracy?" Marks demanded.

"Doing what you told me to do. Working on that Armitage case. It's just what I thought. The case is riddled with Mafia types. I haven't questioned anyone yet who doesn't look like a gunslinger. I hired a detective agency to protect me. You'll be happy to know I'm still safe and sound."

"Overjoyed," Marks said sarcastically. "I'm sure you're more than a match for the Mafia. Hit them with your expense account. That would crush anyone."

"You don't think they're anything to worry about?" Trace said.

"Come on. I wasn't born yesterday. Mafia. Pfff."

"I'm glad you feel that way," Trace said.

"Why?" Marks's voice suddenly reeked suspicion.

"Because I've been worried. So I've been giving everybody I talk to your business card and telling them my name is Walter Marks. If some guys carrying a violin case come to see you, just stare them right down."

"What? You gave them *my* business card?"

"Listen, Groucho, I have to go now. But I'll

check in every so often to see if you're still around. Oh. Another thing. You ought to let your wife start the car in the morning before you get in it. Just a precaution. You can't ever be too safe."

15

"Welcome to Alphabet City," Sarge said.

"So what is this place that was so important that I come to?" Trace asked his father. They had parked Sarge's car half in, half out of a bus stop, a few doors shy of a Lower East Side tavern named The Security Blanket. A cutesy-poo neon sign with those words inscribed inside what was supposed to look like a blanket stuck out over the front door.

"What it looks like," Sarge said. "Nick Armitage's security blanket."

As they got out of the car, Trace asked, "Is that old police shield in the window still saving you from getting parking tickets?"

Sarge nodded. "Except you get some of these new bastards on the force. They ticket the mayor so they can get on the six-o'clock news. Publicity hounds. You got traffic cops now who hire public-relations men."

"You're being bitter. Maybe they just think the job's on the level."

"Nobody who thinks anything's on the level ever applies to join the NYPD," Sarge said.

"God, what a cynical old man."

"Mark it well. It's the only thing I've got to leave you when I go."

Trace said, "Then don't go until you can leave

something better. So why is this Armitage's security blanket?"

"When he moved over from Brooklyn, where he was a real small-timer, this was the first place he opened in Manhattan. That must be twenty, twenty-five years ago. Then he opened a bunch of joints and now that big nightclub, but he keeps this one like he doesn't want to let it go. It's . . . I don't know."

"I know," Trace said. "When I was an accountant, I used to deal with this guy who did income-tax returns for people. He'd charge them ten, fifteen dollars. Then he got into a different business and got to be a millionaire. Hell, the interest on his interest was a millionaire's interest. And still every April fifteenth, he'd sit down and fill out people's income taxes for ten and fifteen dollars. I asked him why once and he said, 'They can take all the money away, but this is my skill, they can't take that away from me. As long as I've got that, I always have something.' "

"What'd you think of that, Dev?" Sarge asked.

"I thought it was dopey," Trace said. "If I were making a million dollars a year, I'd be damned if I'd be filling out somebody's freaking income tax for ten dollars."

"Me neither," Sarge said. "Anyway, I guess you're right. That must be the way Armitage feels about this place. He won't let it go. And I thought you ought to take a look at it. Maybe somebody here knows something that you might not find out uptown. Hey, look at this."

Two young men were walking down the street toward them. They were about twenty years old, and they wore neat tweed jackets and knit ties and button-down collars, and they looked like Jeff and John, the Preppie twins. They were jabbering excitedly at each other, all smiles and orthodontia.

Sarge said angrily to Trace, "It's like this all the time. This is the most murderous vicious drug-dealing part of the city, and these rich kids who don't know any better, they come over here to score drugs. They don't even have enough sense not to go flashing a big bankroll. They think it's some kind of gentleman's game, buy a little nose candy for the boys back at the dormitory. Like it's neat and civilized and they're not dealing with the degenerate scum of the world. There's people around here who'd kill them, who'd slip ice picks into their hearts, if they just got wind that somehow these two twits have an extra couple of hundred in their pockets or hidden in their socks. Men of the world always hide their extra money in their sock," Sarge said.

He shook his head. "These assholes just don't know. They think this is panty raids and giggles. There's one or two of them killed every week or so, and they still keep coming back because you can buy anything you want down here."

Trace knew that "down here" referred to what Sarge had called Alphabet City, a section of Lower Manhattan that covered Avenues A through D. The streets were named with letters, in contrast to New York City's usual system of numbering its main north-south avenues.

"Cops can't stop it?" Trace asked.

"They control it. When they see raw meat like these two, they try to chase them so they don't get hurt. But if they really tried to stop the drug-dealing, they'd just wind up scattering it all over the city again. At least if they keep it here, they can keep hoping that someday there's a federal grant and they can blow up these blocks and get rid of the problem once and for all."

"Until the next week, when it opens up again somewhere else," Trace said.

"Yeah. I know."

Trace saw the bitter hurt on Sarge's face. He knew how his father hated criminals. He could talk like a world-weary sophisticate about smart money, about cops on the take, about the system being designed only to help the rich, and all the rest of the fashionable saloon talk of cynical losers, but Trace knew that in Sarge's heart, the old man wanted the system to work and was upset when it didn't. He remembered every arrest he had ever made in twenty-five years on the police force. He was proud of every one of them too.

The two Preppies were now almost up to them, ignoring Sarge and Trace, violating the first rule of life in Alphabet City by not continually checking on their surroundings—who was on the street, who was behind them. Sarge was right, Trace thought. These two were hamburger.

He heard his father growl a little deep in his throat and then step out in front of the two youths. They were of average size, but Sarge was tall and broad, and with his shock of white hair, his anger-reddened face, and hands the size of canned hams, he had a tendency to be terribly imposing.

The two young men stopped short, startled by this burly apparition that loomed in front of them.

Sarge pulled out his hip-pocket wallet and snapped it open, showing his old gold New York City police sergeant's badge.

"What are you two doing here?"

The two hesitated. "Just walking around," one of them finally said. His voice almost broke in the middle of the sentence.

Sarge nodded, then snarled, "Bullshit." His face twisted in anger. "I've been watching you since you got here and you're on your way to buy drugs." The two started to protest, but Sarge snapped at them and cut them off. "Don't deny it, you two piss-willows. I want you the hell out of here. Right fucking now before I run your asses in for vagrancy."

"You can't—" one started.

"And resisting fucking arrest. And assaulting an officer. My partner over there . . ." He nodded toward Trace, who was leaning against their car. "He saw you try to take a punch at me." Sarge paused a beat, then leaned his face in closer to the two young men. "Listen. I'm giving you a break. There are special raids going down around here tonight. We've got three hundred cops in the area. Buy something and you'll be bagged." He straightened up again. "Now you get your little lily-white asses out of here or you'll have to call Daddy in Westport to come and make bail for you. You understand?" The last two words were a vicious nasty snarl.

The two young men nodded. Neither spoke.

"Then move it. If I see you two again, you're in deep shit." The Preppies looked at each other, turned, and started to walk away.

"I said move it," Sarge yelled. "This ain't no fucking boulevard stroll."

The two men started jogging down the block, away from them, and Sarge replaced his wallet. "Come on, I'll buy you a drink," he said to Trace, his voice totally calm.

Trace pushed himself away from the car. "You did good, Pop."

"No, I didn't. They'll go back to their fancy campus and tell their friends, who'll say, 'Why, that pig violated your civil rights, he can't chase you off the street,' and they're going to wind up back here and maybe dead. Did you see them? They were wearing gold watches. Gold watches, for Jesus' sake. In Alphabet City. God save the children."

"Maybe you did," Trace said. "Maybe they'll

live now and grow up just like their daddies. To be advertising writers and bank presidents."

Sarge looked at him, then at the vanishing figures of the two young men. Mockingly, he called out softly, "Come back. Come back. I was only fooling."

The tavern was spotlessly clean. From the outside, it looked like a local bar and Trace had expected to see a scene out of *Walpurgisnacht*: degenerates, junkies, pushers, prostitutes, pimps. But instead the half-empty bar looked as normal as any New York City bar could be. Which meant that there was no one there with hair dyed pink.

The bar ran straight along one wall of the building to a partition that led to a backroom that was a combination dining room and cocktail lounge, where a woman singer was working under a small spotlight. Trace saw that she was a small redheaded woman in jeans, sitting on a high stool in front of a microphone, accompanying herself on a guitar.

The bartender nodded at them as they came in and sat at the bar. He was barely thirty, Trace guessed, an open-faced young man, but he looked as if he had already begun to suffer from the ravages of his profession. His face was getting a little fatty in the cheeks, the skin of his neck was loosening, and the whites of his eyes, while not really red, were an unwholesome pink. Trace thought that the bartender had started to go to seed a little earlier than usual. Most of them seemed to be protected from aging by the alcohol they lived with, until about their fortieth birthday, and then they went to hell all at once. This one seemed to have a ten-year head start on degeneration.

Sarge told Trace, "I'll be right back. Phone call."

As the bartender approached him, Trace thought

of ordering vodka. He hadn't had a real drink in a long while, and what the hell did Chico expect of him anyway. It wasn't part of the bet that he would stop drinking totally, only that he would moderate his habits. He thought about it for a moment, then decided reluctantly that it was too early in the evening to start on vodka. He would stick with milder stuff until late in the night and then have a vodka as a reward. The thought gave him something to live for.

"Draft beer for him," Trace said. "I'll have red wine straight up."

The bartender nodded. A speaker system was mounted over the bar and the young singer's voice filled the room. When Trace and Sarge had walked in, she was singing "Streets of London" and now she was singing "Willie McBride," another depressingly sad song, but her crystal-pure soprano voice gave the song a beauty he had never heard in it before.

The bartender brought the drinks back. "Start a tab?"

"Sure." Trace sipped at the red wine.

"You like that shit?"

Trace looked to his right. The man who had spoken was big, with a chain gold necklace, a marine crew cut, and a pullover sweater that bared his neck so you could see the necklace. He was big. The crew cut made him look like a marine drill sergeant on furlough.

"What's that you're drinking?" Trace asked, nodding at the man's shot glass.

"Sour mash. Straight," the man said.

"I like this shit better than that shit," Trace said, and turned away. So much for good intentions. If he had ordered vodka, instead of being sanctimonious and drinking wine, this creature would never have spoken to him.

The man's voice followed him. "Only fairies drink wine at a bar. Faggots."

"Hey, Ernie," the bartender said, "cool it."

"Shut up. I drink here. I can talk if I want. Everybody knows faggots drinks wine. Madison Avenue fairies. Dress designers."

"Sounds right to me," Trace said amiably.

"Which are you?" Ernie asked sullenly. He obviously did not want Trace agreeing with him.

"I design ladies' underwear. You've heard of Frederick's of Hollywood? I'm Frederick's of Ohio."

"Fairy. All designers are fairies. What do you think of that?"

Trace beckoned the bartender. "What's your name?" he asked.

"Brian," the bartender said.

"Is it that this asshole wants to hit me? Is that what it is?"

"What?" asked Ernie. "Who you calling an asshole?"

Trace raised a hand for silence. "Time out, asshole. One conversation at a time. You're next. First I'm talking to Brian here. Does he want to hit me?"

"Does the Pope say Mass?" Brian answered.

"Who'd you call an asshole?" Ernie demanded, and since it seemed to be important to help Ernie find himself in this world, Trace turned and was about to answer when Sarge's voice said, "He's not calling anybody an asshole. But I am, you asshole. Now shut up your big ugly face."

Trace saw that Sarge had his big hand upon Ernie's shoulder and was squeezing with his thumb and fingers deep into the trapezius muscle between shoulder and neck.

"Ow, goddammit." Ernie wrenched away, jumped to his feet, and faced Sarge.

Sarge was a lot older, but just as big and wider and burlier, and his face was a lot meaner.

"Who the hell are you?" Ernie demanded.

"Hold on, Sarge," Trace said, getting off the bar stool.

"Why?" Sarge asked.

"You promised me that I'd get the next ugly one. It's my turn."

"Well, I was talking about ugly human beings," Sarge said. "I don't think this thing counts."

"It's human," Trace said. "I heard it try to talk before."

"Real words?"

"Yes. I definitely heard it say wine. And fairy. It said fairy better than wine."

"Probably it's had more practice saying fairy," Sarge said.

"Maybe, Sarge. But it's mine anyway."

"What is this shit?" Ernie snapped. "Why you calling him Sarge?"

"Because he's a cop, and after I punch your ugly fucking face off, Ernie, he is going to book what's left of you and throw you in the can. There are a lot of fairies in there on a Friday night. You should really enjoy it."

Ernie's mouth moved.

"Here it comes," Trace said. "Now it's going to say, 'Yeah? Says who?' and you're going to have to hit it to shut it up."

"Aaaah, you two are nuts. I'm getting out of here," Ernie said.

"A wise decision," Sarge said. "If the nuts are here, can the fruits be far behind?"

Ernie snatched his money from the bar and left, and Sarge and Trace both sat back down.

"Boy, he had me frightened for my life," Trace said. "I'm glad you were here to protect me."

"What are fathers for?" Sarge said. "Thanks for the beer."

"My pleasure. Your phone call go through?"

Sarge shook his head. "Nobody home."

The bartender came over and apologized for Ernie. "He's not a bad guy, but he's kind of a local. Doesn't like strangers."

"Bars are filled with them," Trace said. "Looks like you run a pretty tight ship."

"We try," Brian said.

After he walked away, Trace told Sarge, "It *does* look like a pretty clean bar."

"Don't let it fool you," Sarge said. "Armitage sells drugs uptown, and I bet when he started this place, he sold them here. Maybe he doesn't anymore, probably doesn't need to, but if he needed a buck, he'd sell drugs here or in a damned schoolyard. Don't let that tuxedo and that Chez Nick crap con you. He's still a goddamn knee-capper."

"That's what annoys me about this whole thing. Nick ought to be out kneecapping somebody right now about his kid. Tearing his hair out. Shooting people. It doesn't figure."

"Unless he already knows who killed his kid and he's just waiting for the right time to get even," Sarge said.

"That's not bad, Sarge. Not bad."

Sarge finished his beer. "Order me up another," he said, and walked toward the telephone again.

Trace ordered two more drinks, then watched in the mirror as Sarge was talking to someone. He could see Sarge smile when he said hello and then some pleasant conversation that he could not overhear but that ended with another large smile and a nod of the head.

When he came back, he still did not volunteer anything about the telephone call.

"You got any plans with this case?" he asked Trace.

"I've got nothing going for me, so I think I

might go back to the school and look around up there some. Maybe Tony's roommates are worth another try."

"When there isn't anything else, you do what there is," Sarge said.

"That's either profound or really dumb," Trace said.

"Really dumb. Your mother told it to me."

"How is she?" Trace asked.

"She's okay. I talked to her today. It turns out that she's been in Vegas more than anybody else in the club, so that gives her some kind of pecking rights. Of course, she never goes anyplace but Circus Circus and their slot machines, but they don't have to know that. And I think she has cabdrivers go past your condo. She tells them that that's her son's building. I think she wants them to believe that you're a big real-estate developer."

"Whatever makes her happy, as long as it keeps her out of town," Trace said. "Was she ticked that I wasn't in Vegas?"

"A little, I guess. But she got happier when she figured out that Chico was gone too. So I guess it all evens out."

"I ought to marry Chico just to spite her," Trace said.

"No, you ought to do it for your own pleasure and because it's what's best for you. Spite only lasts a little time, but what you do about it can stay with you forever. Only do what you want to do, for yourself. The hell with everybody else."

"See, Sarge? You're really going to make it as a private detective. Already I've got you thinking big thoughts. As soon as I can improve your cooking, hell, they'll put you on the cover of *Time* magazine. Detective of the Year."

Sarge sighed. "Well, it'll have to wait until tomorrow. I think I'll go home and catch a few.

I'll be in the office tomorrow." He drained his drink and stood up from his stool. "You want to go back now?"

"No, I think I'm going to hang out here."

"You'll be able to get home all right?" Sarge said.

"I always have. Have a good night's sleep."

"Okay. I'll probably unplug the phone so if you call and I don't answer, don't act like your mother. I leave it plugged in and she wakes me up at night. I unplug it and she panics. Don't you panic."

Trace nodded, and after his father left, he wondered where he was really going. Then he put it out of his mind and turned on his stool to watch the redheaded singer.

16

Trace heard a brief patter of applause and turned to see the singer turn off her sound system, flick off the overhead spotlight, and then walk through the small lounge toward the bar.

She stood at the end of the bar, next to Trace's seat.

"You're very good," Trace said.

"Thank you. It's nice to know that somebody listens once in a while. Where's your bodyguard?"

"My . . .? Oh, that was my father. He went home. I always bring him with me when I go into tough places like this."

"I don't really think you need him," the singer said.

"Can I buy you a drink?" Trace asked.

"Not on duty. Thanks." Without being asked, Brian, the bartender, put a glass of orange juice on the bar in front of her.

Trace caught a flash of movement in the mirror behind the bar and looked up to see a young man in a white shirt without a tie come from an office door on the far side of the room. He moved to the bar between Trace and the young singer and said to her, "Last set?"

She nodded.

"Okay. I think you ought to take it downtown this set."

"I don't think so," she said.

"Liven the place up."

"Paulie," she said, with a note of asperity in her voice, as if she were a teacher repeating a lesson again for the dumbest child in the school. "I don't sing up-tempo. These people are used to the fact that I sing slow music. Ballads. That's what I do."

"Sing up-stuff, you'll have them dancing. Drinking more. We've got to do something about improving business."

"I sing ballads. If they want Def Leppard, let them go home and watch MTV."

"Better be careful that one of these nights *you're* not home watching MTV," the young man said ominously. He hitched up his white suspenders and walked away.

"Moron," the singer said softly under her breath, then asked Trace, "That offer still stand?"

"My pleasure."

"Brian," she called out. "Dewars, rocks, splash."

"Art versus commerce," Trace told her. "The story of the world." He gestured to Brian that the singer's drink be put on his check.

"I wouldn't mind so much," the young woman said, "if commerce made any sense. But this isn't commerce arguing with art. This is stupid arguing with sense. That's what you get when you let waiters rise above their station in life. Pfff. They call him a manager."

"An overachiever?" Trace said.

She snorted. "He was an overachiever when he learned to use the potty."

Trace reached under his jacket and turned on his tape recorder. "I guess he hasn't been here long," he said.

"How'd you guess that?"

"Because you're here. If he'd been here long, I don't think you'd have been."

148

"Yeah, that's true," she said. She thanked Brian as he put the drink in front of her, then turned back to Trace. "They came up empty of a manager about three weeks ago and so they get this giboney to fill in. And now he thinks he's Conrad Hilton."

"He was a waiter?"

She nodded and Trace asked, "Why'd they pick *him*?"

"Who knows? They could have picked Brian here. He makes sense and people like him and he's honest. Instead, they get that thing. Thanks for the drink."

"Anytime. Who's they? The ones who picked him?"

"I guess it was the big boss himself. Armitage."

"Armitage?" Trace repeated.

"Nick Armitage. He owns a big nightclub in Midtown. Chez Nick."

"Sorry," Trace said. "I'm from out of town. I never heard of it. If he owns a big nightclub, what's he got this place for?"

"I think this was his first bar or something," she said. "Sentimental reasons, I guess."

Trace chuckled. "Sentiment? In a saloon owner? That'll be the day. You ever meet him?"

"Sometimes. Sometimes he stops in for a bite to eat or something. His son used to be here a lot. Paulie, that's the manager, and his son were friends. Maybe that's how he got the job."

"They're not friends anymore?" Trace asked.

"The son died. Got murdered. Didn't you read about it?"

"I don't think so," Trace said. "I live three thousand miles away."

"Yeah, well, he was found shot alongside a highway in Connecticut. He was wearing a Richard Nixon mask."

She apparently decided that she had talked

enough and looked down at her drink. Trace realized that she was older than he had thought at first. He put her age in the late twenties.

"Hey," he said, "I think I remember reading about that. The Richard Nixon mask. Yeah. They ever find out who did it?"

She sipped at her drink. "I guess not. I never heard anything more about it."

"So that guy was this guy's friend." Trace nodded toward the manager's door.

"Yes," she said.

"I guess that *is* how he got the job. Were they real close?"

"Kind of. I think Paulie sort of kept an eye out for the father. The way I hear it, the father didn't want the kid here drinking or anything, so if Paulie heard that Mr. Armitage was coming down, he'd tell Tony and Tony'd beat it quick. You think if I told Mr. Armitage that, he'd fire this nerd?"

"Might be worth a try," Trace said. "How'd you get along with the last manager?"

"Like a charm. He managed. I sang. He left me alone. So he was talky once in a while and you had to listen to him, but he wasn't bad."

"Sounds like a good manager. I guess he got a better offer."

"I don't know. One night, he just didn't show up for work."

"No notice? That's a helluva way to quit," Trace said.

"Different strokes, I suppose."

"You think he'd at least stop back in and say hello," Trace said. "How long's he been gone?"

"About a month ago, I guess. Let me think." She played on the fingers of one hand with the fingers of the other. "Yes, just a month ago."

Trace imitated her, pressing his fingers together. "I could do that and I still couldn't remember what happened yesterday."

"I've got a good memory," she said. She suddenly bolted down the rest of her drink and said, "Back on. Break's over. You going to stay awhile?"

"Wouldn't leave now," Trace said.

"Good."

"Don't forget to take it downtown now," Trace said with a smile.

She smiled back and said, "Dirge time. Waiters don't tell me what to sing."

There were only a couple of customers left at the bar when Brian came down to refill Trace's glass.

"You've got one vote for manager," Trace said.

"Oh, Alicia? Sure. She doesn't care much for Paulie."

"Why not try for the job?" Trace asked.

"Not me," Brian said. "You get to be the manager and you start hiring and firing and worrying about stock and who's cheating, and then you've got to deal with the owner. Me? I just show up, make my drinks, take the money and run. I leave this place behind the minute I walk out the door. My name's Brian Dennehy, by the way." He extended a hand and Trace shook it.

"They call me Trace."

"That was your father in here with you before?" Trace nodded.

"Not a man to tangle with," Brian said.

"I'm going to knock him on his butt," Trace said, adding with a smile, "but I think I'll wait until his ninety-second birthday. The girl was telling me the tale of the mysterious disappearing manager."

Brian shrugged. "Maybe somebody made him an offer he couldn't refuse."

"I had a cousin like that once," Trace said. "Just vanished off the face of the earth. But I knew it was happening. A couple of months beforehand, I could see him twitching around and looking off into space and like that. He was like a bomb waiting to go off."

Brian glanced down the bar. Satisfied that no one was waiting for a drink, he said, "Not Dewey. He was here one night, talking about how he was moving up in the world, and then he was gone. Not a worry in his mind that I could see."

"Maybe he was on something," Trace said. "People get that way, they get juiced up or something, start talking about conquering the world. Was it like that, maybe?"

"I don't know. He was talking about Mr. Armitage moving him up, maybe going to make him manager of the uptown place. I laughed at him and told him he'd get the job as soon as I got to be the manager of the Waldorf Astoria. 'A lot you know,' he said. 'It's going to be mine. You'll see.' Then he never came back. Funny, you know, because Armitage used to call him once in a while and I thought maybe he *was* some kind of fair-haired boy. He and Armitage even went out together a couple of nights before that and . . . aah, who knows?"

"Maybe all the plans got fouled up when Armitage's son got killed," Trace suggested. "That was right around then, wasn't it?"

"Yeah. It was just a couple of nights after that that Dewey was talking big. I remember 'cause Dewey said maybe we should close the place for the funeral and I said that was stupid, you don't go closing saloons for funerals of silent partners' relatives, and Dewey said, well, that maybe I was right. Where you from?"

"Las Vegas," Trace said.

"Just visiting relatives?" Brian asked.

"Mostly. And trying to avoid the ex-wife and

kids," Trace said. "Maybe if I have to meet them, I'll do it over here. You run a nice clean place."

"We try to," Brian said. "That's why I got so bent before when Ernie started acting up."

"Yeah," Trace said. "My old man's got eyes like an eagle. He's been a cop forever. And that's what he was saying. He said, this whole neighborhood is swimming in dope and there just isn't any in this bar."

"It'd be my ass if there was," Brian said. "Armitage wouldn't let it happen. He runs this place clean as a whistle. Funny story. One night, Armitage is here for dinner and some guy in the dining room lights up a joint and starts to smoke. Well, Armitage had his two . . . I don't know, assistants, I guess you could call them . . . throw him out. Then a month later, Armitage is in again and the same guy is in, minding his own business, not doing anything, and Armitage threw him out again. He never forgets. He told me, 'Don't let that guy in here again.' "

"Alicia said he wouldn't even let his son hang out here," Trace said. "That Paulie'd tip off the kid if the father was coming."

"That's right. They were close, him and Tony." He looked along the bar again, then left Trace to go pour a drink.

A minute or two later, the singer finished her final set. As Trace watched, she packed her guitar in a case, then came and stood by him at the bar.

The manager stuck his head out of the office door and called her name.

"The eagle poops," she said to Trace. "Excuse me."

In the bar mirror, he saw her talking to Paulie. He handed her a slip of paper, then talked some more. Trace saw her shake her head. Then, almost as if on a rehearsed beat, they both turned away from the other.

Alicia came back to the bar. "Nerd," she said.

"What'd he say?"

"He didn't like the last set. Much too depressing."

"What'd you say?" Trace asked.

"I told him if he thought that was depressing, be sure to be here tomorrow night. I'm going to sing Schumann Lieder, my own arrangement of the 'Volga Boatman,' and famous Italian death arias." She was slowly folding a piece of paper that she put into her purse.

"Now I've seen everything," Trace said.

"What's that?"

"A musician getting paid by check. Will wonders never cease?"

"I tell you, this is a strange place. They pay me by check and they send me a ten-ninety-nine at the end of the year. Can you imagine that? I never filed a tax return in my life until I started working here. Now I'm stuck, the IRS knows I exist. I'll have to work here forever. Good-bye, La Scala."

"I knew that voice was too good to have learned in a saloon," Trace said.

"Mannes School of Music. Do you know, I always thought that good golfers were tripping over each other and that there were too many world-class tennis players. That the world was filled with ballroom dancers and piano players. But you want to see surplus, go look at mezzo-sopranos. Go out on the street and scratch any woman, and nine out of ten of them are going to scream contralto. This is a tough business."

"When I buy my own opera house, Alicia, you're hired," Trace said.

"Is there any chance of that?"

"Not unless I hit the New York Lotto twenty-one weeks in a row. Or my ex-wife pays back what she stole from me. She spent it on marksmanship lessons for my kids."

"Well, they're both small chances, but they give me something to hope for."

She went to the ladies' room and Trace wondered if he should call Chico. It was after midnight and he was concerned that she had gotten back to the room safely. But if he called her, she would know that he had been worried about her. It would give her an extra little handle on him. It would be best not to call. Let her know that he didn't really care that much. If she wanted to traipse all over New York at night, she was on her own. He surely wasn't going to be worried about her. That'd show her. Of course. That's exactly what he would do. He wouldn't call.

He got up and dialed the Plaza. The telephone in his room rang four times before Chico answered. She had been sleeping. Her voice was a quiet, groggy "Hello?"

"This is Trace. My American Express card. Did I leave the room without it?"

"Trace," she repeated, as if trying to place him. "Oh, yeah. Trace. Listen, I'm back safely. I had a nice time. It was nice of you to be worried and call. Have a good time with Sarge. *Oyasumi Nasai.*"

And she hung up.

So much for subtlety, Trace thought. There was just no way to outwit the insidious little Eurasian. He went into the men's room and put a new tape into his small recorder.

When he came back out, Alicia looked ready to leave and Trace was happy that she had no problems about leaving without him. He hadn't cheated all night. He had drunk only wine. He hadn't cheated smoking either, unless one wanted to be a nitpicker and count the nine cigarettes he had borrowed from the bartender. He didn't want to cheat with a woman tonight either.

"That time of the evening," she said with a smile. "See you again?"

"I'll be back. I like this place. Have you got a car?"

"Yeah. I'm parked just a few doors down."

"I'll walk you out there." Trace looked at Brian, who was beginning to tote up customer's checks from the now-closed dining room. "Brian, I'm taking the lady to her car. I'll be right back."

"I'll be here until Wanda comes."

Trace hoisted the singer's guitar case. He was surprised at how light it was. "Wanda?" he said to her.

"The lady who comes in for the money at night," Alicia said. "Tough lady. We call her 'Wanda Whips Wall Street.' Brian's butt is suet if he's a dollar off."

"Is Wanda her real name?"

Alicia shrugged. "I don't know. I don't think so."

He walked with her to her car, a ratty old Dodge Dart with so much body rot it looked as if it ought to be a lobby display at the Sloan-Kettering Institute for Cancer Research.

She put the guitar in the trunk and he stood with her while she unlocked the driver's door.

"It's been nice meeting you," she said. "You have a good time?"

"I did," he said.

"Did you find out everything you wanted to know?" Her smile was bright in the overhead streetlight.

"Was I that obvious?" he asked.

"No. Of course not. Everybody comes in and asks me five hundred questions a night," she said. "What's it all about?"

"My father and I, we're looking into Tony

Armitage's murder. We're investigators." He turned on the tape recorder again. The singer opened the door, sat behind the wheel, and lowered the window. He closed the door behind her.

"I figured it was something like that," she said. "Was I any help?"

Trace shrugged. "Every little bit helps."

"You working for the family?" she asked.

He nodded.

"Anything I can do . . ." she said, leaving the sentence unfinished.

"Did Tony use drugs?" he asked.

"Grass and coke, I think. Anyway, I saw him with them once in a while."

"What'd you think of him?"

"He was a boy. I think his father scared him a lot," she said.

"Did he get the drugs down here, do you think?"

She hesitated a moment. "I wouldn't know," she finally said.

"You know, when we left the bar," Trace said, "I was glad that you weren't inviting me home. And now I'm sad about it."

"Maybe some night when you're not working," she said. "When I know you're with me and not with what I know."

"You've got a deal, lady," he said.

She reached her arm through the open window and pulled Trace's head down to the window. She kissed him hard, pulpily. She had a nice mouth, Trace thought.

She released him, rolled up the window, started the motor, and drove off. Feeling very noble, Trace walked back into the bar.

He was the last customer left. It was one of the things he had always liked about working for himself. When he had made his living as a gambler in Las Vegas, he worked when he wanted to.

Now, with the insurance company, he worked when he wanted to. It allowed him to drink whenever he wanted to. He never had to be home at any special time. He could close any saloon he was in, and he often did.

But, God, now what was he going to do, now that he had virtually, almost, damned near given up drinking for Chico? He might as well have an office job if he wasn't going to drink. Go back to being an accountant.

He felt a tinge of annoyance. While he was suffering with big questions and problems like this, Chico was back in their hotel room, sleeping. Did she care that he was going through an identity crisis? If she were any kind of friend, she'd be here with him, talking him over this rough spot, helping him to endure in his good intentions. But that was the way with women. Fair-weather friends. Never there when you needed them.

Paulie, the manager, had joined Brian at the cash register, and was putting cash into a bank-deposit bag. Trace called the bartender over and ordered a Finlandia vodka on the rocks. "Make it a double."

"Welcome back to civilization," Brian said as he poured the drink.

"You mind if I close out your check now?" Brian asked. "We'll be closing soon."

"Sure," Trace said. "Just back me up with another drink. And then when you want to throw me out, just nod and I'll go peacefully."

"Fair enough."

Brian poured an old-fashioned glass almost full of Finlandia. "Let me know when you're ready for rocks," he said. He gave Trace a check for twenty-eight dollars and Trace gave him two twenties and told him to keep the change.

The vodka tasted good. It had been how long . . . two months . . . since he had had a drink of vodka, except for a couple of small ones that had been forced on him by social circumstances or by friends he couldn't stand to insult. Not once in those couple of months had he stopped wanting a real drink. So he was allowed this one. He had already proved that he could stop whenever he wanted to. The couple of drinks tonight wouldn't really matter, he thought. They would be kind of a reward for really being good and on the wagon. Tomorrow, he wouldn't drink anymore.

He would start another two months without a drink of vodka and maybe at the end of those two months, he would celebrate again with a couple of pops. He calculated quickly what day two months would be. This was the twenty-first of July. Would it be September 21? No. July and August had thirty-one days each. Make it sixty days instead. September 19. On September 19, he would drink again.

Just another reward for good conduct. Like these two drinks tonight. Tomorrow, he would forget them. He would jump out of bed and do his half-hour's exercise and eat a breakfast that was heavy in bran and complex carbohydrates, and not smoke either. Chico would be very proud of him. He had the willpower of a Buddhist monk.

He bummed another cigarette from Brian.

The manager had just walked into the office with the bag containing the day's receipts when the front door opened and a woman walked in.

It was Anna Walker, Martha Armitage's sister. So she was Wanda Whips Wall Street.

She nodded to Brian, looked at Trace without real interest, and walked into the manager's office without knocking.

"Going to have to chase you, Trace," Brian said. He pointed to the office door and added softly, "Wanda."

Trace nodded. "I'll be on my way." He picked up his glass, nursed it a little with small sips, and turned on his chair. When the woman left the office, she was stuffing the cash bag into her large leather pocketbook. She saw Trace looking at her, smiled a not-sure smile, then walked over to him.

"I know you, don't I?"

"Just hello and good-bye," Trace said.

"That's right. At Nick's apartment. You're the insurance man."

"Devlin Tracy," Trace confessed.

"Is this part of your investigation too?" she asked. She snapped her pocketbook tightly closed.

"Not really. I was out for a night's carousing with my father, and then he got tired and went home. I was just getting tossed out."

"How fortunate that you wound up in Nick's place," she said. "Do you have a ride?"

Trace shook his head. "Pop took the car."

"Where are you?"

"The Plaza," he said.

"I'll give you a lift. I'm heading in that direction," she said.

"You needn't bother. I can get a cab."

"No bother, and no, you can't. Cabbies don't come down here at night. They have a tendency to get dead."

"Then, thanks. I accept," Trace said. He tossed down the rest of the drink, nodded toward Brian, who had been watching them talk to each other, and walked with the woman toward the door, which he held open for her.

"A vanishing art. You can tell you're not from New York."

"What's that?"

"Good manners," she said.

"It's eighty-seven percent of my charm."

"I'm supposed to ask about the other thirteen percent?" she said.

"My vast personal wealth," Trace said.

"All that, and handsome too."

"I just wanted you to know that I'm financially secure. You don't have to worry about me mugging you for the night's receipts."

"I wasn't too worried," she said.

"I'm bigger than you. Not meaner, maybe, because I'm a pussycat. But bigger."

"I didn't come alone." She led him toward a large Cadillac parked two doors down from the bar. Two men sat in the front seat and one of them hopped out when he saw Anna Walker coming toward the car with a man.

"It's all right," she said.

Trace recognized the man as one of the two he had tangled with the night before in Chez Nick. The man backed toward the rear door to open it for Anna, then saw Trace's face.

"Hey, it's you."

"It usually is when it's wearing this suit," Trace said.

"You two know each other?" the woman asked Trace.

"We had the same dance instructor," Trace said.

"A wise guy," the man told Anna. "Caused trouble last night at the club."

"See how stories get around?" Trace said. "As I recollect it, I was sitting quietly, having a glass of wine—wine, mind you—when this person and his friend suggested I was too old to dance. Then one thing led to another, and pretty soon they both wound up on the floor."

"Very funny," the man snarled.

"Please open the door, Frankie," Anna Walker said.

"I don't know," he said. "About this guy."

"I do. It's all right," the woman said again. There was a sharp edge in her voice this time, so Frankie nodded and opened the rear door. Anna entered and Trace started in after her. Frankie tried to slam the door on Trace's foot, but Trace pushed his foot against the passenger armrest and propelled the door back hard with his foot. It hit Frankie in the stomach.

"Careful of the door," Trace said as he pulled it closed behind him.

Trace saw that the driver of the car was the other man who had accosted him and Chico in the club. The man was staring at him in the rearview mirror, until Anna Walker pressed a button on a panel next to her and a one-way glass window moved silently on a track across the top of the front seat, sealing off the two halves of the car.

She turned on a radio that filled the car with loud stereo music.

"Sorry for the volume, but there's more privacy this way," she said.

"Little *pishers* have big ears," Trace said. "That's what Mother always told me. So who are these two guys? Where'd Armitage get them, from some work-release program at Riker's Island?"

"They're twins. The one on the right up there is Frankie the Singer. The other one's Augie the Hand."

"Sweet," Trace said sarcastically.

"Their father was a friend of Nick's. So he put them to work. So?"

"So?" Trace said.

"So just what are you supposed to be doing around here? I know Nick wasn't very happy to see you."

"I'm looking into Tony's death. It's kind of routine before we pay off on a big policy."

"Find out anything?" she asked.

162

"Not a blessed thing," Trace said. "His roommates don't know anything. Armitage doesn't know anything. Neither does his wife. The people in this saloon don't know anything or else they wouldn't talk to me. So, maybe, since you're the newest kid on the block, maybe you'll tell me something."

"What would you like me to tell you?"

"First things first. How'd a nice girl like you get involved in being a saloon manager?"

She laughed. "I'm not. I'm Nick's bookkeeper. I just come down to pick up the receipts and go over them at my place. I've always done that. God, why would I want to manage a tavern?"

"Especially after the last manager vanished," Trace said. "Maybe you can tell me about that."

"What do you mean?"

"What was his name, Dewey?"

"Dewey Lupus," she said.

"Yeah. Don't you think it's kind of odd that he stopped working just a couple of days after Tony's murder? Maybe it's just a coincidence and maybe it isn't. Maybe he took off before anybody found out about what he did. Or maybe he was just put away in the old family lime pit where all bad little murderers go when they get caught."

"That's ridiculous," she snapped.

"You mean those two goons in the front seat wouldn't do that? You mean Nick Armitage wouldn't do that? Are you telling me nobody ever killed anybody for revenge? You mean all those Destroyer books I've been reading were wrong? I'm crushed. I can't believe it," Trace said. He clapped himself on the forehead.

"You just couldn't be wronger. The manager was a drunk. He was dipping into the register too and he probably got wind that Nick was about to can him. So he just got his pay and took

163

off. You think he had something to do with Tony's death?"

"I don't know. For somebody to do murder, usually they have to not like somebody. Did Dewey have any problems with Tony?"

"Nobody had problems with Tony," she said. "He was a good kid. My nephew, you know. I'm Martha's sister. Well, you know that. Tony was a gem."

"Odd," Trace said.

"What's odd?"

"A nightclub owner's kid. Fancy place, big bucks, disco dollies, beautiful people gobbling up drugs in the bathrooms. You wouldn't expect a kid growing up in that atmosphere to be straight-arrow. You kind of figure spoiled, egotistical, life in the fast lane."

"Not this time," she said. "You say straight-arrow. Tony was straighter than that. He was a laser beam."

"Then why'd he get killed?" Trace asked. "Why alongside a highway? Wearing a rubber mask on his face?"

"I don't know. I just don't know."

"Neither do I," Trace said. "But unlike everybody else around here, I want to find out."

"Just what does that mean?"

"I got the impression when I talked to Mrs. Armitage that she was worried Nick might go after the killer himself and get into trouble by taking revenge outside the law. That was my impression anyway."

"It's easy to get the wrong impression from Martha," the woman said. "She's not always able to make sense." Trace detected a touch of disdain in her voice.

"Well, is she right or wrong?" he asked. "Does Nick care or doesn't he care who killed his kid?"

"He cares " she said.

"It doesn't look it. He hasn't pressed the cops about their investigation. He's got money, but he hasn't hired anybody to try to find out what happened, at least not that I can tell. That's why I was thinking about Dewey Lupus. If he *was* the guy and Nick already got him, that'd explain why he's not worried about who killed his kid. All I keep hearing about Nick is he never forgets anything, memory like an elephant, but this elephant looks like he's got amnesia."

Instead of answering, she asked, "You want a cup of coffee? Or something stronger?"

"Something stronger," Trace said. He looked through the limousine window and realized he was somewhere on the East Side, in the Fifties.

"My place is only a couple of blocks from the Plaza," she said. "Have a drink and then you can hop a cab or walk back to your hotel."

"Sounds good. Do Eenie and Meenie come with us?"

"No," she said. She touched his forearm. "I think I can handle you myself. At least for a cup of coffee."

"Something stronger," Trace reminded her.

Anna Walker's apartment wasn't as large as Nick Armitage's, but Trace would hate to have to live on the difference.

"You like?" she asked.

"I'm impressed. I remember when bookkeepers didn't make this kind of money."

"Come on. You know I'm not just an accountant. I'm Nick's partner."

"In life or in business?"

"You've got sharp eyes," she said after a moment's hesitation. "And good ears too, I guess."

"My sense of smell is also highly developed," Trace said.

"What do you mean by that?"

165

"Something about this whole case gives off an aroma," he said.

She looked at him hard. He could see anger reflected in her eyes. While both Anna and her sister were beautiful, Anna had a blade-edged quality to her, unlike her sister, who exuded weakness and helplessness. It was probably inevitable that Nick and Anna would wind up sharing more than just business because, from what he'd heard and seen, they were too much alike to keep apart from each other.

"Maybe we should pass on that coffee or that drink," she finally said.

"I guess you're right. We're just not destined to be drinking buddies," he said.

"Good night then, Mr. Tracy."

"My friends call me Trace."

"Good night, Mr. Tracy."

Trace peeked in the bedroom of their suite to check on Chico. She slept peacefully on her back, content with the world, royally, afraid of nothing, and he thought to himself, What a tiny, vulnerable person she is.

Trace recalled once having told her that everything about her was wee. The furniture she bought was wee and the dinner plates and napkins, and while he didn't expect her to buy things that would fit his six-foot-three, he did expect her to try to accommodate people larger than her barely five-foot height.

She called this a base canard. She was, she insisted, five-foot-three. "It's on my passport. Would your government lie to you?"

"Five feet. Barely. A wee person. You are too wee by half. You even snore wee."

"I don't snore at all," she had said. "You snore. You snore when you drink. I hate when you drink and snore because there is no sleeping with you."

"Well, when you're ripping off those wee snores, you're not so much fun either," Trace had said.

"Snore? *Moi*? Liar."

"You do. You take in a little pull of air. Very soft, but it vibrates. Kind of like Gllllllll. And then you sneak it out like a canary with emphysema. Peeep. You think it's fun sleeping with you? Gllllll. Peeep. Gllllll. Peeep. Murders have been committed for less."

"Try sleeping on the sofa," she had said.

She was peeping softly in her sleep now. A shard of light from the hallway lamp crossed the bed and fell across her face. She looked lovely and he came to the side of the bed and kissed her gently on the forehead.

"Mmmmmmm," she murmured in her sleep, happily.

"It's Trace," he said.

"Oh," she said. She sounded disappointed.

"What do you mean, 'oh,' like that?" he said.

"Just joking, you ninny. Are you coming to bed?" Even as she spoke, she was drifting back into sleep.

"I didn't smoke tonight," he said.

"Mmmmmm," she said.

"I didn't really drink either."

"Mmmmmmm." Her voice was softer now.

"You don't really seem to care," he said, "so let's just drop it."

He turned to walk away, but she grabbed his wrist. "All right," she said. "Let's hear all about it."

"And I turned down the pathetic pleas of a sex-crazed singer. And a sexually frustrated lady accountant. And I walked off alone into the night. Alone. All by myself. To come home to you. Horny and unfulfilled."

She let go of his wrist. "I understand," she said softly. "I'm glad you came to share this with me." She was falling back asleep.

"I'll be in when I do my tapes," he said.

"I'll be here," she tried to say, but she was asleep before she finished the last word, sipping out her tiny little wee ladylike snore.

17

Tape Recording Number Three in the matter of
Tony Armitage, Plaza Hotel, New York. It is late
Friday night—hell, make that very early Satur-
day morning—and I am tired. What kind of day
was it? What did Walter Cronkite used to say? A
day like all days, filled with the events that alter
and illuminate our time. And . . . You Were There.

And I wish I hadn't been.

I have been everywhere, seen everything, listened to thousands of words, and I don't know
anything. If something doesn't happen soon, I'm
going to try to rouse Tony Armitage in a séance
and ask him to explain it to me.

So. Enough self-pity. On with the show. Try to
forget for a while that I'm not smoking or drinking or sexing nearly enough to keep body and
mind together.

I like the Armitages' apartment. I wonder if
they sublet the living room in the summer to the
Cosmos for soccer workouts. However, I don't
like Nick Armitage. I think the feeling's mutual.
He told me to leave and forget the insurance,
that someday *he* would find out who killed his
kid and take care of it his own way.

He and his wife are peas in a pod. They
know all the same things: that Tony wasn't al-

lowed in Nick's nightclub; that nobody knew why Tony was wearing that mask and neither of them ever saw it before. He didn't like my knowing that Tony was sleeping with Jennie for a while or that he told him to cool it.

And no, dear sweet Tony didn't use drugs, according to his father, who also had the ill grace to call Chico a slope. It was nice anyway to let him know that "the slope" dumped one of his two muscles in the disco the other night.

And it was also nice to find out that Nick is very unbrotherly with Anna Walker. Illicit lovers shouldn't kiss and leave doors open so insurance snoops can see.

That was the one good thing from the visit to their apartment. The other was Martha telling me that Nick pushed Tony very hard and it was his idea that Tony be a lawyer. Am I wrong or is it a pattern that Italian gangsters always want their sons to grow up to be lawyers? Is this to save legal fees later on? Or simply an attempt, against overwhelming odds, to teach the kids the difference between right and wrong, legal and illegal? I'll have to think this through carefully sometime when I'm not so tired.

And I went to the grocery store today for the first time in years, but it didn't do me any good because Cheryl, the British maid, wasn't going to tell me anything and she turned me down for lunch and told me if I wanted to see her again, I could wait for her on a street corner. But she was lying when she said that all she knew about Tony was that he seemed like a sweet young man. Why lie? Why wouldn't she talk to me?

Is this what happens when you get to be forty? When women look at you and know you don't smoke or drink nearly enough and are, therefore, no fun at all to be with? In my salad days, I would have gone through Cheryl like a dose of salts. Ahhh, sweet, flown youth. Good-bye forever.

I didn't tape lunch with Sarge. Just as well. It'd make me cry. First he has an office with an unlisted phone so my mother doesn't pester him. Then, when he goes out at night, he has to leave a note on the door so she won't get the neighbors to pester him. What a life. If ever I get married again, I'm going to have written rules of conduct. For the wife, anyway. I'll kind of make my stuff up as I go along. Anyway, Sarge checked his cop contacts and they all say that Nick isn't on anybody's shit list. And Nick didn't even go to the murder scene with the Connecticut cops. I don't know.

Sarge said he met Martha Armitage once on a case, but he didn't volunteer any more about it, and I guess I just don't want to hear about it because I don't ask him and I should.

I didn't even ask him tonight when we went to Armitage's other joint, that saloon in Drugville. Well, I didn't have much chance to ask him 'cause he only hung around long enough to save me from that moron, Ernie, and until his telephone call went through. Who's he cavorting with tonight?

But Sarge said something interesting. Suppose Armitage isn't really running around wild over his kid's death because he knows who killed the kid. And maybe it was that Dewey Lupus, the vanished manager of the tavern. It might not have turned out to be much of a security blanket for him.

I might have found out more if I wasn't so transparent to that girl singer. She knew that I was pumping her all night long. Still, she told me some stuff: that Tony used to sneak down there and that Paulie, the new manager, was his friend and would warn him when Nick was coming in. I wonder if they were really friends or if Tony had other reasons for going down to Alphabet City. And she told me Tony used some drugs.

And then Wanda Whips Wall Street. If you're listening, Chico, only fooling. That's Anna Walker, Martha Armitage's sister, and she is very hard and very smart, but not nearly so smart as she thinks she is.

Sarge thinks that Armitage keeps that saloon for sentimental reasons. Scratch that. Maybe once, but not now. They pay their singer by check and Anna comes down and picks up the receipts and then takes them back to her apartment, instead of dropping them off in a bank deposit somewhere. And they're cooking the books. She takes the receipts up to her apartment, phonies them up, shows a lot more money coming in than is really coming in, and then they make up the shortage by using the money Nick is making uptown by selling drugs in his joint. It's a laundry operation, to turn dirty money clean.

She told me that the missing Dewey was a drunk and a thief and left before Nick fired him. Well, maybe. And maybe not. I didn't believe her eyes when she told me that.

She got upset with me when I told her something smelled about this case. Probably all for the best. If I'd have hung around, she probably would have torn off my clothes and I'd have the devil's own time explaining to Chico.

By the way, Chico's going to be happy to know I met our two friends again tonight, our dancing partners from the disco. The Ugly Twins. What's their names? Oh, yeah, Frankie the Singer and Augie the Hand. God save us every one.

And so to bed. Tomorrow, I think maybe it's time to look after Dewey Lupus a little bit. Find out how he was going to move to the top of the world and wound up on top of the missing person's list.

A job for Sarge?

Maybe, if he can find room in his busy social schedule.

I've got a whole lot of tapes in the master file. I can't remember a case when I've used this many recording tapes before. I must be getting stale.

Expenses? Call them the usual. Ahh, you say, what's the usual? I don't remember. Say five hundred dollars. I'll itemize them when I go into retirement. I'll have a lot of time then.

I know what I need. I read about one of those devices that you can play a tape recording in and somehow it plays the tape twice as fast as normal, but without making the voices all sound like Alvin the Chipmunk. I think they somehow electronically take out the spaces between the words and nibble out a little bit of the words, but not enough so you can't understand them. If I had one of those, I could go through my tapes in half the time.

I wonder what they cost. Probably expensive and maybe I'd better wait for a cheaper case to work on, before I buy one and try to slide it past on my expense account. Or maybe Tony Armitage had one in his shopping bag of electronic junk. I'll have to ask that hillbilly the next time I see him. Maybe I can buy it secondhand, cheap. If you want to strike a bargain, deal with a dead man.

18

The telephone rang. Chico reached for it, listened for a moment, then covered the mouthpiece and shook Trace to wake him. "For you."

"Who the hell calls at this hour?"

"I'm sure I wouldn't know. What quiff are you boffing who has a phony British accent?"

"Phony? British? Oh, I think I know who she is," he said.

"I'm sure you do," she said sweetly.

"Give me the phone."

"How would you like it between your eyes?" Chico asked.

"In the open palm of my right hand will be sufficient," he said.

She slapped the phone down across the palm of his hand. If it had been a riding crop, it would have cut flesh and reached bone.

It was the maid, Cheryl, who identified herself as Cheryl Britten.

"Hello, Trace," she said. "Sorry if I'm disturbing you." Her accent was still veddy veddy, but her voice sounded a little shaky to him.

"No. Not disturbing. That was my mother. She always travels with me."

Chico snickered, reached her hand under the sheet, and grabbed him.

"Yes, she's very possessive," he said. Chico

tickled him. He tried to swat her hand away with his left hand. She responded by slipping her head under the sheet and going to bivouac with her hand.

"I've got to see you right away," Cheryl said.

"Sure. Important?"

"Yes. I'm leaving town and I want to talk to you first."

"You want to meet me here? For breakfast downstairs?" Trace asked.

"Bring her up," Chico mumbled from under the sheet. "We can have an orgy. Tell her to bring her yardstick and her tweed suit. I'm into English disciplines."

Trace hit her on the back of her head.

"No," Cheryl said. "I'm not . . . well, there's a delicatessen at Fifty-seventh and Sixth. Southeast corner. I'll meet you there."

"Okay. Forty-five minutes?" Trace asked.

"Righto."

"By the way," Trace said.

"What?"

"My mother says your accent's a fake."

"Your mother's right," Cheryl said as she hung up.

Chico reappeared from beneath the sheet. "What'd she say?"

"She said she was born in London and has the papers to prove it. The accent comes from living forty-eight years in the islands before moving here. She's quite an old lady actually," Trace said.

"You lie, God, how you lie. And her too. The accent's a fake."

"Whatever you say," Trace said patronizingly, not wanting to give her the satisfaction of knowing she was right. But he knew she was right. Chico spoke a half-dozen languages reasonably well and had an ear like a spy satellite: it missed

175

nothing and sorted out everything. If she said fake, it was fake.

"I take it we won't be having breakfast together," Chico said.

"No. Sorry. I'm really annoyed too."

"Why?"

"Today, I was going to make you a big gourmet breakfast," he said. "I was going to have the kitchen send up the fixings and a hot plate and really do it for you. The way us big detectives always do."

She shook her head. "What a shame that something came up. Will you cook breakfast some other time?"

"Certainly," he said reassuringly.

"Will you promise to schedule it for a day that I'm sure to be out of town?"

"Bitch," he said. He dived at her, but she escaped for the bathroom. He heard her lock the door behind her.

He importuned that he was in a hurry, but she would not relent. She was already stepping into the shower, she said.

"I have to go to the bathroom," he said. "And I know you're just too nice a person to leave me out here suffering."

"Flatulence will get you nowhere," she said.

"I have to take a shower too," he called out.

"You can come in and co-shower. There is no way you can have the shower first. No way that I am going to step out of this shower now that I'm in it, soaking wet, soapy, my breasts smooth and creamy from the excellent body soap I always carry with me, rippling with youth and vitality. . . ."

It sounded very good and he tried the doorknob again. It was unlocked.

As he stepped into the shower enclosure, he said, "Move over. And keep your hands to yourself."

"Nothing gives me greater pleasure. I just wanted to taunt you."

He showered quickly, dressed quickly, and put on his tape recorder. "I'm off now," he called through the again-closed bathroom door.

"Good."

"For breakfast with that old English lady."

"Liar," she said.

"Someday, you'll see," he said.

"Spread jam on her crumpet for me," Chico said.

Trace had noticed that there were two kinds of delicatessens in New York City: those that charged a dollar and a half for a sandwich and had surly help, and those that charged four dollars for a sandwich and had surly help.

This was the second kind. He arrived early, before Cheryl, sat at a table, and when the waitress growled at him, he ordered, "Two menus, black coffee, and a clean table."

"You don't know what you want for breakfast?" the waitress snarled.

"An incorrect assumption," Trace said with a bright smile. "It's breakfast time for you, but since I just arrived from Kuala Lumpur, I'm ready for dinner. Will you ask the chef if he has pickled camels' bladder? But it's got to be fresh. Frozen just isn't the same somehow."

"I'll get you the menus," she said with great disgust.

Cheryl arrived before the menus, before the coffee, before the clean table, but just as she sat down, the waitress arrived with a cup of coffee, two menus, and a cloth that looked as if it had been stolen from a car wash. She slapped the wet rag around the table, rearranging and dampening dirt, then slammed the menus down on the table. She put the cup of coffee in the back corner of the table, near the paper napkins.

"I don't need the menu," Cheryl told her. "I'll have coffee, toasted bagel, cream cheese, and nova."

"Hold the camel's bladder," Trace said. "I'll have the same."

The waitress looked upset at having been forced to carry the heavy menus so far, on a wild-goose chase, for people who didn't really need menus. She glanced over her shoulder as if looking for the chairman of the union's grievance committee, then grunted and walked away. She left the menus behind.

Trace dropped them on a chair at a nearby table, took a wad of napkins from the dispenser, and dried the table. He dumped the napkins in the middle of the adjoining table.

They heard the waitress bellow into the kitchen, "Burn lox twice."

"Burn lox twice," Cheryl said. "The voice of America. Speaking of which"—she dropped her accent and in a flattish Midwestern voice said—"I'm leaving town and I wanted to say good-bye."

"The accent was pretty good," he said.

"Not bad for a kid from Cleveland, huh?"

"Why are you leaving?" Trace asked.

"Well, now that you've gotten me fired, I thought it was time for a change."

"Me? How'd that happen?"

"I went in to work this morning and the head maid handed me my paycheck and said my services were no longer required."

"No notice?"

"No. They gave me two weeks' severance, and that's better."

"What did I have to do with it?" Trace asked.

"I asked the maid what was wrong with my work, and she said that Armitage said something about my hanging out with the wrong crowd."

"I resent that," Trace said. "I'm wrong, but no crowd."

"When I pressed her, she said I was seen with an undesirable yesterday, going to the market."

"Hey, kid, I'm sorry," Trace said.

"Don't be. Tell you the truth, I'd just about made up my mind to go anyway. Getting into the theater here is no easy business, and hell, I'm twenty-five, I don't think I want to go through it anymore," she said. "But I didn't do anything wrong and I didn't spill any family secrets to you, and that ticks me off. I don't like Armitage. If I had crawled into the sack with him the way he wanted, you can be pretty damn sure I wouldn't have been fired."

"He was after you."

"I've been there about seven months," Cheryl said. "For the first three months, I couldn't get him off my tail. If I stopped short, he'd bump into me."

"Well, I can't fault his taste," Trace said.

"If his loving sister-in-law, sweet Anna, had her way, I'd have been long gone. She must have known he was chasing me because she was always giving me the old dagger eye."

The waitress came with their orders. True to form, she had brought Trace an additional cup of coffee. He resisted the impulse to tell her that he could only be charged for one. The waitress looked around, snapped up the menus from the other table, then lifted the wad of wet napkins Trace had used, and carried them away between thumb and index fingers as if they were a particularly loathsome dirty diaper.

Cheryl sipped at her coffee and Trace asked how she happened to get with the Armitages.

"I thought New York would be a piece of cake," she said. "After all, I graduated from the Cleveland Academy of Dramatic Arts, didn't I? I couldn't even find work as a waitress. Or driving a cab. Why do you wear that frog on your tie all the time? It's ugly."

"It happens to conceal a secret but powerful microphone which is recording this entire conversation," Trace said with a smile. "You were saying you couldn't find work."

She smiled back and said, "So I went to a temporary agency and I put on the phony Brit accent and faked up a background and got the job with Armitage. When I found out who he was, I thought it might be real good, because, well, with a nightclub he's kind of in show business, and I thought he might be an entrée to something. But nothing came of it."

"Did you ever mention it to him?"

"Yeah," she said. "I was there a couple of months and I guess he figured I wasn't going to sleep with him. Then I told him I was interested in a show-business career, and he said that I ought to concentrate more on getting my act together in the kitchen. Prick."

"You probably did right," Trace said consolingly. "The way to become a household word is hardly ever to become a locker-room joke."

"Very profound," she said.

"Detective talk," Trace said. "You should see me cook."

"Anyway," Cheryl said, "I'm leaving, so I figured I don't have any loyalty to those people. I thought if there was anything you wanted to know and I could help. I'd tell you."

"Like that you had an affair with Tony?" Trace said.

She put down her coffeecup. "How'd you know that?"

"It was in your eyes when we talked yesterday."

"Okay. So much for my skill as an actress," she said. "Tony came on to me and by that time I was so ticked at the old man that I let him."

"Did it last long?"

"A month, six weeks, four or five dates," she said.

"When was this?" he asked as she started to eat

She answered him with a big bite of bagel, cream cheese, and lox in her mouth. "About four months ago, I guess," she said.

"No chance of the family finding out? Weren't you worried?"

She shook her head and gulped down her food. "No. Tony wouldn't talk. He couldn't stand his father. And we went up to my place. Once we went to an apartment he rented near the college. He wanted to show off, I think."

"And what happened?"

"The novelty wore off," she said. "I'm not really into spoiled college boys."

"That was Tony?"

She nodded, her mouth full. She was a good eater, Trace decided. She held her bagel in both hands like a hamburger and took a good man-sized mouthful. Maybe not a great eater, like Chico, but a good one.

"Yeah" she said, swallowing almost desperately. Trace moved his fish around atop the cream cheese. "He was spoiled rotten, by his mother, by his aunt. Not by his father, though. The old man always kept a tight rein on him. Like when he was romancing that black chick up at the school, Armitage told him to knock it off."

"Armitage didn't like it, huh?"

"Better believe it," she said. "Anyway, he leaned into the kid, and Tony, I told you, he didn't have a lot of backbone. I was with him that night."

"What happened?"

"A lot of big talk mostly. He told me he'd get even."

"What do you think he meant by that?"

"I don't know. Maybe big-shot talk. A lot of kids talk that way about their father."

"You keep calling him a kid. Wasn't he your age?" Trace asked.

"A couple of years younger. But I've been on my own for a long time. Tony wasn't. He liked Toys. Whoopie cushions. He was just a kid. We'd be going out or something and he'd almost cry because he didn't have any smoke with him. So he'd go to that downtown tavern and get some. He wanted to be a big man."

"Where'd he get it down there?"

"He had a friend who worked there who always had drugs."

"Paulie sound like a familiar name?" Trace asked.

"That's right. That's who it was," she said.

"Did Tony use drugs a lot?"

"He always had grass or coke on him." She hesitated. "All right. The truth. I think he might have been pushing some dope on campus. Little stuff, though."

"Do you think maybe that's why he was killed?"

"I don't know."

"You said you once went to his apartment in Connecticut. Would you remember where that was?" Trace asked.

"Not the address. But it was just outside the main entrance to the campus, a funny-looking green building. Hey, that's something," she said. "Tony rented that just after Armitage told him to split up with the black girl. He said it would be their little love nest. He talked like that a lot, though. He thought it made him sound like a big man."

"How'd you like the bagel?" Trace asked.

"It was okay."

"You want mine?"

"No. I've had enough," she said. He nodded.

Good but not great. Chico would have wolfed his down even before he invited her to take it.

"What else can you think of?" Trace said.

"You know that Armitage and that Anna Walker are getting it on."

Trace nodded. "I figured it."

"And you know that Mrs. Armitage is a drinker."

"You don't work for her anymore. You can call her Martha. A bad one?"

"Bad enough. She's got a little buzz on most of the time and sometimes a big buzz. That orange juice she was drinking yesterday morning, those were really screwdrivers. Loaded with vodka. She sits around most of the day drinking them. At night, she's blotto."

"I knew that's what she was drinking," Trace said.

"How'd you know? I thought I was pretty discreet," Cheryl said.

"You were. But she said, 'Cheryl, make me another orange juice.' No one says 'make' an orange juice. You make a screwdriver; you pour an orange juice."

"You're smarter than you look," Cheryl said. "I thought, well, the way you chatter, I thought you were sort of a halfwit."

"It's always good when people think you're stupid," Trace said. "It makes them careless. Like you're deaf so they don't have to whisper to keep their secrets."

"Not bad," she said. "I'll remember that. There was one more thing I wanted to tell you about."

"What's that?" he asked.

"It was the night Tony got killed. It was the regular maid's night off and I was filling in for her. Mrs. Armitage, Martha, was sitting in the television room chugging a glass of straight vodka. She was whacked out of her gourd. The phone rang in the television room and she didn't even get up to answer it. So I did and it was Armitage. He asked me how his wife was, but I didn't want to get her into trouble, she looked like a zombie, so I said she seemed to be all right. Then he tells me, 'Listen, Cheryl, I want you to make sure that the apartment doors are double-locked.' There are two entrances, you know. And he said, 'Don't open the door for anybody but me and Miss Walker.' That's Anna, the sister-in-law. I said okay, and he said, 'And make sure that Mrs. Armitage doesn't go out.' "

"What'd you do?"

"Well, he told me to do it right away, and in the meantime, let him talk to Martha. So I gave her the phone and I went and locked the doors. When I went back inside, she was just sitting in the chair, with this wild look on her face. She had dropped the phone on the floor. I picked it up but Armitage wasn't on the line anymore."

"What happened then?"

"Martha wanted to take a nap. She was really drunk now. I told her I'd help her into bed, but she wouldn't move. It was like she didn't know I was there. She just kept talking about napping, but she wouldn't move. Finally, I just let her sit there by herself and I went outside. Anna came over about twenty minutes later and then she went in and was with her sister."

"Did she say anything to you?"

The young woman shook her head. "A cold woman, that one. But she came out into the kitchen later and asked me to make tea for everybody. She put her purse down on the table when she told me and I saw she had a gun in it."

"What time was all this?"

"It was before ten o'clock," Cheryl said. "Because I made the tea, and after I did, Anna told me that she would take care of everything and I could go. And I did, and I was home before ten o'clock 'cause I saw *Falcon Crest* on television. Oh. Another thing. When I left, that goon who works for Armitage, he was in the hallway outside the apartment."

"Which one?"

"Frankie? Is that his name? And the other ugly one, his brother, was sitting in a chair down in the lobby. They didn't say anything to me, though."

"What do you think it all meant?" Trace asked.

"I don't know. Maybe it meant that there was something wrong, I guess, but I don't know what. It was just that the next morning they found Tony's body."

"Who'd you tell this to?" Trace asked.

She shrugged. "Who's to tell? And what's to tell? That the lady I work for is a drunk, the man I work for is a nut? Nothing to tell."

She finished the last sip of her coffee and glanced at her watch.

"So now you're leaving," Trace said. "Isn't it kind of in a hurry?"

"No. I've really been thinking about it for a long time. You can keep the Big Apple. Give me Cleveland. Unless, of course, I got a better offer. You a millionaire, looking for a young wife with a great phony British accent?"

"Afraid not. My mother wouldn't allow it."

"I guess not. I talked to your mother on the phone before. She sounds wonderfully young."

"She is."

"I think it's great that you two still sleep in the same bedroom."

"I never told you I was a nice person," Trace said.

"No, that's right. You didn't."

19

Chico had already left the room when Trace returned to lay in a new supply of recording tapes. She had left him no note so he left her one that said:

"You didn't leave me a note, but that's all right, I hardly noticed. I will be out on this case today. Working. I'll call before dinnertime and maybe we can have dinner together if you can fit me into your busy New York schedule of fun in the sun."

The front desk had no messages and he called Sarge at his home and office, but got no answer.

He ransomed his rental car from the parking garage near the hotel and reflected that parking the car each day in Manhattan cost him almost as much as it cost to rent the car itself from Hertz. Somehow O. J. Simpson and Arnold Palmer had forgotten to mention that. As he was driving downtown, he thought that that might be his million-dollar breakthrough. Suppose he could sell some car-rental company the idea of providing free parking with each car they rented. Of course, it wouldn't work in New York because the garages were always full and each of them seemed to set its own price, all of them confiscatory. But maybe they could make a deal in a city that nobody visited. It would work in Tulsa. Nobody ever visited Tulsa. Trace had spent a lifetime there one day. He was overwhelmed by the brilliance of his scheme: renting a car when you went to a lousy city and having parking included in your rental fees. Garages in Tulsa were always empty. They'd jump at the chance.

He knew right off that it was one of his better ideas, ranking right up there with the C.B. Bible of the Air, and the reversible signs for the front of everyone's car so that a driver could move people off the road from in front of him. The one he had liked best was OUT OF CONTROL, printed backward so that drivers up front could see it in their rearview mirrors. He had tried to convince Walter Marks to invest ten thousand dollars in the plan, but Marks—a mean little man of no courage and small vision—had insultingly declined.

Not that Trace had needed Marks's ten thousand. He had money of his own, quite a few thousand saved from his gambling days, and he had a good retainer from Garrison Fidelity insurance and somehow he managed to save them a lot of money on cases he investigated and he got a percentage of that. He could have financed the plan himself, but when he was in accounting and business school at the Jesuit college in New Jersey, he had learned the first and most important rule of business: never invest your own money. Get other people to put up the cash. Keep control, but don't lose a nickel of your own.

He had just not had much success in getting people to invest in his plans. He thought that it might have had something to do with the fact that he drank like a fish, smoked like a chimney, and according to Chico, dressed like a creature who had found his wardrobe in a Volunteers of America collection basket. Maybe that would all change now that he was becoming sober and unsmoky. All at Chico's behest. Maybe he would let her pick out some new clothes for him so he looked neater. And then he would repay her for all her kindness: he would borrow money from her for his next great idea.

He had already rejected the Tulsa car-rental-cum-parking scheme. To set it up, he'd probably have to go to Tulsa and he had already been to Tulsa once in his life.

But there were plenty of ideas where that came from. Plenty for Chico to invest in. He expected a little resistance. Chico was, as were many beautiful women, obsessed with the future and its perils. She was only twenty-six years old, but she was sure that cellulite, wrinkles, and varicose veins were only moments away and she wanted to have something laid by for that day when her beauty would no longer get her over on the world.

Trace, for his part, figured that day would not come for another quarter-century, if then. Chico had that luminous, always youthful Oriental skin, a shining Eurasian face, and a body that was kept young and vibrant by constant exercise.

But he would work on her. If she would put some of her money—and he knew she had a lot of it—into one of his good plans, why, the two of them could be rollickingly wealthy in just a matter of months. A year at the outside.

He turned onto West Twenty-sixth Street and parked at a fire hydrant outside his father's office. Sarge wasn't in the office, nor at the restaurant on the ground floor, and in the conviction that his father was more likely to visit the bar than his office, Trace left a note there for his father, telling him what he had heard about Dewey Lupus and asking Sarge to check out anything he could learn about the man, and meet Trace at six P.M. at the restaurant.

Then he drove up to Fairport. He had trouble restraining his laughter when he drove through the Bronx and saw the latest in lunatic New York City programs. Somebody had gotten the bright idea that one way to dress up New York was to take the crumbling old buildings of the Bronx and put decals on them. The decals were supposed to depict scenes of solid, middle-class life. They were slapped on the buildings, over gaping glassless windows that had long been broken by vandals, and were supposed to make it look as if there were plants in the window, people in the abandoned apartments, and life going on as usual. Typical for New York, he thought. Solve the slum problem by sticking decals on it. What would you expect from a city whose police department gave classes for the elderly in how to be mugged and survive?

The small home where Tony Armitage had lived with LaPeter and Jennie Teller seemed to serve as a background sound module for the street it was on. The street could have come from any college town. It was packed with head shops and stereo repair parlors, designer boutiques, and karate studios. And thumping over it was the musical racket coming from the small house.

This time the front door was locked and Trace banged on it with both fists and one foot for a full two minutes, before he heard the lock being turned.

"Oh, it's you, what's your name?" LaPeter said, looking like a bamboo pole with hair.

"Tracy. Who were you expecting?"

"That girl said she's moving her stuff back in, she is. I figured it was her."

"So she's not here now?"

"Maybe working," LaPeter said.

"Thanks," Trace said. He turned to leave, then

stopped. "Why do you have that music on so loud all the time?"

"It's my work," LaPeter said. "I fix stereos for people or give their sound systems more power, I give them. Can't do it without turning up the volume."

"Thank you. I've misjudged you."

"How's that?"

"I thought you were just crazy and deaf."

LaPeter seemed to take umbrage at that. He said, "*I'm* not the one who does W. C. Fields impersonations."

"I can attest to that," Trace said, waving his hands over his head, pulling his head down into the collar of his shirt, and rolling his eyes wildly.

"I love it," LaPeter said. "I love it."

Trace drove to the front entrance of the college campus and found the small green garden-apartment building that Cheryl said she had once visited with Tony Armitage. He stopped his car, glanced at the doorbells, and found one that listed the name of Teller. He rang the bell a long time but got no answer, then drove to the diner where the black woman worked.

He stopped in the parking lot, left his motor running, and walked to the restaurant's door. He saw Jennie Teller working behind the counter, which was packed with diners, so he went back to his car and returned to the green apartment building.

Like most apartment buildings occupied mostly by college students, the security was negligible. The front door was unlocked, and while he passed two people walking up the stairs, neither of them asked him what he was doing there.

If Jennie Teller had a deadbolt lock on her door, she hadn't used it that day. It only took him a few seconds to slip open her front door,

190

step inside the apartment, and close the door behind him.

He waited inside the door for a few moments, listening for sounds, just in case the woman had a roommate, but the apartment was silent.

He was in a bright living room whose furnishings were bland and spare. Some dance posters and two African masks hung from the walls. The furniture was varnished rattan, with nubby tweed cushions, and Trace decided that the apartments came already furnished. Except for the wall hangings, nothing in the apartment looked as if Jennie Teller would have bought it, and if Tony Armitage had rented the apartment as a little love nest, the chances are he would have chosen a furnished apartment. To the right, he found a small kitchen and, on the left, Jennie's bedroom. The closets showed him that she lived there alone. Only woman's clothes were hanging up.

As he often did when he committed a burglary, he started to wonder exactly why he was there, exactly what he hoped to find, and was annoyed when he could not answer those questions to his own satisfaction.

He went to the tall Formica dresser in the room. There was a box of Sweet'n Low envelopes on top of it, which struck him as passing odd. He rooted around in the dresser drawers for a while, feeling uncomfortably perverted as he continued to find nothing but ladies' undergarments. Stuck in the back of a bottom drawer, under a pile of woman's T-shirts, he found a bankbook.

The account was in the name of Jennie Teller and her balance was $4,809.27. All of it had been deposited in the three months before Tony Armitage's death. There had been no deposits in the last thirty days.

He repeated the number aloud so that his tape

recorder would pick it up, then put the bankbook back.

He didn't know what else to look for but idly opened the box of Sweet'n Low packs. He counted twenty of the small packs inside the box, but all of them were empty. The packs had been neatly slit across the top, probably with a razor blade, and their contents of artificial sweetener poured out.

He reclosed the box and left the apartment. Tony Armitage had lived there with the woman, but no traces of his existence were left.

"Back again, huh?"

"Came to talk to you some more."

"What's your name again?"

"Call me Trace."

"That's right. Tracy. What'd you want to talk to me about, Mr. Tracy?"

"Same thing. Tony's death."

"Same answer. I don't know anything about it," Jennie Teller said.

"When's your break?" Trace asked.

She glanced at her watch. "Fifteen minutes. I don't want to spend it with you."

"I was going to buy you lunch," he said.

"Lunch comes with the job."

"Then you buy me lunch. I'll make it worth your while."

"How's that? You going to make me rich?"

"Even better than that," Trace said.

"What's better than rich?"

"Alive."

They sat at a metal table in a far corner of the diner's big kitchen. Jennie Teller had a long-shoreman's breakfast in front of her, even though it was past noon. Trace had coffee.

"So how you going to keep me alive?"

"I'll get to it," Trace said. "I hear you're moving back into the old house."

"That's right."

"Where you moving from?"

"Ho, ho. The detective is a shrewd one. Trapped me right away, tripped me right up."

"Can the Aunt Jemima shit," Trace said. "You don't do it all that well and I've seen it before."

"Giving the audience what they want to hear."

"What I want to hear is where you're moving from?"

"Why should I tell you?"

"No reason, I guess, so I'll tell you. You're moving from the apartment that Tony Armitage rented for you."

"Who told you that?"

"It didn't take a lot of work. You haven't been staying at the house with Rufus Redneck. Tony's old man leaned into him to break it off with you, and then right after that, you moved out of the house. You had one pair of jeans in your closet there and an old pair of boots. That sounds like a lady who's living somewhere else."

"Guilty. Any law against that?" she asked.

"No. And now, I figure that with Tony dead, you can't make the rent, so you're moving back with Rufus."

"I'm listening," she said.

"Good. Now, I'm not telling Nick Armitage about this. He's no friend of mine and I don't care if you and Tony rented the top floor of the World Trade Center and played body-slide there sixteen hours a day. No skin off my nose."

"You're just being my friend," she said.

"You're being sarcastic, but that's closer to the truth than you know," he said. "So now I'm going to tell you some more things and you're going to chime in at the correct intervals with pieces of

193

knowledge that I should have and that will enrich and beautify my life."

"Maybe I will and maybe I won't," she said.

"You will."

"You are one pushy man."

"Jennie, I don't have time to be sweet and charming, so I think we ought to go right to the main point."

"Go to it," she said.

"Tony was selling drugs on campus," Trace said.

The patronizing look in her eyes vanished. An overreaction, Trace thought.

"He was getting them from New York and he was making a few bucks selling them around here. How'm I doing so far?"

"I don't know anything about it," she said. She looked down at her iced tea and stirred it, staring as if there were something in the ice cubes that demanded her immediate attention.

"Could I have more coffee?" Trace asked.

She took his cup to a large urn in the center of the room and refilled it. When she put it in front of him, she automatically pushed a sugar bowl in front of him.

"I'd rather have Sweet'n Low," he said.

"It's with the sugar."

"One of those from your pocket," he said.

Her face turned ashen.

"We both know who was helping Tony sell drugs, don't we?" Trace said.

She pushed her ice tea away angrily. "I don't have to sit here and listen to this nonsense."

"No, you don't. I'm sure Nick Armitage would like to hear it. Maybe it'd give him a lead to who killed his kid. I think Nick might like to talk to you about it." She wavered and he snapped, "Sit down, girl."

"You're a mean bastard," she said, but she sat

"You got it. Anyway, the diner is a good place to sell drugs from. Nothing big. Students wander in and out all day long. A few bucks here, a few bucks there. Like that, right? Just slip them their pack of Sweet'n Low."

She looked at him and he let the silence hang heavy over the table until it became almost palpable and painful, and then she glumly nodded.

"So you were making a couple of bucks and so was Tony, and it was nice and enough to pay for the apartment where you and Tony shacked up after the old man told him to drop you. And now the nose candy's gone because Tony was the supplier and the rent money's gone and you're moving back in with LaPeter." She looked woebegone and he reached across the table and touched her hand. "Jennie, I don't give a damn. It's no skin off my nose, nothing that I care about."

"I'm glad," she said with heavy sarcasm. "If you cared about it, you might really have gotten nosy and dug around." She essayed a small smile and he patted her wrist and smiled back.

"When Nick told him to drop you, Tony told people he was going to get even with his father."

"So?"

"Was it just the drugs or did he have something else planned?"

"Like what?" she asked.

"Dammit, Jennie, don't keep answering questions with questions. Like anything."

"I don't know. Honest, I don't know."

"He wasn't planning to expand his drug dealing?"

"He never mentioned it."

"I thought that might be a reason for getting him killed," Trace said.

"No. Truth. He never mentioned it. He was just moving a little stuff. You're right. It paid the rent. It was like selling to just friends. There was no real drug dealing, nothing that would get him chilled."

"Were you really out of town that weekend?"

"I was gone the whole weekend."

"Could it be checked?" Trace asked.

"I've got a hotel receipt from Atlantic City. I was there with half a dozen people. You want their names?" She started to sound confident again.

"No. I believe you. Something happened the night before Tony got killed."

"Well, I was away. I wouldn't know," she said. She stopped and Trace waited. "Like what happened?" she said.

"Something that upset his family. You don't know what that was?"

"No. Did the family say what?"

"They're not talking to me a lot," Trace said. "Tell me, was Tony a big romance in your life?"

She hesitated and he said, "The truth."

"All right. The truth. He was a guy that I lived with in the house with that crazy redneck and his stereo systems. Tony had money, all the time, and I never had any. So we played house. I got another year of school to go here, and then two more years of graduate school at least. I don't have two nickels to rub together. And Tony did."

"That why you got into the drugs with him?"

"Had to make some money someway."

"You could keep working here," Trace said.

"At minimum wage?" she said. "Anyway, working sucks."

"Sucking works," Trace said.

"I don't do that kind of work," she said.

"Peddling drugs isn't a lot different," he said. "And it's dangerous. Too many people know. Too many records. You put money in the bank and someone wonders how a counter girl in a diner can get a lot of money together. You talk to the wrong people or the wrong people talk about you."

"I'm done with it," she said. "The supply's all gone and I'm not interested anymore."

"I hope you're in time," Trace said.

"What does that mean?"

"That black guy who was in here the other day? The one who wanted to throw me out?"

"Yeah. Barker's his name."

"I saw him the next night going into Nick Armitage's office in New York."

"Oh, no," she said.

"Afraid so. Does he come around much?" Trace asked.

"Only a couple of times," she said. "Not in a while."

"Were you romancing him?"

"No. He wanted to, but I wouldn't," she said quickly, searching Trace's face, as if looking there for reassurance.

"Did he know what you were doing here? With the little sideline business?"

"No. I never told him. We were never that close."

Trace shrugged. "Then you're probably all right. Maybe the best he could tell Nick was that you're clean."

"I hope so."

"If I find out different, I'll let you know," Trace said.

20

Trace and Chico were waiting for Sarge at the restaurant below his office. Chico had spent the day shopping.

"I don't understand how somebody can spend the day shopping," Trace said.

"You could if you put your mind to it," she said.

"What do you do when you shop?" he asked.

"That is well up, even on your elevated list of dumb questions. What do you do when you eat?"

"Eat is usually a transitive verb," Trace said. "Transitive verbs are specific. Shop is an intransitive verb. By definition, they are vague and dangerous. Tell me what you do when you shop."

"You shop," she said.

"What is it that *you* need that you shop for?"

"You might not need anything," she said.

"You can spend a day walking around, looking at things that you don't need or want and usually can't afford?" he asked.

"That sounds about right."

"That's idiotic," Trace said. "My mother may not have much to recommend her . . ." he began.

"Hear, hear," Chico said.

"But she knows how to do one thing."

"If you're going to tell me that that woman

knows how to shop, I'm going to pour Roquefort dressing in your hair."

"That woman really knows how to shop."

"Where's the Roquefort dressing?" Chico asked.

"She goes to Shoppers' City and she finds whatever is cheap and she buys it."

"Suppose she doesn't need it," Chico said.

"She buys it anyway. You never know when you might need it."

"Suppose, to interject some humor into this insipid conversation," Chico said, "suppose she found something that was too ugly, even for her so-called taste, something she really didn't like. What would she do then?"

"If the price were right, she would buy it and give it to somebody as a gift. If it was cheap enough, she'd buy two and give them both away so people could marvel at her generosity. Now, that's shopping," Trace said.

Chico said, "If I were back in the womb and had a choice of being an Irish Jew like you or a Japanese Italian like me, I think I'd stay the way I am."

"I don't care what you pick as long as you pick August again to be born in," Trace said.

"Why?"

"Because I think it's wonderful that your birthstones are peridot and sardonyx. Imagine if you were born in April and your birthstone was a diamond. You'd never get a birthday gift. But, hell, I can buy a basket of peridots and sardonyxes for seventeen dollars."

"I don't get diamonds and I don't get peridots either," Chico said.

"The hell you say," Trace said.

"The truth I say."

"Didn't I give you them last year? Oh, no. I'll tell you why. I remember going into Tiffany's on one of my trips East and asking them for the biggest peridot they had in the place."

"What happened?" Chico asked.

"You know Tiffany's. Always trying for the fast buck. They only had second-rate peridots and they tried to stick me with a sardonyx instead. I wasn't going for that."

"So you wound up getting me nothing for my birthday."

"That's hard for me to believe," he said.

"It's true."

"I gave you nothing? Not even a sweat shirt?"

"The sweat shirt was the year before last. It was the one with Uncle Sam on it. It said, 'Join the Army. Travel to faraway lands. Meet interesting, exotic people. And kill them.' "

"I remember that. Nothing last year, you say?"

"No. You gave me a gummed address label for my belly."

"I don't remember that at all," Trace said. "Who was I trying to send you to?"

"It didn't have an address on it. It said, 'Caution. Danger. Keep Out. This area patrolled and protected by Devlin Tracy's attack tongue.' "

"You never wore it either," Trace said.

"I threw it out."

"You dummy, what did you expect?"

"What are you talking about?" she said.

"You probably didn't realize that there was a thousand-dollar bill stuck on the back of that gummed label. And you threw it out. What a pity."

"That thousand-dollar bill? Was that yours? Was that from you?" she asked. She looked very cheerful.

"Why?"

"I found it loose one day in my dresser drawer. I didn't know how it got there."

"Shouldn't you have offered me half?" he asked. "We share the apartment."

"Ho. Ho. Ho," she said. "So where's Sarge? He's late."

"It didn't stop you from ordering dinner."

"A girl's got to eat, doesn't she?" Chico said without shame.

"I don't know where he is," Trace said. "I left him a note to meet us here and he picked up the note."

"Has he been any help to you so far?"

"Well, he hasn't hurt, and as long as he's working, maybe he can help. I'll take help from anybody on this case."

"That bad, huh?"

"There's nothing here. I've got the kid as a low-level drug dealer who didn't like his father much. I've got the father washing drug money through a tavern he owns downtown. I've got the mother a drunk and the father banging his sister-in-law. I've got a missing manager from the downtown saloon. What I don't have is a murder suspect. You want to hear my misery?"

"Go ahead. Just don't expect a lot of responses. I want to eat."

"Can I drink?"

"Stick with the wine. You're doing well."

Trace grumbled some, then slowly and carefully told Chico about his breakfast meeting with the Armitage maid, his burglary of Jennie Teller's apartment, and then his interview with her in the diner kitchen.

"What do you think?" he asked.

"Let me listen to some of it," she mumbled through a mouth full of bread.

When he was sure no one was looking, he unbuttoned his shirt, untaped the recorder, and put it on the table. With a small personal earphone from his pocket, he let Chico listen to the tapes of the interviews.

She went "ummm" a lot before she turned off the recorder.

"Now what do you think?"

"I think you didn't sleep with either of these women," she said.

"Of course I didn't. I tried to tell you that last night too, but you wouldn't listen. If it's not eating, it's sleeping. You're really just a creature of your instincts," he said.

"I'm impressed. I don't know what to think. Except for these, I haven't heard any of your tapes and you haven't filled me in a lot. Martha Armitage? She's the one Sarge had the affair with?"

"So *you* say," Trace said.

"Why would that girl get fired for being seen with you?" she asked.

"I don't know. Armitage doesn't like me. And the only reason he's got not to like me is that I want to find out who killed his kid. The maid talks to me and gets fired."

"It doesn't make a lot of sense, does it?"

"I don't need somebody else who doesn't understand," Trace said. "I don't understand enough for all of us."

Chico ignored him and was talking as much to herself as to him. "I don't fathom why the kid was wearing that rubber mask when he got killed. That's got to mean something, Trace. And I don't know what that phone call was from Nick Armitage the night before the killing. The chickie with the phony British accent sounded like a nice kid."

It was a mark of her maturity, Trace thought, that she would characterize as "a kid" a woman only a year younger than herself.

"She was," Trace said.

"And Jennie's a liar, of course." She looked at him mockingly. "Heh, heh. 'Working sucks. Sucking works.' Aren't you cute?"

"You noticed she's a liar," he said.

"She oozes lying," Chico said.

"I know. She's too quick with the answers, just a little too pat. I wouldn't trust her at all."

"A lot of questions, Trace, and no answers. Maybe you ought to work a different way."

"I don't have any deep emotional commitment to the old way 'cause it hasn't done me a freaking bit of good so far," Trace said.

"Forget the people involved," she said. "Concentrate on the killing instead."

"Okay. I'm concentrating. I still don't know anything."

"Maybe you would if you stopped talking for a while," she said. "The Armitage kid was killed where they found his body, right?"

"That's what the police say."

"All right. Why there? Did somebody take him there to kill him? Was he there waiting for a bus? Maybe he went there himself?"

"What the hell for? It's in the middle of nowhere."

"Come on, pal," Chico said. "I'm thinking out loud. Don't challenge me now; it's inhibiting at this stage of the process."

"I'm sorry," Trace said.

"Suppose he went there himself. Suppose he was going there, I don't know, to meet somebody. Maybe he got a ride with somebody and got off there to get a lift."

"Still, why the mask?"

"He wasn't going to a party?" she asked.

"Nobody knows anything about any party," Trace said.

"And they don't know if the mask was his?"

"Nobody ever saw it before."

"What was he wearing again?" she asked.

"Black shirt and pants. They were his."

"If he *was* going to a masquerade party or something, that doesn't sound like the outfit to go with a Richard Nixon mask," she said. She stared off at the wall and shook her head.

"I know." Trace touched her arm. "It doesn't parse for me either."

The waitress came to tell them the kitchen was out of scungille salad. Chico ordered a shrimp cocktail and fried clams instead.

Trace thought that before they left, he would show her the strip of pictures on the wall behind the bar. If she threw up on the spot, as he expected she might, there might be merit in his diet-through-vomiting plan.

He told Chico he was going upstairs to see if Sarge had returned to his office. The door was still locked, and when he came downstairs, Chico said, "Sarge just called. He's not coming."

"Why not?"

"He said something came up and he was going to be busy."

"Why didn't you hold him on the phone?" he asked.

"I tried. He said he was in a hurry. He almost hung up on me."

Trace sat back down and sipped at his wine. "You know, it used to be that if he said something like that, I'd say, okay, he was going to be busy, in a hurry, something came up."

"And?"

"And now that you've poisoned my mind against him, making me think my own father's the playboy of the western world, all I can think of is that he's got a chick on the side somewhere while my mother's out of town and he's too busy rolling around in bed to come and have dinner with us."

"To which I say, hooray."

"Hooray for cheating husbands? My, my, my, how the worm turns."

"Hooray for some nice sweet old man who's sixty-five years old or some such—"

"Sixty-seven," Trace said.

"Sixty-seven and maybe being happy for a change. Trace, stay off his case. Leave him be."

"I want to ask him about it," Trace said.

"Why?"

"Because I want to see him sweat when I grill him. I want to see little beads of perspiration run down his guilty red face when he finds out the jig is up and I know all about it."

"You take this very hard for someone to whom Fidelity is only the name of an insurance company," she said dryly.

"Hold, woman. Holdest thou thy tongue, wench. That was all in the past. I have been a model of purity for God knows how long now. And now that I've finally gone straight, I find out my father's twisted. This makes sense to you? Did it ever occur to you that I might have a genetic flaw, some inbred inability to stay out of strange beds? Don't you think I should know this? Don't you want to know it before you get involved with me?"

"Involved with you? I've lived with you for three years. There have been a hundred and fifty women in that time. A hundred and fifty that I know about. Double it, triple it for the times you sneaked around and I didn't find out about it."

"I don't want to talk about it," Trace said. "I just find the whole matter slightly repulsive."

"God, I hate it when you don't drink. I hate it when you drink because you're a lunatic, but when you don't drink, you're a petty, vicious, nasty, carping hypocritical nag. Buy a bottle of vodka and get ripped, will you?"

"Not until you pay me the five hundred dollars you're going to owe me," he said. "Unless you want to concede and pay up now."

"Don't hold your breath, ace," she said.

When they finished dinner, Trace asked her, "Do you want to hang out with me tonight?"

"Might as well. It's too late to do anything else."

"I know a great place," he said. "You'll love it."

When they left the restaurant, he showed her the bank of portrait photos high on the barroom wall.

"What do you think?" he asked her.

"That fellow, second from the right, looks pretty nice. I might like to know him."

"The hell with him. What about the others?"

"Degenerates, obviously. Enough to make you want to throw up."

"Good girl," he said. "You've made my night."

"How?" she asked.

But Trace would not tell her. First, he decided, he would have to figure out how to get her to invest her money. Then he would tell her.

21

They were at a restaurant off University Place
that featured opera music.

Trace said, "You're going to love this place."

"Why didn't we eat here, then?"

"Because I don't like the food, but the drinks
are good and it's the best entertainment in New
York. And they're not snobs here. They don't
care if I hum along, unlike some people I know."

"My bel canto hummer," she said. "I wonder
if God, in His infinite wisdom, knew what He
was getting me into."

They sat at a table in the far corner of the
room. Chico ordered Perrier and Trace smugly
ordered white wine. When the waiter left, Chico
said, "Remember, I told you, go ahead and drink
vodka. If you're going to be miserable with wine,
I don't want to hear about it."

"When I get my five hundred from you," Trace
said. "And when I finally figure out what I'm
going to do with my career. If I decide I'm going
to be a big detective, I want to come in pure. No
drinking hard stuff, very little smoking, exercising each and every day. Soon I'll be running
miles each morning and lifting tons of dead iron
around."

"Exercise? You did one pushup tonight before
we left the room," she said.

"That's because you wouldn't get under me for inspiration. It's not much fun exercising alone."

True to his word, Trace hummed. He hummed when the bartender played the Anvil Chorus on the cash register and on an assortment of bottles, and he hummed when all the waiters, the cigarette girl, and the maître d' took turns standing on the stage in the center of the room, singing arias.

"That guy used to sing *Carmen* standing on his head. I remember that," Trace said.

"I don't believe it," Chico said.

"It's true. Of course, that was fifty pounds ago. He might have trouble standing on his head these days."

Another waiter came from the kitchen wearing a chef's hat. He began to twirl pizza dough over his head, then threw lumps of the dough around the room. When people threw them back, he caught them in his mouth, all the while singing *Figaro*.

Chico was laughing so hard tears ran from her eyes. "I don't believe this place. It's priceless," she said.

"See. You're so busy dealing with the seamy underside of New York life, Bloomingdale's and Saks, that you don't get to see the good parts of the city. If you like this, there's some decals up in the Bronx that you have to see."

"Huh?" she said.

"Never mind," Trace said. "You had to be there."

The house lights dimmed. A few moments later, the doors to the kitchen opened and four waiters, carrying candles and wearing bull masks over their heads, came charging out and wended their way about the room, singing a chorus from *Carmen* while other waiters on the stage joined in.

Trace started to say something but Chico shushed him. She was watching the waiters as they moved about the room, stopping to play with young children who were with their parents among the late dinner crowd.

He started again and she shushed him again. So he poured another glass of wine from the bottle and hummed until the waiters vanished into the kitchen and the lights brightened.

"Now can I talk?" he said.

"Go ahead, say something."

"Nothing."

"I figured as much. You know, think about this." She still looked at the kitchen door. "Nobody put that mask on Tony Armitage."

"No?"

"He put it on himself so that nobody would recognize him," Chico said.

"I don't think that's such a big breakthrough that you have to be rude and tell me to be quiet," Trace said.

"It gets you on a different track. You don't have to think maybe about why somebody else put that mask on him. If anybody wanted to hide him or fix him up so nobody'd see him or notice him, they weren't likely to do it by having him wear a Richard Nixon mask. Or a King Kong mask for that matter. They'd just put him in the trunk of the car. Or on the floor of the backseat. Put a bag over his head. A Nixon mask is the kind of the thing he might put on himself. Especially a college kid. And a druggie."

"It might be right," Trace conceded.

"So then, ask yourself why?"

"All right, why?" Trace said, although his heart wasn't really in it. He liked the music and the wine. He didn't want to think about Tony Armitage tonight. He wanted to drink a little and hum a lot, and when Chico wasn't looking, pour a few spoonfuls of his white wine into her Perrier water and reduce her to a state of drunken paralysis, then take her back to their room and punish her body in a sexual frenzy. Or, maybe, just kiss her good night and fall asleep holding her.

Either sounded pretty good.

"Why didn't the kid want to be recognized?" Chico asked. "And recognized by whom?"

"I like the way you always say 'whom' correctly. I could never be in love with a woman who used 'who' when she should use 'whom.' I used to go with a woman who said terrif. The first time, I dismissed it as an error, and the second time as a lapse in judgment. The third time, I knew I had to get that woman out of my life."

"You mean if I say terrif, I can be rid of you?"

"Yes," Trace said.

"Terrif," she said. "Just the breakthrough I've been looking for."

"On the other hand," Trace said, "I don't like the way you end sentences with prepositions."

"You've got that look in your eye. I don't think you'd be satisfied with any sentence that didn't end in a *prop*osition."

"Hah. You wish," Trace said. "If I get to be a big detective, that's another thing that goes. No more wasting my precious body fluids with meaningless casual sex. From that moment on, I'm only making it with lady social workers who make me listen to their sophomoric ideas of life before giving me any, if I'm still unlucky enough to be awake."

"Good. Then take me home. Now that I know I'm safe, no need to spend the night out, watching you hope that I'll pass out."

Trace went into the bedroom to tell Chico there had been no messages at the desk from Sarge. She was already in bed.

"Can I whip you up something in the kitchen

for breakfast?" he said. "An avocado soufflé, maybe?"

"You know," Chico said, "I've read novels about big fancy private detectives. It's not that they cook complicated things."

"No? What is it, then?"

"No, they cook things like omelets or fried bacon."

"The hell you say."

"True," Chico said. "But what they do is they make a big deal of it. They sprinkle tarragon on top of their omelets. Or they coat the underside of the bacon with mustard before they fry it. Stuff like that. Bullshit stuff that only fools people who've never really stood in a kitchen cooking."

"Lady social workers," Trace suggested.

"Exactly. People too involved with the big, the really, really big issues of life." She spoke those words with her jaw jutting out, her lips tightly compressed, in a wicked parody of a Westchester County private-schoolmarm. "People who can't be involved with food or its preparation because it's not creative, or who feel guilty about it because as long as one person is starving in India, they're supposed to hate escargot."

"You may have something. As I was told today—and I'm always willing to pass along a compliment—you're smarter than you look."

"Thank you. Come to bed. Savage me."

"Okay," he said.

He was using alcohol to wash away the adhesive tape that held the tape recorder around his waist, when Chico sat up in bed as if she were a zombie called back from the grave.

"Trace, I think I've got it."

"I'm glad you told me *before* sex." He kept rubbing at the tape marks. "Got what?"

"Remember what the maid told you about Martha Armitage? She was drunk and her husband talked to her on the phone the night before the kid was killed and she was talking about napping. Napping. And then Anna Walker came over?"

"Yeah, so?"

"And then when the maid left, those two gunmen were hanging around, in the hall and in the lobby. Trace, they were standing guard."

"What for?"

"Because she wasn't talking about napping. She was mumbling about kidnapping. Suppose Tony Armitage was kidnapped. Does that make any sense?"

He set the alcohol bottle on a dresser, then sat down on the edge of the bed and kissed her forehead.

"It sure does," he said. "It sure does."

"Hello, darling," the woman said.

"Hello, sweetheart," Trace said.

"Who is this?" Anna Walker demanded.

"Devlin Tracy. You didn't know that?"

"What do you want? It's three o'clock in the morning."

"If I wanted the time, I would have called the special number. Only twenty cents to reach out and touch a tape recording."

"I was getting ready for bed. Talk or good-bye."

"I have to talk to you, Miss Walker."

"About what?"

"About a kidnapping in Connecticut a month ago."

There was a long silence on the telephone and then Anna Walker's voice again, much less imperious, said, "Can you come over? Say in a half-hour?"

"Say fifteen minutes," Trace said. He waited thirty seconds, dialed again, and her phone was busy.

*　　*　　*

No, he didn't want coffee. What he really wanted was a drink, a large drink. He told Anna Walker the first but kept the second to himself.

She insisted. "Come on, it'll only take a moment. Conversation goes better with coffee."

Trace thought of what Chico had said about tarragon omelets and he said, "Okay. With cinnamon."

"Coffee with cinnamon?" Anna Walker said.

"That's right."

She left Trace sitting on one of the four sofas in her auditorium-size living room. "I'll only be a minute," she said.

Trace wondered how long it would take Nick Armitage to arrive. That he was coming was obvious, since Anna Walker was wasting time. She either wanted to talk to Trace, in which case she would have talked, or she didn't want to talk to him, in which case he wouldn't have been invited up. The coffeemaking was to buy time until someone else arrived.

Ten minutes later, the coffee arrived, but Nick Armitage still had not.

"Here you are, Mr. Tracy. With cinnamon." She put a small tray on the end table before them. A silver service held cream and sugar. The coffee was in two fine, small porcelain cups. "I've never heard of coffee with cinnamon," she said.

"A special way I have of making it," Trace said. "I make it a lot when I have eggs and tarragon."

He sipped the coffee. It tasted like effluent. He said, "Yummie," and poured a lot of milk into the cup. He sipped it again and put in three spoons of sugar. He could no longer taste the cinnamon. When he went back to the hotel room, he promised himself to be sure to tell Chico that she had stupid ideas about what big detectives ate and drank.

"Now it's just the way I like it," he said. "When is your brother-in-law coming?"

She looked startled at his bluntness, then said, "He should be here any minute. Do you mind?"

"Not unless I have to sit here and talk about coffee and tarragon and everything else except what I came to talk about. Why don't we get started? We can catch him up when he gets here."

"I'd really rather wait."

"I'd really rather not," Trace said. He pushed the coffee away. "There are other people I can talk to," he said. He started to rise, but she reached out and put a hand on his wrist.

"Please sit down," she said softly. She left her hand on his wrist longer than was necessary. "Did I tell you last night that I think you have a terrible disposition?"

"I always kind of looked at myself as a pussycat," Trace said. "But we can talk about that some other time, too. Now that we're going to be such great friends, we'll probably meet a lot for dinner and drinks and coffee and chatter. But right now, Tony Armitage."

"All right," she said. "What do you want to talk about?"

He decided to run a large bluff. "I know about the kidnapping. I don't know who."

"I really don't know what you're talking about," she said.

"Good. Perhaps the police will. It was nice sharing this time with you, but I'm leaving. I have to get some sleep."

He stopped when he heard a voice from the room entrance behind him.

"I wish you wouldn't, Tracy." Nick Armitage was there, wearing his business tuxedo, and Trace thought that brother-in-law, sister-in-law relations had made major strides with these two since Nick obviously had his own key to the front door, which Anna had locked behind Trace.

"If we talk, I'll stay," Trace said. "We were just talking about the kidnapping."

"What do you know about it?" Armitage asked.

"Enough. Now I want to know what you know about it. I want to know who."

He was still skirting around, trying to sound definite and authoritative, but he did not want to make a flat statement that would show that he knew nothing and was only guessing. Still, the trip was already a success; both had conceded that there had been a kidnapping.

Armitage came into the room slowly. With the familiarity born of practice, he went to an oak cabinet against the far wall, opened it, and poured himself a Scotch in a water tumbler. He squeezed in a splash of soda from an old-fashioned seltzer bottle. He took a lot of time, then walked over to a sofa facing Trace, who had lit a cigarette and put his feet up onto the marble-topped coffee table.

"Who?" Trace mouthed silently.

"We don't know who." Armitage sipped his drink and sprawled back on the sofa. "Don't you think we'd like to know who?" As he spoke, tendons swelled in his thick muscular neck. Was this what he would look like if he started lifting weights, Trace wondered.

Armitage leaned forward again. "Maybe it's time that you and I talked a little bit."

"About time," Trace said.

"For instance, I'd like to know just what business any of this is of yours. Who the hell invited you here to look into anything? Just who do you think you are, Tracy, you and your old man nosing around, pestering us?"

"You said all that before," Trace said. "And I thought I explained. My insurance company invited me here. They told me to look into it before they pay up five hundred very large ones."

"And I told you once before that you can tell your insurance company to stuff their money. I don't need it."

"You never know," Trace said. "Most people could use an extra half-million usually. Keep it around to tip the paperboy. Or in case the money-laundering saloon downtown goes up in a fire."

Armitage stared at him angrily for a moment, then looked at Anna Walker. Trace saw her shrug.

"I wasn't born yesterday, Armitage. But I don't give a damn about your business or how you run it. Just your son."

"We want to be left alone," Armitage said.

"So you can just forget that somebody murdered your kid? Just wash it off, forget it. What do you call it? A business loss? A deduction you don't need anymore? Is there a special line on your ten-forty: murdered Kids, removed from dependency status? What the hell kind of father are you anyway?"

"What do you know about it?" Armitage said. "You've got no right to judge. You don't know what I'm doing or not doing."

"Yes, I do. The only thing you were doing was having that black guy keep an eye on Tony's old girlfriend in Connecticut, and he didn't find out spit. You haven't done a damned thing else. Tell me about the kidnapping."

"There's nothing to tell."

"Good," Trace said. "Tell it to the cops." He rose to his feet and turned toward the front door of the apartment. He wanted a drink really badly now and he hoped Armitage would try to stop him. He would not mind hitting the man.

He was almost at the door when Anna Walker's voice, soft and calm, reached him.

"At nine o'clock that night, Nick received a telephone call at his private office," she said.

"Don't," Armitage snapped.

She ignored him and went on. "The man on the telephone said that Tony had been kidnapped and Nick had to come up with two hundred and fifty thousand dollars. He had to take it to that spot on the Merritt Parkway. He delivered the money as he was instructed and came home to wait for word from Tony. The next morning, Tony's body was found at that spot. The money was gone. Those are the facts, Mr. Tracy."

Trace came back into the room and went to the bar to pour himself a drink. He splashed a lot of vodka into a glass as he asked Armitage, "Why didn't you tell this to the police?"

"Would it have made any difference? They didn't find the people, did they?"

"Would it have hurt to have them look?" Trace asked.

"I didn't trust them to look very hard," Armitage said. "They had a killing to investigate. Why complicate it?"

"What do you think happened that night?" Trace asked.

"I think some kidnappers got Tony and beat me out of money and never planned to release Tony. Probably because he could identify them. And I think they took him there with them to pick up the money and then they killed him."

"Why was he wearing that mask, do you think?" Trace asked.

Armitage just shook his head. He was staring into his whiskey glass, as if it were a lens, looking at a country long ago and far away.

"I don't know," he said finally. His voice trembled a little.

"Haven't you ever thought about it?" Trace asked.

"Maybe they didn't want him to be recognized or something."

"Who called with the ransom demand?" Trace asked.

"Some guy I never heard before."

"He called you at the club?"

"Yeah."

"What did he say? Exactly?"

"He said something like, 'Just listen and don't talk. We've got your son and if you don't want him chilled, you'll do just what we say.' And he told me to get two hundred and fifty thousand dollars in cash and he told me where to drop it along the Merritt. That spot where the litter basket is."

"Why did you believe him?" Trace asked. "It could have been a hoax."

"I thought that for a minute," Armitage said. "But he called on my private line and nobody has that except family. I was waiting to hear from Tony because we were supposed to get together for dinner that night. I told him he wouldn't get anything unless I knew Tony was all right, and he said, 'You'll find that out soon enough.' So I hung up the phone and ten minutes later Tony called. He said he was being held prisoner and that I should do what they said or they'd kill him."

"How did he sound?"

"He sounded upset. How the hell do you think he sounded?"

"So you came up here then and got the money—" Trace started.

"I didn't say that," Armitage snapped.

"You didn't have to. You came up here and got the money and delivered it. Did you wait? Did you hang around? Did you see anybody?"

"No, no, and no. I did what they told me. It was my son, remember, that they were holding. I dropped off the money and I beat it. Then I went back to my apartment. Anna was there with Martha. We waited for a message but there wasn't any message except from the cops in the morning that Tony was dead."

"Where were your two bodyguards during all this?" Trace asked.

"I had them watching the apartment. I didn't want anybody to try anything with Martha. And that's all I know."

"Well, maybe just a couple of other things," Trace said. "Who has your private office number?"

"Just family, I told you."

"Who knew that Tony was supposed to have dinner with you that night?"

Armitage thought a moment, then shook his head. "I don't think anybody did. We made the date that afternoon on the telephone. He was going to call back at nine."

"What happened to Dewey Lupus?"

"Anna told you and I'll tell you again tonight. He was a thief and a drunk and that kind always winds up getting lost someplace. He quit before I had a chance to fire him, that's where he is. And you and your father nosing around about it isn't going to change that. I don't like you hanging around."

"What are you going to do, Mr. Tracy?" Anna asked.

"With reference to what?"

"Are you going to the police?"

"Not yet. I don't have anything to tell them yet."

"Then. . . ."

"I'm just going to keep looking," Trace said.

"I don't want you looking. I want you out of this," Armitage said.

"In life, you don't always get what you want."

"We've answered your questions now, Mr. Tracy. Will you answer one of ours?" Anna Walker said.

"Try me."

"How did you find out about the kidnapping? We thought—"

"You thought that the only other people who knew about it would be the kidnappers," Trace said.

She nodded.

"I'm sorry. I learned this from inside your camp. I don't think it'd help anything to tell you exactly how I learned it."

"I understand," she said. "I'll walk you to the door."

"First things first." He turned back toward Armitage, who was still sitting on the sofa nursing his Scotch.

"Where's Tweedledum and Tweedledee?" he asked.

"Who?"

"Your two trained apes, Frankie and Augie, the Happiness Twins."

"I sent them home. Why?"

"I didn't want them sneaking up on me from behind when I leave here."

"They went home, I said."

"Me, too," said Trace.

When Trace returned to the Plaza, he went directly into the bedroom and woke up Chico.

"You were right. Tony *was* kidnapped."

"Good. Did you figure out who did it? Who killed him?" she asked groggily.

"No."

"We will," she said.

"We?"

"I've decided to help," she said thickly.

"I'll let you get your rest, then," he said. "I've got to do my log."

"Okay. Leave it out for me so I can hear it," she said.

"I will."

"There's a present for you on the living-room table," she said as he was leaving the room.

The present was a pint bottle of Finlandia and a note from Chico. "Trace. I bought this a couple of days ago. Have it if you want. It won't count against our bet." She had signed her name in Japanese symbols.

He kissed the note and poured a drink.

22

Trace's Log:
Very early Sunday morning. The one bird in
New York City is already up peeping and the
left-wingers are skulking to the newsstands to
buy the *New York Times* to get this week's party
line and I ought to be in bed, so this will be very
short.

Chico, I'm leaving this out for you and so I'm
presuming you're listening to this while I'm
sleeping, and since I never tell you in person,
"close up and personal," as Howard Cosell says,
let me tell you that I think you are a very excep-
tional lady. You are beautiful and funny and
smart and you're economically self-sufficient.
About the only thing wrong with you is that you
really don't put your money to work for you in
the best way, and perhaps one day soon, you and
I will talk about that and see what we can do to
make you more secure in your old age.

You know what happened when I met Cheryl,
the cashiered maid, 'cause you listened to the
tape in the restaurant tonight. Martha's a drunk,
Tony was pissed because Nick told him to break
up with the black chick, Tony had a secret apartment near the school, and that business with
Martha talking about napping, which turned out

to be kidnapping. And Tony got drugs from Paulie, the manager downtown who was a waiter then.

And you listened to the Jennie Teller tape. I should have spotted that she was selling a little dope when I was at that diner the first time and she gave that kid Sweet'n Low from her pocket, instead of from the sugar bowl. Being sober too long, I find, clouds one's mind so that one cannot see. That's the only reason Lamont Cranston lasted so long as The Shadow. If he had ever tried that trick on a bunch of drunks, they would have seen him right away. By the way, this vodka is good, but next time, please try to put the bottle on ice. So anyway, I found the Sweet'n Low packets in Jennie's room and the bankbook with the big balance from the time she and Tony were living together. I guess she's just been selling the leftover drugs since then. And she confirmed that Tony was going to get even with the father. Was he going to deal more drugs? I don't know. Maybe he was going to open a competing restaurant and disco.

Anyway, then you and I went to dinner and to that opera club and we had fun even if you were rude to me and didn't let me talk when I wanted to.

I'm leaving you the tape of my pleasant kaffee-klatsch tonight with Anna Walker and Nick Armitage. It will explain everything about the kidnapping, or at least everything they told me, and I still don't know whether I believe them about anything or not.

It occurs to me that the reason Nick Armitage didn't tell the police about the kidnapping was that he didn't want anybody to ask how he could get his hands on a quarter of a million dollars in cash at night on just a few minutes' notice.

Still no clue why Tony was wearing that mask. Maybe there's something in the tapes that you can find, but I don't have anything right now. I still think Dewey Lupus counts for something, and maybe Sarge found out something about him. If I ever hear from him again.

Actually, although I don't have one single damned answer, I don't feel too bad. The fact that there was a kidnapping changes the whole thing. It could bring a new investigation by police and they might solve all these riddles and save Gone Fishing some money. That should make Walter Marks happy, if any man smaller than you can ever be said to be truly happy.

I like this vodka a lot.

I am going inside now, Chico, to go to bed with you. If, by chance, you should try to seduce me during the night and I resist, remember this: it was not because I loved you less but because I loved sleep more. I am very tired. Good night to one and all.

Yes. This vodka is very good.

Oh. I'll do my expenses some other time. Be sure to give me a receipt for the vodka. Make believe it was a half-gallon bottle.

23

It was noon when Trace awoke. It felt like old times. His throat was raw from cigarette smoking. The membranes of his nose were dry and his head felt as if it were packed with cotton. It hurt to move his body quickly. His teeth felt loose and the inside of his left arm itched, but he knew from experience that if he scratched it, his whole body would begin to itch, so he just lay there in bed, trying to ignore the irritation on his left arm.

It felt wonderful to be hung over again.

Alleluia. And Hallelujah, too, in case the Protestants were right.

He noticed that Chico was not in bed with him and he bellowed, "Chico. Get in here. Your man awaits. Attend me."

There was no answer and he shouted again, then waited, and when there was still no answer, he went back to sleep some more to give her a chance to come into the room and apologize before he had to call her again.

It was another hour before he woke once more. When Chico did not respond to his renewed bellowing, he finally got out of bed and went into the living room of their suite.

There was a fresh note on the table. It read: "Trace. I think maybe I've got a handle on this.

I've taken the car and am checking a couple of things out. I'll be back before dinner. Good job on the vodka. I hope you're back to normal."

The empty vodka bottle was still on the table, and Trace picked it up and held it to the light. It was empty. He tried an old army trick, holding the bottle at an angle, then running his cigarette lighter back and forth beneath the glass at the bottle's lowest point, then quickly upending the bottle. He was rewarded by a dribble of six drops of vodka into his glass.

Not bad, he thought. A man could live on six drops of vodka, if there were enough six dropses. All he had to do was to make sure he never ran out of empty vodka bottles. A noble ambition, he assured himself as he drank the six drops.

He lit a cigarette. When he finished coughing, he called the front desk to see if there were any messages for him. There weren't.

He wondered where Chico had gone and then he wondered where Sarge was. He called his father's office and then his home. No answer either place.

Some silent alarm bell went off inside his head. Sarge had said he was working on something good, but he had been out of touch too long. Usually when Trace came to town, he and Sarge spent most of their time together. A rare father and son, they got along with each other, genuinely liked each other, equally disdained Trace's mother, and were more like friends than kin. For Sarge to get lost this way was highly unusual.

Trace thought of calling his mother in Las Vegas to find out when she had last spoken to her husband, but he quickly rejected that idea. The woman would pry, complain if things were wrong, pester all of New York on the telephone, and wind up coming home from Las Vegas four minutes earlier than scheduled and claim that

Sarge had ruined her vacation. Forever afterward she would call it "the vacation I cut short when Patrick got lost."

No, thanks.

He went and looked in his luggage and found two airlines bottles of vodka that Chico didn't know about, which he always carried for emergencies, and poured both of them into his glass.

His worrying fluctuated between Sarge and Chico. Where would she have gone with the car? She was a terrible driver, her foot so heavy on the accelerator that she mashed it into a concave shape. The thought of her tooling madly around Manhattan was horrifying. He reminded himself to be sure to catch the hourly radio news to see if there had been a wave of traffic deaths among surly cabdrivers, run into brick walls by the Yellow Avenger.

And where was his father? What the hell was he up to?

Trace showered, shaved, and stepped outside the bathroom every few minutes to sip his vodka, which he had left on a small end table near the door, because he thought it was disgusting to bring a drink into a bathroom.

He finished the vodka about the time he finished dressing. He called his father's two numbers again and there was still no answer. Now he was more than a little worried, and he called the bell captain to get another rental car, and while he waited, he hooked up his tape recorder.

His parents lived in Queens, just across the river from Manhattan's East Side, on a quiet tree-lined street that looked more New Jersey than New York.

Trace had not been to the house for more than two years and most of the homes on the block looked alike with identical brick fronts, but he recognized Sarge's instantly by the large decal set in the glass of the front porch door.

It showed, in straight-on perspective, a gun facing anyone coming up the stairs and it bore the legend: "Forget the dog. Beware the owner."

As he leaned on the doorbell, Trace glanced up and down the street, but he did not see his father's beat-up old Plymouth.

When no one answered the door, he walked along the narrow alleyway to the back entrance. That was locked too, but there was an old unused milk box inside the back porch door—who delivered milk anymore?—and Trace found a house key taped underneath it.

He went into the house nervously, calling out, "Hey, Sarge, you here? Sarge? Hey, Pop. Where the hell are you?"

He walked through the first floor, room by room, then up to the second floor, checking all the rooms, the tub in the bathroom, feeling vaguely like a peeping Tom when he looked into his parents' bedroom, but relieved nevertheless when he found no body. Sarge's bed was made.

"Nothing is dead here except good taste," he said aloud as he went back downstairs, past the diamond-shaped racks on the stairway wall in which his mother had displayed her collection of inch-long plastic dolls with two-inch-long plastic hair in many colors.

Another rack held a collection of glasses from places they had visited on vacation, most of them at the New Jersey shore, all of them ugly, usually painted red, white, and blue since their vacations in the days of Trace's youth always seemed to coincide with the Fourth of July weekend. It was only years later that he realized that his mother had insisted upon this because she added in the extra weekend, and decided that such scheduling gave them three weeks of vacation instead of two. It had never mattered to her that this forced her husband to spend extra hours driving in the frustration of maniacal holiday traffic.

There were also displayed a lot of plastic stirrers with whistles attached, presumably for blowing at a bartender to catch his attention, so that he would know whose face to punch out for whistling at him.

He saw a set of cheap plastic ashtrays, brightly painted to resemble slightly less-cheap ceramic ashtrays. The scenes usually depicted some woman's legs or some man's rear end or somebody wearing a barrel. They had a lot of snappy, surefire, laugh-getting phrases written on them as well as the name of the dismal resort town in which such dismal words were regarded as humorous.

Downstairs, now that he had a chance to look at it, was much as he remembered it. There was one pattern of flowered print on one sofa; another pattern on each of two chairs; yet another pattern on the window drapes. The carpet was flowered and matched nothing else in either color or style.

There was a little pad on the end table near the telephone, but there were no notes and no message. So Sarge wasn't here. Then where the hell was he?

"Hold it, pal, right there."

The voice barked out from behind him, instantly recognizable as officialdom, and Trace turned slowly, his hands visible before him, and said, "I belong here."

The policeman standing in the doorway to the kitchen was young. The cop who stood behind him, safe for the moment from crazed random pistol fire, was older.

"Yeah? Who are you?" The older one called over the young cop's shoulder.

"My name is Devlin Tracy. This is my father's house."

The older cop squinted at him. "You don't look much like Sarge."

"My identification's in my wallet," Trace said. "My driver's license with my picture. 'Course, that doesn't look much like anybody."

"All right, I guess," the younger cop said. "Show us the license."

Trace slowly handed the policeman his wallet, opened so that the license was visible. The cop nodded as he handed it back.

"What are you doing here?" Trace asked.

"One of the neighbors called. They saw you go down the alley and then not come back out. They thought you were a burglar."

"No. I'm in town for a couple of days and I haven't been able to reach my father by phone. I just came out here to make sure he's all right."

The younger cop looked at the other one and Trace snapped, "What the hell's going on? Don't jerk around with me. Where's Sarge?"

The old cop stepped forward and said, shaking his head, "There's nothing wrong. Don't get upset, okay?"

"Swell, where is he?" Trace shot back.

"He didn't get hurt, but he was in a little accident last night."

"What kind of accident?"

"A car accident," the policeman said.

"Where is he now?"

"He's in Riverside Hospital, but he's okay," the policeman said again.

"How okay is okay?" Trace asked.

"He lost control of his car and hit a bridge railing. A little concussion. No broken bones, no internal injuries, nothing to worry about. He'll be getting out right away."

"That's the truth?" Trace asked. He stared hard at the older cop, then his eyes asked the younger one for a second opinion.

The older policeman answered. "I wouldn't lie to you about something like that."

"Thanks, then," Trace said. "I appreciate it."

Sarge wore a helmet of bandages and Trace said, "You look like a goddamn tight end for Mummy University."

"You come here to yell at me?" Sarge said.

"No. How you feeling?" Trace went to the bed and hugged the old man, who squeezed him back with enough pressure to push the air from Trace's lungs.

"I'm okay. They say when you're my age, you get hit in the head and you gotta hang around for twenty-four hours or so just to make sure there's no hidden complications. But I'm all right. I don't even have a headache."

"What the hell happened?"

Sarge glanced toward the bed to his right, but its occupant was sleeping noisily. "Come closer," he said.

Trace leaned over the bed.

"I got run off the road. On purpose. Somebody tried to kill me, Dev."

Trace looked at him sharply to be sure the old man was not joking.

"It's true," Sarge said. "I spotted the car following me when I left Manhattan."

"When was that?"

"Last night, about one or two o'clock or so. I saw the car following me over the bridge. Then, when I got close to the block near the house, there's that overpass, and the son of a bitch cut me off and tried to run me off the top of it."

"What'd you do?"

"I banged along those railings for a while, but I finally fought it back on the road. I cracked my head on the windshield. I remember trying to look out the window to see the bastard—I was going to peg a shot at him—but he was gone or his lights were out. And then I passed out and I woke up here. I'm okay, though."

"You don't think it was just an accident?"

"No, it was on purpose. Somebody wanted either to kill me or hurt me or give me a warning."

"Who?" Trace asked. "What jealous husband do you have riled up now?" And then he realized what he said might not have been as funny as all that. "Did you recognize who was in the other car?"

"No. Two guys. I saw that much, but I couldn't see their faces."

"Recognize the car?"

"Big old thing, plates muddied up, I don't know."

"The cops told me that you lost control of the car," Trace said.

"That's what I told them."

"Why not the truth?"

"What for?" Sarge asked. "The guys who did it were gone, and cops have too much to do to go looking for them. And I don't want a lot of people nosing around in my business. *Our* business."

"You think this had something to do with Tony Armitage?" Trace asked.

"Sure. I got a lot done yesterday and maybe somebody saw me."

Trace pulled over a chair. "Maybe you ought to tell me about the lot you got done yesterday."

"First thing, I went up to Connecticut real early in the morning and I found a store right near where the kid lived that sold those Nixon masks. And bingo, the clerk remembered Armitage buying one. I had a picture of the kid and he recognized him."

"Why the hell didn't the cops find that out?" Trace asked.

"Maybe it wasn't important to them," Sarge said. "But it *is* important. He bought that mask himself. That's got to mean something."

"That's what Chico says too. She kind of guessed that it was his mask."

"She's eerie sometimes, that woman," said Sarge.

"So anyway, I get back to the city and I get your note at the restaurant and I went to some friends of mine on the city liquor squad and I got a home address and next of kin on that Dewey Lupus. I went to his apartment, but the landlord said he hasn't seen him in a month. He skipped the rent and the landlord was getting ready to rent the place again. He said Lupus left all his stuff and I got him to let me in."

"Find anything?"

"The apartment had been tossed, Dev. It was a mess, with everything thrown all over. I asked the landlord if anybody had been there and he said he saw two guys skulking around about a month ago, but he didn't know."

"Could he describe them?"

"He said they were big and ugly and they dressed like George Raft."

"I think I maybe know who they were," Trace said. "And you got run off the road by two guys."

"Think they were the same?" Sarge asked.

"I think so because I was someplace last night where they should have been and they weren't there. I think they were out taking you over the hurdles."

Sarge shrugged. "Anyway, I went through what was left of Lupus' apartment, but I didn't find anything that counted for anything."

"Think about this. We found out that the kid was kidnapped the night before he was killed. Anything in Lupus' apartment that goes with that?" Trace asked.

Sarge squinted his eyes, and Trace knew that under the bandages his brow was furrowed. He thought for a full minute, then shook his head. "No. Nothing there meant anything. It was just another bachelor's apartment. A lot of copies of *Playboy.* I was going to steal the centerfolds for my office wall."

"All right. Keep going," Trace said.

"I had the address of his family in Jersey. It's down near Freehold by the harness track, so I decided to drive out there just to check it out. I talked to his mother. She said they hadn't heard from him in a month. They didn't know where he was."

"Were they lying?"

"No," Sarge said. "I checked some neighbors and the gas station on the corner, but he wasn't around. I would have known if she was lying anyway. Dev, he just vanished. One day he was around and the next day he wasn't. And somebody came and went through his apartment right after that."

"Complicateder and complicateder," Trace said. "Then what'd you do?"

"I was in Jersey when I called the restaurant and missed you. Then I just nosed around some more. Nothing important."

He seemed ready to let the matter drop there, and after a moment's hesitation, Trace said, "Hey, Dad, are you afraid to tell me you were with Martha Armitage? That you two have an affair going?"

Sarge's eyes looked startled at first, then narrowed to hide all expression.

"What'd you say?"

"You and Martha, you heard me."

"Where'd you hear that?"

"Hey, Sarge, this is Devlin, your son. Don't give me that answer-a-question-with-a-question routine. I've done it too many times myself. Who told me? Who told me was the look in your eyes when you two met in your office. Who told me was your going out and borrowing plants and cleaning the joint. Who told me is all of a sudden you've very busy at night. Who told me . . . well, who told me was Chico. She figured it out without ever seeing the lady."

"I told you that woman's eerie," Sarge said. "Okay. I was with Martha the last couple of nights, but it's not like you think."

"Where were you with her?" Trace asked.

"Jesus," Sarge said. "This is real tacky crap, trying to talk to my son about what he thinks was an indiscretion."

"We're talking, maybe, about your attempted murder. Where'd you meet her?"

"There's an apartment near Columbus Circle, belongs to a friend of Martha's. The friend's out of town and we met there."

"Any chance Armitage found out?" Trace asked.

"I don't think so," Sarge said.

Trace noticed that his father had his head turned away and was keeping his eyes averted. "How'd Martha get there?"

"By cab," Sarge said.

"How'd she get home?"

"I dropped her off." He shook his head quickly. "Not at her house. Near her house."

"Near enough to be seen," Trace said with a sigh. "Pop, you know she's a drinker?"

Sarge nodded. "She's on a lot of pills too. She isn't a well woman."

"The sauce is enough. It was something she said one night to a maid, a freaking maid, mind you, that led us to the kidnapping. You know damned well she probably dropped your name around too when she's in her cups."

"I don't think so," Sarge said.

"I know so. Last night, Armitage and his sister-in-law both knew you were working with me. But nobody knew that except Martha. You can't trust a drunk, Sarge. Why'd you meet with her?"

"I don't know. Dev, it was her idea, but then we'd get together and we'd just talk. I thought maybe it was doing her some good, but I never could figure out why she wanted to talk."

"Maybe she was trying to build up her courage to tell you about her son's kidnapping. She hasn't been playing square with you, Sarge."

"I know that. I'm sorry, son. She's not all there anymore. She was once, well, she was a helluva woman."

"Is that when you two got it on?"

"You make it sound shabby," Sarge snapped angrily. "It wasn't like that. It was just once, a lot of years ago, and it wasn't like that. You want to know how it was?"

Trace was silent for a moment. "No," he said, "I don't."

He looked down and saw that his hands were gripping the rail on the side of the bed so hard, his knuckles were white. With an effort, he relaxed, then reached over and squeezed his father's shoulders.

"When do you think you'll get out of here?"

"Tonight, if I'm lucky," Sarge said.

"Should I call Mother? Run interference for you or tell her about the accident?"

"Don't say that or you'll see me die before your eyes. She doesn't have to know anything and I'll have the car fixed before she gets home. I'll call her tonight myself."

"All right," Trace said. "Then I'm going to be moving along."

"What have you got planned?"

"Chico's out. I want to check on her, and then . . . well, I don't know, I've got some other business."

"You think you know who put me here?" Sarge asked.

"Yes."

"Don't do anything dumb," Sarge said.

"I won't," Trace said. He started toward the door. "I'm your son."

"Devlin."

When Trace turned around, Sarge said, "With Martha, it wasn't like you think. It wasn't cheap or dirty."

"I know that, Pop. It couldn't have been."

"Why not?"

"Because you were involved in it," Trace said. "Thanks, Dev. Be careful."

24

Trace had been back in his hotel suite only a few minutes when the telephone rang.

"Is this Devlin Tracy?" asked a man's voice that he had never heard before.

"Yes."

"If you're wearing boxer shorts, I'll give you a million dollars."

"Huh?"

"If you have a birthmark on the inside upper part of your right thigh, I'll double it."

"Who is this?"

"If you live with a Eurasian beauty who is the picture of sweetness and grace and all that is good in life, you will be happy forever," the man said. "Unless you try to poison her with Veal Surprise."

"This must have lost something in the translation," Trace said. "Who are you?"

"I'll be right up," the man said.

Three minutes later, there was a knock on the door. When Trace opened it, Chico stood there, grinning obscenely, holding a plastic bag in her hand.

"I give up," Trace said. "What was that all about? Who was that?"

"I cannot tell a lie," Chico said as she breezed into the room. "C'est moi."

"The man who called, I mean," Trace said.

"Me. Don't you understand? That was me."

"Your voice changed," he said, still not understanding what she was talking about, but she nodded and said, "And I can change it anytime I want. Here." She handed him the plastic bag.

"What is it?"

"Look," she said.

He looked inside and saw a gray plastic device that looked like a small telephone-answering machine.

"What is it?" he said.

"The answer to the Armitage kidnapping," Chico said.

"I expect you're going to explain all this," Trace said.

"I am. Did you hear from Sarge?"

"Yes. Somebody tried to kill him, but he's all right. He found out that the kid bought the mask himself," Trace said.

Chico nodded. "I know," she said. "And now I know why."

25

When Trace answered the knock at their door
shortly after midnight, Armitage, Anna, Martha,
and the two bodyguards stood there. Trace had
an impulse to jump through the doorway, grab
the two goons, and smash their heads together,
and he restrained it only with effort.

Armitage's face was flushed. "You got a hell of
a nerve, Tracy, ordering us to be here. It better
be important."

"And you came anyway, not knowing," Trace
said. "What a friend. Come on in."

They began to come through the door into the
living room, where Chico sat at a writing table in
the far corner, near the windows that overlooked
Central Park.

"Just you three," Trace said. "Bonzo One and
Two can wait in the hall."

Frankie the Singer and Augie the Hand snarled
in unison in Trace's direction, then looked at
Armitage for instructions.

Armitage paused in the doorway, then nodded.

"All right, boss," one of them said. The other
one nodded.

Trace slammed the door in their faces. "Sit
down, won't you all?" he said. "I'd offer you a
drink, but I ordered a case of Polish beer and it
hasn't arrived yet. Sorry about that."

"Can the chatter," Armitage said. "What do you want?"

For the first time, Trace noticed that Martha Armitage was wearing a hat with a veil. She kept it on as she sat on the couch. Her sister sat at the other end of the sofa, and finally Armitage sat in the middle.

"This is my assistant, Miss Mangini. You've met her, Armitage, but the ladies haven't."

"I'm going to take a nap," Armitage growled. "Why don't you call me when all the introductions are over and you're ready to tell us what you want."

"I thought you'd want to know what I found out about Tony's kidnapping and murder. Before we tell it to the police," Trace said.

"You've figured it out?" Anna Walker said.

Trace nodded. Martha Armitage moved forward in her seat. The veil was heavy and he could not see her eyes, but he knew the woman was staring at him.

"Well, go ahead," Armitage said. He lit a cigarette and sprawled back on the sofa.

"I won't bother you with a lot of the details," Trace said, "because I don't think you'd be impressed by how much effort I put into this, Armitage. So I'll just hit the high points."

Armitage stubbed out the cigarette.

"The rubber mask was the key," Trace said. "It didn't make any sense when this was just a murder, and then when we found out it was a kidnapping, it made even less sense. Why would kidnappers put that mask on him if they were going to kill him? A Richard Nixon mask? It sure wasn't the sort of thing not to draw attention to him. That was the big question. Why the mask?"

"All right, why?" Armitage asked. He started

to fumble in his shirt pocket again for another cigarette.

"We found out that Tony bought the mask himself in a store near the school."

"That still doesn't answer why," Anna said.

"It didn't for us either, at first," Trace said. "But when we figured out that Tony planned his own kidnapping, then it made all the sense in the world."

"Ohhhh." The sound came from Martha Armitage.

"Quiet," Armitage snapped at her. "That's horseshit, Tracy. Why the hell would he do that?" He had an unlit cigarette in his hand and he rolled it between his thumb and index finger while waiting for an answer.

"No, it's not horseshit," Trace said. "We found the person who helped him pull it off." Trace had been standing and now he pulled around an easy chair to face the sofa, and sat down. When he glanced at Chico, she nodded encouragement to him.

"Think about it, Armitage. You were always pushing the kid. You wanted him to be a lawyer and he didn't really want to. He was having his romance up on the campus and you made him split with Jennie."

"Jennie?" Anna Walker said.

"The black girl he roomed with," Trace supplied. "So Tony was ticked at you. He went around telling people, a lot of people, that he was going to get even with you. You didn't know it, but he rented an apartment near the campus and was living there with Jennie."

Armitage's eyes narrowed and he searched Trace's face.

"And he started dealing a little drugs on campus to help make the rent money," Trace said. When Armitage began to speak, Trace said, "Don't argue. We know his partner and we know his supplier. You ought to be flattered, Armitage. You know, imitation is the sincerest form of, and like father, like son. That kind of thing."

"I've about listened to all of this I want to," Armitage said. He rose to his feet.

"You're going to leave without knowing who killed him?" Trace said. "But that's right. You're really not terribly interested in knowing that, are you?"

"Sit down, Nick," Martha Armitage said suddenly.

Armitage hesitated, then sat and lighted the cigarette he had been holding.

"So back to the mask. It was part of Tony's kidnapping plan. He must have hated you, Armitage, because he planned to beat you out of a lot of money. The mask was so that nobody would identify him when he went to pick up the ransom money."

"Why Richard Nixon?" Anna Walker asked, and Trace shrugged. "Why not? He was just a kid. Kids do funny things."

"This is still crap," Armitage said.

"No. We found his accomplice, I told you. The one who called you at exactly nine o'clock that night in your office. With the private number that came from Tony and exactly when you were expecting your son to call. The accomplice gave you the ransom message, then called Tony and said it had been done. Ten minutes later, Tony called you and said it was true."

Armitage pursed his lips in disgust.

"Who else would know that you had access to a quarter of a million dollars in cash, at night, on short notice?" Trace said. "Tony did. He knew that you kept your money up at Anna's place and that you could get it right away. That's why it was all done at such short notice. He knew you didn't need a lot of time."

"You keep saying 'accomplice,' " Anna Walker said. "Who was this accomplice?"

"Jennie Teller," Trace said.

"Boy, are you stupid," Armitage said. "I told you, it was a man who called."

"You should have paid more attention to what your son liked," Trace said. "He was a tinkerer with electronic things. He had this gadget that changes a person's voice on the telephone. We found the advertisement for it in Tony's room, in his junk. It made Jennie sound like a man." He nodded across the room. "It even made Chico sound like a man," he said.

"*Star Wars*," Armitage said in disdain.

"Don't forget. Jennie's admitted it. She *was* in Atlantic City that weekend for a convention, but she called you from a pay phone. She just basically read the script that Tony wrote for her. Then she called Tony and told him it was all right for him to call you. And he did."

He stopped to light a cigarette and Martha Armitage said, "Go on, Devlin."

"Tony must have figured that the tight time limits would make it impossible for you to try anything," Trace told Armitage, who again snubbed out his cigarette. "I guess he just didn't understand you. You got the money and sent Anna and your two dimwits to go guard Martha. Then you called Dewey Lupus and made plans for him to go to Connecticut with you."

He paused as if waiting for Armitage to comment, but the man was silent.

"The way I figure it is that you took two cars up. First, you went up and parked near that place—on the Merritt, there's an exit just a couple of hundred yards away—and then went back and hid in the bushes right near there, so you could see what happened. Then, at the regular time, you had Lupus drive up, drop the money in the basket, and drive off, probably back to New York. And you waited. When Tony showed up, he was junked up. He had taken some Quaaludes. I figure he showed up, wearing the Nixon mask just in case, picked up the money, and you jumped out of the bushes and fought with him. And then you killed him."

Martha Armitage's face swiveled toward her husband as if on a tight spring. Trace stopped for a moment. Armitage stared at him and Trace said, "Any comments?"

"Keep going," Armitage said. "This fairy tale is getting good."

"Nick?" his wife said. "Did . . . did you?"

"Of course I didn't. Let him talk. He's full of shit."

The woman stared at him a moment, then relaxed and sat back.

"The next day," Trace said, "Dewey Lupus must have figured out what happened. Probably he finally realized that he could blackmail you into taking care of him forever. That's when he started talking a lot about moving up in the world. I guess he didn't figure that you'd put him away. He should have known. But that's why you weren't any help to the cops and why you got so upset with my nosing around."

"Anyway, you shot Tony and then you took the money back and gave it to Anna, and she's probably still got it in your little love nest . . . oops, her apartment."

"That's vicious, Tracy," Armitage snapped.

Martha looked at Trace through her veil, and Trace said, "Sorry, Martha. But I think you knew that these two were an item."

"You're very cruel," she said.

"And *you* jerked my father around for a couple

of days and you never told us the truth about the kidnapping and you damned near got him killed when he was seen taking you home. Probably by Nick's two goons. What's under that veil, Martha? Take off the hat."

The woman paused, then slowly complied. There was a large bruise around her left eye. Both eyes were bloodshot from drinking.

"At least it's nice to know he beat it out of you," Trace said. "Last night, Nick was complaining that my father and I were getting on his nerves. But he'd never met my father and didn't have any reason to know he was helping me on this case. Did you set him up last night? Is that the way it was?"

She shuddered and closed her eyes. "Is Patrick all right?"

"No thanks to you," Trace said.

"I didn't know it. I didn't know they would try anything on him," she said.

"You seem to have forgotten. You married a vicious man," Trace said.

"What are you going to do with all these stupid theories?" Armitage said.

"I'm going to the police," Trace said. "What did you expect?"

"Go ahead," Armitage said. "They'll laugh in your face about all this. You don't have a shred of evidence. Nothing. Zero."

"No, you're right," Trace said. "But that's the nice thing about my job. I don't have to. I've got enough to give the cops. I can prove there was a phony kidnapping that Tony engineered. His accomplice will swear to that. I've got that you got the ransom demand. You and Anna both told me that you went up there with the money and left it—when you told the cops you'd never been near the place—and that Tony was found dead there the next morning. That'll be enough to start the cops looking. And then there's Dewey Lupus. The cops probably have an up-to-date list of lime pits and things like that; they'll find his body pretty quick.

"And then you've got the Happiness Boys out in the hall. They're pretty stupid. The cops won't have to talk to them too long to find out anything they know. After Lupus vanished, his apartment was broken into and searched. That was their handiwork, and the cops'll find that out pretty soon and start asking you interesting questions about why you sent them there and what they were looking for. And why they tried to run my father off a bridge last night. And then there's Anna's records. There'll be a warrant and people will go through the records of both of your joints and they'll find out you two were cooking the books to hide your drug income, and that should lead to a lot of interesting questions from the feds, the IRS, the Justice Department, everybody else. Maybe somebody'll want to know how you were able to get your hands on two hundred and fifty thousand in cash in just a few minutes. I've got enough," Trace finished.

Armitage was silent a long time and Martha turned her head to search his face with dull, confused eyes. But he looked at Anna before speaking.

"It doesn't have to be that way, Tracy," Armitage finally said.

"What do you mean?"

"Look. This is a closed case. Tony's dead and nothing will bring him back. Why do we need the cops looking into a phony kidnapping? Why do we need the cops at all?"

"You have something in mind?" Trace asked.

"We're due to get a half a million from your insurance company," Armitage said. He tried a smile that involved only his mouth. "It doesn't have to go to us, you know. It could go to you just as easily. In advance."

"Nick," his wife said, "what are you saying?"

"We don't want trouble, is all," Armitage said. He looked at Trace again. "What do you think?"

But Martha spoke before Trace could answer. "Is it what he said? You killed Tony? Is that how it happened?"

"No, it's not like he said. What about it, Trace?"

"Don't talk to him," Martha said. "Tell me. What happened, Nick? What happened?"

Armitage shook his head as if the memory pained him. "I was there. This guy came with the mask and got the money and I jumped out and I said, 'Where's my boy? Where's my son?' And he looked at me, with that stupid mask on, and his voice was all muffled, and he said, 'Your son's gone, Armitage. You're never going to push him around again. He's gone. Dead and gone.' And he laughed. He laughed like a maniac and I saw red and I shot him. And then I started to take the mask off and it was Tony. And he was dead." He buried his chin on his chest.

"You killed him. You killed our son," Martha said.

"It was an accident. I didn't mean it." He stopped speaking and the silence hung in the room.

Anna Walker looked at her sister and brother-in-law, then turned to Trace and said coolly, "What about it, Mr. Tracy? I think Nick has an offer on the table."

"And you knew too, didn't you?" Martha Armitage snapped at her sister. "You knew that Nick had killed Tony. You knew and you never told me."

"Shut up, Martha. Stop your whining. We've listened to it all our lives, and it's about enough. You can go home soon and drink yourself unconscious and forget everything." Anna looked again at Trace and raised her eyebrows quizzically.

"Not a chance," Trace said. "Not a fucking chance."

"Why not?" Anna said, the picture of sweet reasonableness. "Nick's offer makes sense to me."

"You know, that was one of the things that smelled bad from the beginning. Nick didn't seem to want anybody to try to find out who killed Tony, and yet everybody was telling me how tough he was, how he never forgot, how he had a memory like an elephant. Well, Nick's two goons almost killed my father, and I'm not an Armitage. I don't forget. When elephants forget, us Tracys remind them. No deal."

Armitage looked up at the mention of his two bodyguards. "There's another way I can go, you know," he said.

"What's that?"

"All I've got to do is nod, and Frankie and Augie will put you and the little missie here asleep forever. You can go join Lupus. He tried messing with me too."

"Maybe we ought to ask them what they think about that," Trace said. He rose from his seat and went to the suite's front door. When he opened it, Frankie and Augie stood there. Behind them stood Sarge with a pistol in his hand. He prodded one of the twins with it.

"Inside, you two giboneys," he said as he pushed them into the living room. Just then, the door to the bedroom opened and two more men came out.

"Did you get it?" Trace asked.

One of the men nodded.

"Get what?" Armitage said, his face snapping back and forth from his two bodyguards to the two men who had been in the bedroom.

"I told you before," Trace said. "You should

have paid a little more attention to Tony and what he was interested in." He reached under the coffee table and removed a shiny piece of metal about the size and thickness of a stack of three quarters.

"This was Tony's. A little transmitter. The two policemen here have you all on tape." He smiled at Armitage. "What do you think?"

"I'm not talking till I see my lawyer," Nick said.

"Too bad you don't have one in the family," Trace said.

They were in a small bar a few blocks from the Plaza. Chico had been disappointed that the bar's kitchen was closed and she ordered three bags of peanuts and two Slim Jim smoked sausages from the bartender. Trace ordered a double Finlandia and Sarge a bottle of beer.

Sarge said, "I don't know how your figured out the girl, Jennie, was involved."

"It was the ransom message," Chico said. "Armitage said that the guy who called warned that he had to pay up or Tony would be 'chilled.' And I remember one of Trace's tapes when he was talking to her and she used the same word about killing, 'chilled.' That was a lead, and I remember Trace talking about Tony's electronic junk, so I went to the house and his roommate, the big scarecrow, showed me Tony's bag of stuff. There was an ad in there for that electronic voice changer. LaPeter said that Tony had one. He said Tony liked to play around with it, but he hadn't seen it since his death. He didn't know where it was. But he knew somebody else that had one and he got him to lend it to me." She paused to dump half a bag of peanuts into her mouth.

"Then when I went to see Jennie and I showed

her the machine, she just folded. So I convinced her that the police would go easy on her if she cooperated, and she said she would."

"She's probably skipped by now," Trace said.

"Police can find her," Sarge said. He savored a large drink from his beer mug. "My agency's first case. A roaring success," he said. "I'm very proud of me."

"So am I," Chico said, spraying peanut chips across the bar. She patted the top of Sarge's bandaged head.

"It's all right," Trace said. "I'll just sit here and drink while you two big detectives congratulate each other."

"Chico," Sarge said, "you want to be a partner in a detective firm? I was thinking of Dev, but he's a little slow on the pickup. I think he spends too much time trying to think big thoughts."

"We'll talk about it," Chico said.

"Promise?"

"I promise."

"Good," Trace said. "Get her off my hands."

Daylight was peeking into the city when they got back to their hotel room. Trace was feeling pleasantly high, and as he lay in bed next to Chico, he said, "A nice day."

"And tomorrow will be nicer," she said.

"Oh? How's that?"

"You drank tonight. Without permission. Tomorrow, you call your kids."

"I can't believe you're saying that to me," Trace said.

"It was our deal. No heavy drinking. You lost when you started sucking it up tonight," Chico said.

"You're hateful," Trace said.

"You told me once you loved me. You remember that?"

"I take it back. I regard you as a hateful person, directly responsible for the sneak attack upon Pearl Harbor. You are a woman who will live in infamy."

"And you are a man who will call his two children tomorrow."

26

Trace spent a lot of the next day on the telephone.

He told Walter Marks that the Armitage case had been cleared up, Trace had personally saved Garrison Fidelity a half-million dollars, and his expense account would probably be a little high.

"You know how carefully I watch things, trying to keep costs down, but this one, well, expenses were heavy. Me and my staff, you know."

"What staff?" Marks said.

"The private detective I hired. And Chico. She did a lot of work too. And we used the latest in electronic surveillance equipment. It's going to be a big bill. I just thought I'd let you know."

"You better have receipts," Marks said. "Without receipts, I don't pay for anything."

"It's nice to know that in a world of changing values and mores, some things are constant," Trace said.

"What are you talking about?"

"You're too goddamn cheap to live, Groucho," Trace said.

"I don't care about that. I want receipts."

"You will get them," Trace said.

"When?"

"As soon as I have time to write them."

He hung up and called Robert Swenson, the president of the insurance company.

Swenson congratulated him when he heard that the Armitage killing had been solved. "Good work."

"Thanks. Listen, Bob, does your brother-in-law still have that factory in Brooklyn?"

"Yeah. He still doesn't make a nickel at it either. Somebody once told him that tax losses are good, and he can't seem to get it through his head that they're only good if you've got some kind of plus income to apply them against. He is a total minus."

"I want to make him more minus," Trace said.

"I don't think I should talk to you anymore," Swenson said.

"No. Seriously. Sarge has opened up a detective agency and he needs some clients. How about your brother-in-law hiring him? To stop thefts or something."

"Sarge need the money?"

"He needs an excuse to get out of the house," Trace said.

"I've met your mother," Swenson said. "Consider it done."

"And, of course, it didn't come from me. Or you. Have the brother-in-law say he read about Sarge in the papers or something," Trace said.

"All right," Swenson said. "Anything else?"

"Tell Groucho to get off my back about my expenses on this case."

"Just send in the receipts. I'll see that he pays them."

"You're a big help," Trace said.

He waited until late afternoon, trying to build up his courage to call his ex-wife and children. Finally, he realized that Chico would be back soon from shopping, so he hooked up the electronic voice changer to the telephone and dialed the New Jersey number.

When his ex-wife answered, he said, "Let me talk to the daughter."

"Who?"

"The daughter. The girl," he said.

"She's not here. Who is this?"

"Let me talk to the son, then."

"Who is this? Whose voice is this?" his ex-wife demanded. "I don't know you. Who are you?" Her voice sounded like glass cracking.

"The son. Let me talk to him."

"He's not here either."

"You'll have to do, then," Trace said. He began to breathe heavily into the phone. "Haaaaaa, haaaaaaa, haaaaaaaa."

"Creep," his ex-wife said, and hung up.

Quickly, Trace disconnected the electronic device and put it back in the bedroom.

When Chico came back, she said, "Did you call?"

"Call whom?"

"Your kids, of course."

"Of course, I did. I promised you I would, didn't I?"

"And?"

"They hung up on me," he said.

She shook her head. "Well, at least no one can say you didn't try," she said.

Trace's mother was due back in New York Thursday afternoon. He and Chico returned to Las Vegas aboard a Thursday-morning plane.

JOIN THE *TRACE* READERS' PANEL

Help us bring you more of the books you like by filling out this survey and mailing it in today.

1. Book Title: _____

   Book #: _____

2. Using the scale below, how would you rate this book on the following features? Please write in one rating from 0-10 for each feature in the spaces provided

POOR		NOT SO GOOD			O.K.			GOOD		EXCEL- LENT
0	1	2	3	4	5	6	7	8	9	10

RATING

Overall opinion of book .... _____
Plot/Story .... _____
Setting/Location .... _____
Writing Style .... _____
Character Development .... _____
Conclusion/Ending .... _____
Scene on Front Cover .... _____

3. About how many Private Eye books do you buy for yourself each month? _____

4. How would you classify yourself as a reader of Private Eye books?
   I am a ( ) light ( ) medium ( ) heavy reader.

5. What is your education?
   ( ) High School (or less) ( ) 4 yrs. college
   ( ) 2 yrs. college   ( ) Post Graduate

6. Age _____   7. Sex: ( ) Male ( ) Female

Please Print Name_____

Address_____

City _____ State _____ Zip _____

Phone # (___)_____

Thank you. Please send to New American Library, Research Dept., 1633 Broadway, New York, NY 10019.